Accidentally Working Class

Karly Lane

All rights reserved. No part of this publication may be reproduced, stored or transmitted in any form or by any means, electronic, mechanical, photocopying, recording, scanning, or otherwise without written permission from the publisher. It is illegal to copy this book, post it to a website, or distribute it by any other means without permission.

This novel is entirely a work of fiction. The names, characters and incidents portrayed in it are the work of the author's imagination. Any resemblance to actual persons, living or dead, events or localities is entirely coincidental. The author asserts the moral right to be identified as the author of this work.

The author has no responsibility for the persistence or accuracy of URLs for external or third-party Internet Websites referred to in this publication and does not guarantee that any content on such Websites is, or will remain, accurate or appropriate.

Designations used by companies to distinguish their products are often claimed as trademarks. All brand names and product names used in this book and on its cover are trade names, service marks, trademarks and registered trademarks of their respective owners. The publishers and the book are not associated with any product or vendor mentioned in this book. None of the companies referenced within the book have endorsed the book.

This edition published 2022

Copyright © Karly Lane

Chapter 1

Quinn Appleton heard Bryson's small gasp from beside her as they emerged from the dense, tree-lined drive to be greeted by the sprawling, two-storey stone mansion hidden at the end. She was used to the effect it had on people seeing it for the first time and, to be honest, it still managed to take her breath away too.

It was a mysterious place. A landmark, for sure, built in the early 1900s by her great-great-grandfather, made to replicate an impressive country estate manor he'd always loved back in Scotland, near a village he'd grown up in as a small boy. Most people weren't even aware of its presence in busy inner-city Brisbane, hidden from the street behind tall iron gates and large trees. It was as much a local icon as the brand, Appleton's, named after her family, which was a household name even today.

The house was home to her grandmother, the matriarch of the Appleton dynasty. It was a home fit for royalty, and Elizabeth Appleton was a queen in every sense—except title. She ruled the business as though it were her kingdom and the family her subjects.

Quinn sighed, bracing herself as they climbed from her sleek Audi convertible parked on the circular white drive to head inside. The crunch of gravel beneath her feet echoed like a funeral march with each step.

Today the house looked festive, with Christmas trees either side of the entrance and wreaths hung merrily. It was very much a Christmas card scene—that is, if you ignored the searing summer heat around them.

Bryson issued a low whistle as they walked past the luxurious and very expensive vehicles already parked, and Quinn could feel a small bead of perspiration run down her spine under her bright yellow sundress. She hated making an entrance—especially here—and it looked like there were already quite a few family members inside.

'I still don't understand why it's taken three months to introduce me to your family,' Bryson murmured in a low, almost awestruck tone as they climbed the front stairs to the massive entrance.

'You'll soon find out,' she said with an apprehensive glance at his handsome, model-like face. She really liked Bryson. They'd met at a yacht party a few months before, and Quinn had been smitten ever since. He was an up-and-coming tech genius with dreams of starting his own business. She could listen to him talk about it all day—in fact, that's what she usually did. From anyone else, she would have grown bored, but not Bryson. His passion and drive were infectious. When she was around him, she felt as though she could do anything and succeed, and it wasn't only her; everyone was drawn to him, like moths to a flame.

'Come on now, babe. You know how charming I can be,' he said with a wink. 'I'll have your grandmother eating out of my hand by the end of the first course.'

Quinn tried to hide a wince behind a wide smile at the visual of her gran docile and compliant. It was impossible to even imagine, and a heavy lump formed in the pit of her stomach at the thought of the lunch ahead.

There'd been no way to back out of the Christmas lunch. It was tradition. It was the one time of the year the entire family came together. All of them. Every. Last. One.

'Miss Quinn.' A tall, narrow-faced man in a grey suit greeted them inside the front door with a small bow, and she saw Bryson's eyes widen, no doubt finding the fact her grandmother had a butler rather impressive.

'Merry Christmas, Lionel,' she said with a genuine smile for the older man. Lionel had been with her grandparents for as long as she could remember—for as long as anyone could remember, in fact—and Quinn knew behind that rather intimidating persona was a gentle, loyal man. He'd often played outside with her and her brother and their cousin when they were younger, once the adults had gone into the office to talk business. He'd always been adaptable to whatever role Lady Elizabeth, as she liked to be called by her staff, needed him to play. As were they all.

'Lady Elizabeth is awaiting your arrival in the main parlour,' he said, extending his hand towards the set of large doors at the end of the foyer, before leading the way.

'Thank you, Lionel.' She gave a small nod, taking a calming breath as the butler opened the doors with the usual dramatic flourish. The only thing missing was the sound of trumpets announcing their arrival, just to complete the charade.

Stepping into the parlour was like stepping into some French palatial court. The furniture was antique, brought over from Europe, giving the impression you were standing in a castle somewhere far away from the inner suburbs of Brisbane.

Quinn led Bryson across the room to where her grandmother sat in a gold embossed armchair, a gin and tonic on the small table beside her as she listened to the man and woman seated across from her.

'Grandmother. Mother. Father,' Quinn announced, hoping her voice sounded level and confident as she waited for them to turn and face her. 'I'd like to introduce you to Bryson Stonebridge. Bryson, my grandmother, Elizabeth, and my parents, Jethro and Lyla.'

Bryson turned his thousand-volt smile onto her parents as he shook her father's hand. Quinn held her breath as she watched her father, always looking impeccable, as if he'd just stepped from the pages of a men's fashion catalogue, slowly sizing up her boyfriend. The two men seemed close in height, just shy of the six-foot mark. Her father had the rounded belly of a man who spent far too much time on the golf course in a buggy, or at the clubhouse, rather than chasing the little white ball on foot, and his greying hair was almost silver nowadays.

When Bryson turned, he reached for her mother's hand, placing a lingering kiss to it. Lyla Appleton was as different to her husband as night was to day. Where Jethro happily succumbed to putting on a little weight, Lyla waged a personal war on ageing and spent the majority of her life working out and attending maintenance work at a beautician clinic.

Botox was her mother's weapon of choice, and Quinn often worried that one day she would go too far and end up with a permanent muscle-freezing abnormality that would result in her looking like some zombie-faced freak show. While it hadn't happened yet, there was always that possibility. However, it was more than a little annoying when people asked if she and her mother were sisters. No matter how attractive they were, *no one* wanted their mother looking hotter than they did.

And Quinn grudgingly had to admit her mother looked particularly hot today. Her long, platinum-blonde hair—a Kim Kardashian replica cut—hung down almost to her waist, and the tight yellow satin cocktail dress clung to all her gym-moulded curves. *Damn it. Yellow? Really?* She needed to start checking what her mother was wearing to events.

Lyla wore a satisfied, cat-who-ate-the-cream kind of smile as Bryson stepped away, before he turned to reach for her grandmother's hand, only to give a small start when he encountered a cool, calculating expression as Elizabeth ignored his extended offering.

'It's a great honour to meet you all, especially you, Mrs Appleton,' he said, regathering his earlier confidence and trying another smile.

'Always nice to meet one of Quinn's...*friends*,' Gran said with saccharin sweetness. 'She's a very popular girl.' And by popular, her dear grandmother didn't bother hiding the fact she meant Quinn was a bit of a hussy. At least, that's what the women's magazines that loved nothing more than to follow her around and report on any hint of a scandal thought.

So, she liked men—big deal. And she liked to party—so what? She was young, popular and, well, let's face it, *rich*. Besides, it was a full-time job preparing for and attending all the social events she was forever being invited to. And Gran couldn't complain about her partying habits when the company sponsored more than a few of them. It was *required* that she attend race days and fashion events.

'Oh, look,' Quinn cut in. 'There's Felix. Come and meet my brother.' She didn't give Bryson time to protest.

The key to surviving this family lunch would be to limit the conversations and keep moving.

Quinn accepted the tall flute of champagne her brother, Felix, handed her as they approached before knocking back the entire glass in one go.

'Going that good, is it?' Felix drawled, raising an eyebrow at the empty glass.

'I just got here and already I'm exhausted.'

'There, there, it'll all be over soon,' he said with mock sincerity.

Quinn turned at the sound of a throat clearing nearby and remembered Bryson. 'Sorry. This is Felix.'

'Good to meet you.' Bryson shook hands with the other man and waved over a passing waitress with a tray of drinks. The action wasn't entirely out of line, but something about the proprietary manner with which he did it annoyed her. He was a guest in her grandmother's home.

'Well, you certainly act as though you fit in here,' Felix said with a dry chuckle.

'All this meeting the family is a bit overwhelming,' he said, taking a sip of the champagne and savouring the taste.

'Don't look at me for sympathy. You were the one who wanted to come,' Quinn reminded him, helping herself to another glass. It was going to take quite a few of these to make it through lunch.

'The things you do for women, am I right?' Bryson winked at Felix

and ignored her small frown. Why was he making this out to be some kind of favour to *her* all of a sudden?

'How's the racing circuit this year?' he asked Felix, turning the conversation back to her brother. 'I'm a big fan.'

'Well, thanks, but we've had a run of bad luck lately.' Felix shrugged, downplaying the actual degree of bad luck that put their Formula One racing team almost at the bottom of the ladder. Her brother was following his dream of becoming a professional race car driver. Despite the fact he was almost six years older than her, the two had always been close. Lately, though, they'd drifted apart. Felix was now a celebrity and the up-and-coming poster boy for Formula One. He was moving on with his life and leaving her behind.

'And just who do we have here?' a sultry voice purred from behind her. Quinn didn't have to turn to see who it was.

Chapter 2

'Greta.' Quinn forced a smile back on her face before greeting her cousin. 'This is—' she started, before Bryson leaned across and took her hand.

'Bryson Stonebridge,' he said, lowering his voice. 'I see beauty runs through *all* the women in the family.'

Quinn was a little perturbed by the rather suggestive wiggle of her cousin's hips as she moved in closer, nudging Quinn aside.

It was becoming more than a little crowded in their corner now, so Quinn excused herself to find something stronger than champagne.

She nodded at the bartender as he reached for the bottle of Scotch, and whirled her finger in the air, indicating he could continue when he looked up at her after pouring no more than a small nip. 'Keep going,' she said irritably, when his concerned expression deepened as the liquid neared the rim of the glass. 'That'll do.' She took the glass and a hefty sip. 'Don't bother putting that bottle away. I'll be back in a minute.'

'Oh my, this doesn't bode well for the remainder of the day, does it, Ducky?'

Quinn glanced sideways at the man in the plaid suit as he handed over a tray of round coconut-covered balls to a passing waitress before ordering his own drink. 'Wow, gracing us mere mortals with your baking prowess? Someone's in the Christmas spirit,' Quinn murmured as the waitress took his tray away.

While Tobias was renowned for his culinary skills, and in any normal family would have gone on to be an actual chef, he usually only cooked for his own fancy dinner parties.

'I was feeling generous,' he said with a shrug.

'Well, thank goodness you're here, Uncle. I'm not sure I'd survive.'

'Of course you would, but it's more fun when I'm around,' he agreed, brushing away the idea that a party without him would be in any way acceptable. 'So, we brought the boyfriend...very brave of you.'

'It wasn't my idea.'

'Oh, I see.'

'You see what?' she asked, frowning.

'Nothing. He looks rather tasty,' he said, lowering his voice into a seductive drawl.

'Uncle Tobias, he's not on the menu. Besides, where's Claude? I thought you'd be bringing him along tonight?' Her uncle was a scandalous heartbreaker of men, and the occasional woman, depending on his fancy at the time, but over the last few weeks he and his new fling, Claude, had seemed inseparable.

'It's over,' he said with a dramatic sigh.

'Why?'

'Why do you think?' he asked, arching an eyebrow.

Quinn's frown grew as the implication set in. *Grandmother*. 'That's not fair,' she said, placing a sympathetic hand on his arm.

'It is what it is.' He shrugged, but Quinn could see through his blasé act.

In this family, there were certain rules, and everyone had to play by them—including her parents and her uncle. Everyone knew her uncle was a raging party animal with little to no morals and quite the drunk. While his mother allowed him to indulge in whatever extracurricular activities he chose, when it was time to be pulled into line, she used the reins—with force.

For whatever reason, Gran had clearly thought his fun with Claude had to come to an end. It used to confuse Quinn, until she got older and understood: she who controls the purse strings controls those who depend upon them.

Quinn hadn't realised all families weren't the same for a long time—an *embarrassingly* long time. She'd just assumed this was the way families worked. But more and more she was starting to realise just how messed up *this* family was.

'Don't fret about your boy toy, my darling,' Tobias said, patting her arm. 'I'm sure everyone will be nice and chilled by the time we sit down to lunch.'

She didn't get a chance to scoff at the notion before more finger food was brought out and she hovered over a selection of Christmas sweets.

'Ah, I wouldn't suggest the rum balls,' Tobias said, making a vulgar expression. 'Ghastly. Try the brie and pecan bites,' he suggested, before sending her a wink and bustling off to see who he could upset before lunch was called.

By the time Quinn headed back to the group, Bryson was partway through telling a story—one she'd already heard three times this week—but her gaze landed on the manicured hand that was currently sitting on her boyfriend's knee as he spoke. *Greta, the sneaky cow.* Her eyes narrowed as she took in the smug little smile her blonde-haired, blue-eyed cousin sent her. It had always been like this. Whatever Quinn had, Greta wanted. More often than not, being a year older than her, Greta had just taken it. It didn't matter what it was—a lollypop, a doll, a boyfriend. She hadn't changed since they were children.

It was hard to deny that Greta was stunning. She'd moved to New York two years ago and was now a professional model. It didn't hurt that the family business was a huge investor in a number of fashion houses both here and overseas, Quinn often told herself. Although Greta *had* gone on to become one of the most sought-after models in the business, so she obviously had *some* kind of talent.

As children, they'd once gotten along quite well, although Greta's mother, her aunt Davina, had an annoying habit of always talking up her children, which in turn put a lot of pressure on them. They always had to be going to the best schools and getting the highest marks and being far more advanced than any other children their age.

Quinn, on the other hand, was always in trouble for getting into fights with kids at school who picked on other kids, and coming home with rescued animals she'd somehow end up finding.

This had never gone down well with her grandmother. The Appleton women were ladies. Always.

Quinn's gaze was drawn to the older woman holding court across the room, and she gave a small internal sigh. She'd always felt like such a disappointment around Gran. Everyone else had found something they were good at. Everyone except her. She'd started university, thinking she would study events management—after all, she'd always been able to throw an awesome party—but she'd missed a few classes here and there and then fallen behind, and before she knew it, she didn't understand any of it and had dropped out by the end of the first year.

She enjoyed a lot of her charity work, fundraising for particular family charities the company supported, and some of which they'd even started years ago, but it didn't earn her any income and Gran didn't consider that a meaningful career choice. She wanted Quinn to get a business degree so she could work for Appleton's, like her father and his siblings did, but Quinn couldn't think of anything more mind-numbing than figures and reports and sitting in on meetings all day long. Besides, if she worked full-time, when would she have time to travel?

Quinn loved to travel. She spent time in the family's homes in France and Italy, and often stayed in the apartment in New York for two or three months of the year. There was something exhilarating about living in a big city; she loved the nightlife and the noise. The mere thought of it made her restless to return, and she began to mentally organise a time she could manage to get over there for a few weeks. Winter in New York was always beautiful. She looked across at Bryson and imagined them hand in hand as they strolled through Central Park in the snow.

The waitress came through with the tray of appetisers once more and eager hands reached for the goodies.

'These rum balls are to die for,' Greta sighed as she stuck the small, coconut-rolled chocolate ball in her mouth and gave a groan. 'Although I shouldn't even be having them. I'm very particular about what I put in my mouth,' she added with a sly smile aimed at Bryson.

'Not what I heard,' Quinn said under her breath. Beside her, Felix chuckled.

The doors of the parlour swung open and Lionel announced that lunch was now served in the dining room.

Her father stood and offered his arm to Gran, leading the procession from the parlour as everyone else fell in behind.

'This is unbelievable,' Bryson said, leaning close to her ear.

'I know. Gran's big on tradition and formalities.'

'You seriously do this kind of stuff all the time?' he asked.

'Yep. All the time.'

His incredulous chuckle caused her heart to sink once more. She knew inviting him here today was a bad move. He was going to see how weird they all were and run for the hills. She just knew it.

Chapter 3

Quinn took a moment to admire the room as she walked in. As usual, it had been professionally decorated and was nothing short of breathtaking. Bright red berries and deep green leaves were draped around the doorways and windows, while the massive fireplace, with its imported, hand-carved mantle, housed the treasured family Christmas decorations, which sparkled and shone behind the delicate fairy lights tucked unobtrusively around them. As it never actually got cold enough in Queensland to use the fireplace, its alternate life as a twinkling shrine to the festive heirlooms that had been passed down by generations of Appletons was nonetheless warm and inviting. In the corner sat a real pine tree, standing almost twelve feet high. The familiar scent of pine and cinnamon took her back to her childhood, when her favourite place to hide during visits to her grandmother's house was beneath the Christmas tree.

Anyone looking in through the window would think how perfect the whole picture was—a big family, a beautiful house—it looked like something out of a Hallmark Christmas movie. But looks could be deceiving.

Quinn and Bryson took their seats, finding themselves across from her parents and next to her grandmother. The head of the table was, as was the traditional custom, left empty but set for her grandfather, who was always included in their family gatherings, despite the fact he'd died when Quinn was ten years old. Her grandfather had been a large man, she remembered. Although maybe he'd just seemed large because she'd only been small. He was very serious; a quiet man who wasn't big on talking, but he listened.

Quinn remembered many times sitting beside her grandfather and telling him all kinds of boring stories about God only knew what. They'd sit side by side on the couch and he'd just listen, nodding his head occasionally and giving a small smile now and again. Of course, looking back, he was most likely thinking about running his empire and not even really listening to her ramblings at all, but he made her *feel* as though he'd been hanging on every word. He'd made her feel important. Her parents had never sat with her and listened to her stories. But Grandfather had. The empty seat always gave her a melancholy feeling.

As she settled into her seat, she found Greta had sat herself down beside Bryson, and the two were now making small talk as they waited for everyone to be seated.

A loud burst of laughter drew her attention towards her aunt Davina, who was normally the epitome of grace and poise. Beside her, Tobias was chuckling, having just told her something hilarious. That in itself should have been even more surprising than Davina's unusual slip of decorum, since the siblings hardly ever got along.

Quinn wasn't exactly sure how they'd managed to get stuck at the grown-ups' end of the table. This was always the place to get as far away from as possible. The added pressure of having Gran close enough to frown at any hint of inappropriate behaviour or lapse of table manners made the already painful family lunch almost unbearable. And yet, here they were. *Fantastic.*

Quinn looked over and tried to catch her parents' eyes, subtly pleading for help, but neither of them picked up on it, both too busy drinking their champagne and glaring at each other to notice her. Clearly, they'd just finished having yet another argument on their way into the dining room. It was good to see some things were still normal around here.

The entrées were brought out by the waitress who had been circling the room earlier and another taller one, who'd most likely been slaving away in the kitchen with the cook. Her gran had a permanent cook, butler and gardener on staff, as well as a cleaning contractor who came twice a week to eradicate the huge house of any dust that might have dared to settle on the priceless artwork or furniture inside. It took a very dedicated, yet relatively small, army of people to keep a manor house like this up and running, and Gran ran a tight ship.

From across the long table, she saw her brother lock eyes with the tall, dark-haired waitress as she leaned across to place his entrée in front of him, and caught the subtle smile that touched the woman's full red lips. Her brother had a reputation with women from all over the world. He was often photographed at nightclubs and parties wherever he went on tour, and always had a different woman on his arm in each one.

Quinn almost felt sorry for the waitress, until she caught her sending a look that could only be described as *smouldering* at Bryson as she straightened and walked away. A woman with ambition, it would seem. Quinn had seen her kind before. They always hung around her brother like bees to honey, hovering in the hopes of landing a rich young stud. Clearly, the dark-haired woman had bigger plans than waitressing. *Well, not today, sweetheart*, Quinn thought, waiting patiently for the woman to look at her before holding her glance with a glacial one of her own.

There was a weirder than usual vibe around the dining table as Quinn eyed her various relatives. Her aunt in particular was a lot more animated; alarmingly so, leaning back in her chair, which was drawing a rather unamused expression from Gran, Quinn noted, as she glared at her daughter, who was waving her hands rhythmically in the air like she was at a Stevie Nicks concert or something.

'We should have music,' Greta said, slapping the table before scrolling through her phone, presumably in search of some.

'Oh yes,' Aunt Davina said, opening her eyes and smiling. 'Something...spiritual.'

'Spiritual?' Quinn's father said, laughing a little too loud. 'What on earth do you know about being spiritual?'

Davina sent her brother a dismissive look before leaning forward to place her folded arms on the table. 'I'll have you know, I'm planning on doing a spiritual retreat to Tibet. My yoga master suggested it.'

'Since when have you been doing yoga?' Greta asked.

'Since it was compulsory on her last little...*forced* health retreat stay,' Tobias said.

'I put myself into that place voluntarily,' Davina snapped.

'If you say so, pet,' he nodded with a sanctimonious drawl.

Her uncle really could be a dick sometimes, Quinn thought, as she watched on from across the table.

'I'm starving,' Davina suddenly announced, as her entrée arrived and she dug in with the gusto of an overworked lumberjack.

Quinn risked a sideways glance at her grandmother and felt an icy shiver run down her spine at the furious look on her face. This was not the behaviour she expected at

Christmas lunch. Quinn had to admit, even she was a little shocked by it all.

Just then, her brother threw a prawn across the table at Greta, hitting her in the face. For a moment, there was a stunned silence before Greta let out a horrified screech and then retaliated.

This is not happening. What on earth is going on? Quinn's stunned gaze swung around the table, noting her parents were actually laughing, before it fell on Tobias, who, although in hysterics, was also wearing a very smug grin as he momentarily sobered and held her glance, before giving a wink and looking away once more.

The bloody rumballs. It had to be. Tobias had gone and spiked the rumballs. *Oh dear God.* Her entire family was under the influence of chocolate and rum flavoured weed! On any other occasion, Quinn might have even found this funny. But today was *not* any other occasion. Today was the day the man she was trying very hard to impress was meeting her family.

'Enough!' Elizabeth said, standing up. Her narrowed gaze zoned in on each of the faces around her. 'Lionel, have coffee brought out at once,' she ordered. 'Make it strong,' she added, her gaze never leaving that of her family before her for a second. 'I don't know what kind of ridiculous game you think this is, but you're all going to need to be quite sober for what I'm about to tell you. So you will drink some coffee. You will eat this food I've gone to all the trouble to arrange for our annual family celebration, and be grateful for everything you have been given. Do I make myself clear?' Her tone was crisp; the atmosphere arctic.

'Yes, Mother,' a chorus of answers mumbled from the table. Quinn noticed the effort it took most to keep a straight face, the effects of their high still buzzing in their system.

Coffee was passed around and within moments the first course came out, and soon the only sound around the table was of silverware on fine bone china as everyone concentrated on eating.

Quinn inwardly shook her head and sighed. She knew she should have cancelled. This was a disaster. What on earth must Bryson be thinking about her crazy, dysfunctional family now?

As the meal dragged on painfully, the earlier silliness had gone. In its place seemed to be a kind of hangover. Conversation was stilted, and the coffee continued to flow.

Quinn glanced at Gran. She was used to disappointment in this family. Over the last few years, her grown-up children had given her a lot to be disenchanted about. There'd been a few scandals; her uncle, in particular, had caused more than a few raised eyebrows over the years with his shenanigans. Today's mischief was tame compared to some of his more famous exploits. He'd once protested the closure of a famous nudist beach, chaining himself naked to the sign post they were trying to pull down. It made national news because he was an Appleton, one of the nation's most famous families. Tobias was no stranger to controversy.

But today Gran seemed in control—more in control than usual. Normally this kind of incident would have caused her to toss down her napkin and leave the room, but for some reason, she seemed to have steeled herself. The others might have been too fuzzy-headed to pick up on the heavy sense of impending doom that lingered around the table, but Quinn felt it and it took away what was left of her appetite. She caught her gran's eye and smiled weakly before dropping her gaze back to her plate, where she continued to pick at her meal.

'So, young man,' her grandmother said, looking at Bryson, breaking the silence. 'Tell me about your family. Where are they from?'

This was Gran's usual method of interrogation. Who your family were often told her everything she needed to know—unless, of course, you came from a family that wasn't from the inner circle of privilege the Appletons associated with.

'My family is from the west coast,' he said. I was the black sheep that couldn't wait to escape to the east.'

'Western Australia,' Gran repeated thoughtfully. 'Stonebridge…doesn't ring any bells. I know quite a few people over there. I'm sure we'd have a few friends in common.'

Which translated to, she knew enough people to ask around if you gave her a dodgy name and would check up on your story.

'My father made his money in car dealerships. He wanted me to go into the family business, but I wanted to become successful in my own field, which I'm doing. I've already been featured in the up-and-coming entrepreneurs to watch list in *The Daily Money* magazine.'

'I see.' Gran nodded, her eyes narrowing. 'I can't say I've heard anything about you,' she said bluntly.

'You will,' Bryson said in that cocky, self-assured tone that usually made Quinn's heart flutter, but now made her breath catch in alarm. No one spoke like that to her grandmother.

'Will I now?' Gran said slowly after a moment's pause.

'I have big plans,' Bryson continued, blithely unaware that even her parents had stopped bickering and also seemed to be fearing for his wellbeing.

'And where in these plans of yours does my granddaughter fit in?' Gran's question cut through Quinn's inner anguish. 'Do tell.' Gran invited with all the grace of a queen allowing a condemned man to speak…one who didn't even know he was condemned.

Bryson seemed caught off guard. It was only for a fleeting moment, but she knew her shrewd gran hadn't missed it. 'I have to admit, I'm completely smitten by your lovely granddaughter, Mrs Appleton.'

'Well, it's easy to be smitten by her beauty; after all, many have been, haven't they, Quinn?' Gran said, glancing at her with an innocent smile. 'But I'm wondering if maybe it's more than that. You present yourself with all the confidence of a self-made man and yet…you're not.'

'Not yet, but once I have some investors behind me…' Quinn caught a flicker of frustration pass across his charming face before he launched into his business spiel— the one where he outlined how his idea would transform the tech world overnight and launch him into the same hemisphere as Bill Gates and Mark Zuckerberg.

Quinn tried to get his attention, squeezing his hand to signal him to stop, but he slipped his hand away from hers as he warmed to his favourite subject. As much as she loved listening to him talk about his dreams, she knew here, in this setting, in front of her grandmother, everything was coming out wrong. He sounded like he was making a pitch to an investor.

Her heart stopped as the truth sank in. That's exactly what he was doing. All these months he'd been hinting, subtly at first and then more insistently lately, about meeting her family. It hadn't been as a boyfriend wanting to move forward. It had been as a wannabe entrepreneur looking for someone to fund his dream.

How could she have been so stupid? Because she'd been worried that her dysfunctional family would scare off yet another guy she liked. If she hadn't been so distracted, hadn't been so blinded by his charisma and the fantastic sex they'd been having, maybe she would have really listened to what he'd been saying.

'I assure you, I'm very much in love with your granddaughter and aim to provide her with an extremely comfortable life one day soon,' Quinn heard him say, coming back to the present with a lurch that almost gave her whiplash.

She stared at Bryson. Had he just said he was *in love* with her? She tried to ignore the excited voice in her head jumping up and down hysterically, screaming with joy as she struggled to remain calm. He'd never once said he loved her before today. Shouldn't that somehow lessen the excitement if the first time he said it, it's to your grandmother?

'Oh? So, marriage is what you're asking?' Gran pressed, seemingly innocent, unless you knew that Gran was anything *but* an innocent, romantic little old lady.

Bryson swallowed and seemed to struggle to reclaim his composure. 'Well, you know, Quinn is a beautiful woman, and a man would be a fool to sit by and let her slip away...'

'Oh my God,' Greta gasped. 'Is he about to propose?' Her raised voice immediately stopped conversation, and all eyes turned upon them.

Bryson's eyes widened in alarm; he spluttered as he tried to form some kind of response.

What the hell was happening? This was supposed to be a boring family lunch.

'Are you asking for my blessing to marry my granddaughter?' Gran asked, undeterred by the rather unbecoming shade of beetroot Bryson was turning.

'Gran, please,' Quinn cut in, humiliated.

'I'm just trying to be clear on Mr Stonebridge's intentions, my dear,' Gran replied, before waving a hand across at Lionel, who stepped forward and produced an envelope from inside his suit jacket, like some grim-faced magician's assistant, minus the fishnet stockings and one-piece swimsuit. 'Because I've had my private detective look into your background, and I'm a little confused at what he discovered, to be honest.'

Quinn's mouth dropped open. *Surely, she didn't*, she thought, shocked by the revelation before common sense kicked in. *Who am I kidding? Of course she did.* It was exactly what Gran would do.

Gran pulled out a large photo of a couple in a very intimate embrace, and blood drained from Quinn's face as she stared at the image. 'Who's that?' she asked Bryson weakly.

She hoped against hope there'd be a perfectly simple explanation, but the fact Bryson was gaping at her doing a remarkable impersonation of a fish right now did little to reassure her.

In the photo, Bryson was wearing the Italian leather jacket she'd bought him only a month ago, and her mind began making all the appropriate calculations. This was taken recently.

'Well, you may want to hold off on the proposal until after you hear what I have to announce,' Gran suggested, clearly tiring of whatever momentary amusement she'd been hoping for, and tapped her crystal glass with her fork. 'If I could have everyone's attention, please.'

I freaking hate Christmas.

Chapter 4

Around the table, the hum of conversation stopped. Quinn found herself unable to look at Bryson, still numb to the incriminating photo on the table before her.

'Firstly, I'd like to wish everyone a merry Christmas,' Gran said. 'You all know that it's been our family tradition each year to gather together at Christmas and celebrate our year—the good and the bad, the highs and the lows.' Her gaze roamed the table as she spoke. 'However, this year it's come to my attention that changes must be made. Considerable and decisive changes. Changes that won't be popular.'

Quinn felt the shift of uneasiness around the table begin to grow.

'Firstly, my three children, Jethro, Tobias and Davina,' she said, her gaze falling on each one in a measured, calculating move. 'You've all been employed and part of the Appleton's business now for a long time. Years, in fact. The company has given you a lifestyle many would envy, and for very little asked in return from you. In fact, all that *is* asked of you is to turn up to the meetings and make a useful contribution to the company that's given you everything.' Gran paused, and her eyes hardened. 'And yet none of you have bothered to come along to a meeting even once this year. In fact, I can count on one hand the number of times *any* of you have even been seen at the office in the last three years. I am sick and tired of dealing with this kind of disrespect.'

Quinn was too scared to look over at her parents' faces, but she could sense the discomfort from everyone present.

'Mother, you know that we've had a number of disruptions this year...' her father began.

Gran cut in briskly. 'Renovations on your house, running three times over budget, is not an acceptable excuse to avoid your responsibilities to the company.'

'Well, I've had health issues,' Davina put in from up the table.

'Darling, a boob job and a stint in rehab are not classed as health issues,' Tobias countered snidely.

'Oh, you'd know, Mr Chin Implant,' Davina retorted. 'And, for the record, it didn't work. You still have a weak chin and now you just look like an ageing Roger Ramjet.'

'You take that back, Crack House Barbie,' Tobias sneered.

Quinn closed her eyes briefly and counted to five, releasing her breath slowly, just the way her therapist had taught her to do in times of stress.

'Enough!' Gran snapped impatiently. 'You've all been fired.'

A chorus of disbelief echoed around the table and Greta glared at her grandmother. 'You can't fire your own children. It's a family company.'

'Oh, I can,' Gran said simply. 'Which brings me to my grandchildren. I'm putting a stop on all the company cards, and your trust funds have been frozen until further notice.'

The what now? Quinn opened her eyes and blinked uncertainly, exchanging a confused glance with her brother. All thoughts of Bryson suddenly vanished.

'All I have asked of any of you over the years was a little respect for your heritage. Attend an event or two,' Gran continued.

Greta gave an indulgent sigh. 'Gran, I'm in demand at the moment. I'm at the pinnacle of my career. I can't just drop everything to show up at some fundraiser.'

'And how did you get to that pinnacle, my dear? Who got you in front of those designers and agents in the first place? It's all very easy to forget where you came from, isn't it?'

Greta shrugged. 'I don't need the trust fund, Gran.'

Quinn's mouth dropped open at her cousin's blatant disregard for...well, personal safety was the first thing that came to mind. Gran was not someone you ever wanted to get off side.

'Oh? You don't get out of bed for less than ten thousand dollars a day?' Gran quipped sarcastically.

Greta gave a derisive snort. 'Try a hundred thousand.'

Gran barely batted an eyelid, but Quinn found herself quietly impressed by her cousin's earnings.

'Then you're right. You clearly won't be needing your trust fund—at all. I can think of a few charities we can direct the money to instead.'

'Now, Mother, just hold on a minute,' Davina protested. 'That money belongs to Greta...'

'My darling, that money belongs to *me*. *I* am the managing director and CEO of Appleton's,' Gran corrected bluntly. 'I allow the grandchildren an allowance against their inheritance, because Henry and I believed the family business should be shared among family. All these years, we've prided ourselves on keeping this business family owned. Do you have any idea how many iconic family businesses are still owned in this country? They've almost all been sold to foreign investors. Your grandfather and I fought hard to keep this company in our family's hands, *for you.*' She looked at her grandchildren sternly. '*For your futures,* and not one of this generation has shown the slightest interest in the company—except when they need it for something. If your grandfather was still alive, it would break his heart.' She paused momentarily, and a shadow passed across her pale, English rose complexion. 'This is my fault,' she said, shaking her head. 'After Henry passed, I loosened the reins too much.' She sat reflectively, before her voice hardened once more. 'I've been too soft for far too long.'

'Mother, I hardly see how you can force the children to work somewhere they don't want to. Besides, they've all found other careers, you can't penalise them for not joining the company,' Aunt Davina said with an exasperated roll of her eyes.

'The company has always been the heart of this family—for generations. The Appletons were synonymous with the products we made, that's what made it special—we had wholesome, family values. But now the only way anyone hears anything about the Appletons is in the gossip magazines.' Gran nodded at ever-faithful Lionel, who stepped forward on cue, turning to gather a stack of magazines from the sideboard to spread out on the table.

Her brother was on some of them; his arm draped across the shoulders of a topless woman on a beach somewhere exotic on one, and standing naked in the doorway of a luxury villa on another, a huge yellow star hiding his groin (which, personally, Quinn thought was probably twice the size of whatever it was supposed to be covering).

On the other covers, Greta was captured at various parties, kissing multiple men *and* women on different occasions; on another, she was holding up a bottle of Scotch with one hand and flipping the bird to a photographer with the other.

Then there were the ones which featured her. Quinn grimaced slightly at the cover closest to her, having been taken after a heavy night of drinking. *Of all the photos Gran could have used*. She was sitting in the gutter out the front of a prominent nightclub, her top sliding off one shoulder, her skirt hitched up to an indecent level and her makeup smudged and hideous. It was unfair that even in drunken debauchery, Greta had never been caught on camera looking that horrific. *Cow*.

Quinn had been featured in way more magazines than that, and had actually looked fricking amazing. Typical that it would be *that* cover they used to highlight her wayward behaviour.

'This is what a once respectable family name has become,' Gran said as her gaze moved around the table.

'Mother, I hardly—' her father started before he was cut off by a glacial glare.

'I blame *all of you* for raising such delinquent children.'

'Just pointing out that I have no children,' Tobias said, with a doleful glance towards his mother, 'and can honestly say, looking at this, that I'm bitterly disappointed in my siblings and their offspring.' He shook his head sadly at the offending magazines.

'Oh, shut up, Tobias,' Gran snapped, and without even needing to look at Lionel, the man dropped another three magazines on the pile, featuring her uncle in varying displays of undress at some questionable-looking parties.

'Oh. Yes,' Tobias murmured with a devilish grin, reaching over to snag the top one. 'I remember *that* night.' The self-satisfied smile vanished from his face when Gran reached over and snatched the magazine from his hands.

'I will *not* have this family's name dragged through any more mud. All of this nonsense stops right now. Until I'm confident that we've rebuilt our reputation back up to a standard we can be proud of, none of you will be getting a single cent out of this company.'

'Mother, I think you're blowing this all out of proportion,' her father tried once more, but bit back a frustrated sigh when she waved off his protest.

'You'll be noticing several changes that will start immediately,' she continued, just as a rumble sounded outside.

'What on earth is that?' Quinn's mother asked, frowning, or what would be frowning if her recently administered Botox had allowed her forehead to crease.

Tobias dropped his linen serviette onto the table as he rose from his seat and went to the window, curiosity getting too much for him. 'Mother, you *wouldn't*,' Tobias gasped, turning a disbelieving stare on Gran.

'Yes, son. I would and I have.'

Chapter 5

The rest of the family exchanged varying looks of alarm before rising from their seats to see for themselves what all the fuss was about.

'Why is there an enormous semi-trailer in the driveway?' Quinn's mother asked, confusion showing in her eyes, if not in her facial expression.

'I believe that's a car carrier,' her father murmured, giving a smug snigger as he patted his brother on the shoulder. 'They're taking your Bentley away.'

'Mother, what are you doing?' Tobias demanded as he watched in horror as the large tow truck driver hooked something beneath his silver Bentley and pressed a button on a handheld winch device.

'Your car is leased. Paid for by the company. You no longer work for the company, so it's going back.'

'But…you can't,' he stammered, his gaze turning back to his beloved car helplessly. 'Not the Bentley.'

No sooner had Tobias's car been loaded than the truck driver turned his attention to the next vehicle.

'Mother!' Davina screeched.

'Sorry, dear.'

'This is ridiculous,' Davina said. 'Jethro! do something.'

'Mother, I really feel this is a little extreme,' her father protested once more.

'Do you, son? More extreme than billing up a three-week Caribbean resort stay to the company as a business expense?'

'I was attending a conference. It was work.'

'It was a golf tournament, don't lie to me, Jethro. This is exactly the kind of behaviour that's brought all this about. For far too long, you've all been bleeding the company dry and giving nothing in return. You are the only two generations of this family who have no idea what it means to do a decent day's work, and it's thoroughly shameful.'

The whine of a winch drew Quinn's gaze back to the window, and she gasped as the tow truck driver headed towards her vehicle. 'Wait!' she called in alarm, tapping the window frantically to get the driver's attention, to no avail. 'That's *my* car! Dad, tell him. It was my birthday present. You and Mum bought it for me.'

'Ah,' her father stammered, looking across at her mother as though hoping she'd intervene.

'Jethro?' Her mother seemed just as confused as Quinn.

'Yes, well...you see, the thing is...' He cleared his throat awkwardly. 'Technically, it's leased...to the company,' he finished weakly.

'You *leased* my car? The one you bought two years ago for my twenty-first birthday present?' Quinn asked incredulously.

'It was just...easier...' He shrugged with a wince. 'Let's not talk about this now,' he added quickly.

'Oh, I think we should talk about this,' her mother cut in scathingly. 'Why don't you tell everyone the truth? I mean, your dictator of a mother has just sacked you, so why don't you explain to me and everyone else here how you plan to live when you've mortgaged everything we own to the hilt?'

Quinn's gaze ricocheted between her parents as she tried to follow the conversation but had a sinking sensation that whatever was unfolding was only going to make today even worse.

'We'll talk about this later,' her father snapped.

'We'll talk about it *now*,' her mother countered. 'Go on, tell them.'

Her father remained stubbornly silent, but her mother was on a roll and, after a small impatient huff, turned to face Elizabeth and launched into a theatrical tirade. 'We're penniless. Your son has a gambling addiction.'

'It's not an addiction. I've just had a few bad investments recently.'

'Since when has horse racing been called an investment?' Tobias scoffed under his breath, but just loud enough to carry.

'Mind your own damn business,' her father said, raising his voice and glaring at his brother.

'Well, I would, brother, but it appears we no longer have one,' Tobias said with an offhand shrug and a widening grin.

'What are you so damn cheerful about? You were fired too,' her father pointed out impatiently.

'Exactly. I've just realised it's actually a relief,' Tobias said, turning to face Gran and taking hold of his glass. 'If we're no longer chained to you by the business, then you no longer have any say in our lives.'

Quinn held her breath in the silence that followed her uncle's blasé announcement. Gran watched Tobias calmly. This frightened her more than if her expression had been furious. Calm Gran, in her experience, meant she already knew something no one else knew.

'This will be an interesting exercise for you, Tobias,' Gran said. 'To be free to make the choices you've always said you wanted to make...and to live with those consequences.'

'Oh, I'll be happy to live with the consequences — freedom.' He toasted her with a caustic grin.

'I'm glad to see you're all taking this like some kind of joke,' Davina snarled, drawing the table's attention. 'I, for one, don't find this in the least bit funny.'

'I can assure you, Davina, I haven't been finding anything about this family amusing for a very long time. I've given you all chance after chance and to no avail. You're all so wrapped up in your own shallow lives that you've forgotten the meaning of family and loyalty. I won't stand by and allow a one-hundred-and-seventy-year family institution be destroyed.'

'So what are we supposed to do?' Davina protested.

'I'd suggest you all go out and get a job,' Gran said simply.

'A job?' Davina gaped. 'Are you insane?'

'Come on, sis, I think you'd make a great bartender—you've always made a mean martini,' Tobias put in cheerfully. 'You'll just have to remember not to drink them though.'

'We'll be fine, Mum,' Greta cut in impatiently. 'You're coming back to New York with me. Come on, let's get out of here.' Greta uncrossed her long legs and stood, dropping the napkin on the table and giving her grandmother a look of disdain. 'I hope this little stunt of yours isn't going to backfire, Gran. I mean, imagine waking up one day in this big old ugly house and realising you don't have anyone left to boss around? How sad.'

'You have a lot of growing up to do, my dear. I hope, for your sake, you do it quickly.'

Ouch. Take that, Greta. Say what you wanted about Gran, but the woman was the poster girl for decorum.

With her aunt and cousin gone, the remainder of the room seemed to be sitting around in shell shock. What was going to happen now? Without her trust fund allowance, and with all the perks of the family credit card, Quinn was more or less...destitute. She no longer had any transport. Her beautiful car. A sob lodged in her chest. How could her father do that to her? She still remembered the night of her twenty-first birthday when her parents had presented her with the silver Ferrari, the same kind Kim Kardashian drove. She loved that car. Oh my God, what was she going to do without a car? *Don't panic,* she told herself, making a conscious effort to loosen the grip on the back of the chair she'd been holding. Mum and Dad would work something out; although, there *was* the whole *penniless* thing her mother had thrown around earlier, but that had to be just Lyla being dramatic...God, she wished her mother had expressions like every other human being on the planet, so she could read her face occasionally.

However, judging from her father's pasty complexion at the moment, she had a terrible suspicion things might actually *be* as bad as her mum had been claiming. *Oh God.* No. Stop it. Bryson would reassure her everything was going to be okay. Strong, charismatic, totally head-over-heels-in-love-with-her Bryson.

Quinn's gaze swept the room. Where the hell was Bryson?

'Sweetie, I think you better hurry and get outside,' Tobias said from beside her, staring out the window.

Quinn followed his gaze and her heart froze mid-beat.

Bryson was heading towards Greta as Aunt Davina got into the back seat, deep in conversation on her phone. *Oh, hell no!* Quinn's inner outraged southern woman yelled, propelling her from the dining room, through the foyer and out the front door in record time. She was slightly out of breath as she called out his name.

'What are you doing?' Quinn asked as she spotted his hand on the passenger-side door handle.

'Quinn,' he started, his voice sounding annoyed. Annoyed! Like he was the one who'd just had his world turned upside down.

'I offered Bryson a lift home,' Greta cut in, stepping closer to him.

Quinn continued to stare at Bryson. The implication of his actions was momentarily lost on her.

'I'm sorry, Quinn,' he started, and gave a sympathetic smile. 'After what just happened in there today, I'm just not ready to be stuck in the middle of all that.'

'Stuck in the middle...' she repeated numbly, before she spotted her cousin's hand snaking its way around her boyfriend's waist. 'Are you *kidding me* right now?' Indignation spewed from within her like a volcanic eruption.

'Quinn, I'm sorry. This is all way more than I'm prepared to take on right now. Your gran, pressuring me into some kind of commitment...your family self-imploding...'

'Oh, and how convenient for you not to have to address the little issue of who the hell that woman was in the photo?' Quinn snapped. 'But I guess the chance to get your hands on all that money has now disappeared, so that's pretty much a moot point.' She shrugged as her eyes narrowed.

'This isn't what I signed up for,' he finished blandly.

'So, you're going with *her?*'

'I'm simply giving him a lift out of here,' Greta said, with a shrug and a sickly sweet smile.

'You were just going to leave without even saying goodbye?'

Bryson shrugged one of the broad shoulders she'd lovingly massaged that very morning. 'I don't do the whole soap opera thing. You have things to sort out and I'd just be in the way, so I thought I'd catch a ride with your aunt and cousin.'

'Speaking of which, we have to go,' Greta put in, sending Bryson a meaningful look that ended in a sexy smile, which no doubt promised him some kind of lustful reward whenever they got to wherever they were going.

Quinn's insides were churning and her palms had gone sweaty.

'Sorry, Quinn. It was fun while it lasted. I guess I'm just not ready for the kind of commitment you're after,' he said, before pulling the door open and climbing inside.

'Rookie mistake bringing a boyfriend to meet the family, little cousin,' Greta said, bringing Quinn's attention back to her. 'I thought you were smarter than that.'

'And you're still not happy until you've taken whatever I have off me.'

'He didn't put up much of a fight,' she scoffed, opening her car door and sliding in behind the wheel with a patronising smile of farewell.

Quinn couldn't move as she stood there and watched the black car disappear down the long drive. Inside, Quinn resembled a deflated balloon, empty of everything she'd been so full of earlier in the day. Before she'd walked through that front door, she'd had a boyfriend. She'd had a life. She'd had a *car!*

What the hell was she going to do now?

Chapter 6

Quinn opened her eyes, soon realising that was a mistake, as the sun felt as though it was burning a hole through her retinas. Her head throbbed; she carefully sat up in bed and cradled it in her hands. Memories of the night before, when she'd finally arrived home and decided on a liquid dinner, crying herself into a drunken slumber, came rushing back.

On reflection, it probably hadn't been the best plan, but coming back to an empty apartment that still smelled of Bryson's aftershave, it had been the only real course of action at the time. She was too angry at her parents to go to their house and too miserable to crash at a friend's place.

He'd left her. *For Greta.* She dropped backwards onto her pillow and swung an arm across her eyes. It was bad enough he'd broken up with her so brutally...but to leave her for her cousin? That hurt far more than anything else. *The bastard.*

Quinn gave a small groan as her head reminded her there were consequences for trying to dull the misery through a mild case of alcohol poisoning. She needed a shower and some pain relief; of the non-alcoholic kind this time.

In the bathroom, she closed her eyes and let the hot water run over the base of her neck as she rested her forehead against the cool tiles, allowing the magic of her Italian-designed chromotherapy shower to take all the stress away. Her mother had been a huge fan of chromotherapy, her own favourite method of embracing emotional, spiritual and mental energies using colour. The shower used coloured lights to reflect your mood, and the gentle rainfall shower head and soft purple hues pulsated inside the shower stall, swirling around her. For all the mumbo jumbo her mother insistently spouted about colour therapy, Quinn had to admit that, within moments, the worst of her hangover started to subside.

Well, she sighed, she might be suddenly poor, but at least she still had her apartment.

Quinn wrapped herself in a thick white towel and headed out to the kitchen. She needed coffee, stat.

Yep, there were decidedly worse places to be left destitute, she thought as the view from her kitchen of an endless blue ocean stretched out before her.

She loved her apartment, located in what real estate agents toted as the 'most iconic building on the Gold Coast'—the Q1 building. Her parents had made the wise investment—clearly their only wise investment—years ago when the building was first opened, purchasing two apartments; one of which they let out as a holiday rental, and the other they had always had as the family holiday home, which Quinn took over full-time two years ago when she left Brisbane. It was close to the trendy Chevron Renaissance precinct, with loads of dining and boutique shops a short stroll away and stretches of sandy beach literally across the road.

Quinn took her coffee out to the enclosed balcony and curled up on one of the outdoor settees, letting the cool breeze blow through her hair, salt and sunshine washing over her as she watched the white frothy waves gently break and gush back and forth against the white sand of the beach below. From her high-digit floor, the scattering of people down below looked no bigger than ants, but it was later in the afternoon and the wind was picking up, so most of the holidaymakers would be heading back to their accommodation for an afternoon nap or to hit the shopping centres nearby.

She was too upset to talk to her parents about what her grandmother's huge announcement meant; she was still in shock that her supposed boyfriend, who'd just pledged his love for her in front of her family, had decided she was now a liability with no trust fund money and had taken off with her cousin, who apparently was making a fortune modelling in New York and Paris.

Well, good riddance then, she thought, as a blistering burst of rage filled her once more. *They deserve each other*. She caught sight of the leather jacket she'd bought him, slung over the back of a dining room chair, and the tears came flooding back. He'd looked amazing in it, she remembered glumly. God, how could she have been so stupid? All this time, she thought they'd been in love; that she'd found a man who loved *her*—unconditionally.

She'd kept him away from her family and their constant three-ring circus of drama on purpose. She hadn't wanted any of that to get in the way of how he saw her. He knew she came from a wealthy family. Everyone knew who she was, especially in the circles they ran in. And Bryson himself came from a family with money—maybe not as much as her family, but she'd never imagined he'd be trying to use her. He was part of the party scene—the young and wealthy. Only, she thought with a frown, she hadn't actually looked into it. He certainly looked and acted the part, but, come to think of it, he'd never really answered any of the casual questions she'd asked about his family. He'd always distracted her with that sensual mouth of his…God, she missed those lips. She closed her eyes against a fresh rush of pain, then gave a small growl of frustration. He could even distract her in a memory!

Quinn reached for her phone and googled his name. Links to Instagram came up, but she didn't bother clicking on those. She already knew what photos would be on that — she'd taken most of them. She clicked on his Facebook account instead, because she suddenly remembered he rarely used it, but the posts only went back as far as eighteen months before she met him. That was weird. There were a few parties from Bali and lots of travel photos, but nothing else. It was as though he only existed from a year and a half ago.

Why had she taken this long to look into it? *Because you were too busy being swept off your feet like a love-sick fool.* He'd disarmed and mesmerised her with his charismatic personality and ability to make her believe she was the most important thing in his life. She'd been in love, and the perfect gullible target. It was true. Her family's money had been the only thing he'd been interested in.

'You idiot,' she snapped out loud to herself. With a renewed swell of self-worth, Quinn got up, grabbed a plastic bag, and walked into the master bedroom. She was going to remove all evidence of Bryson bloody Stonebridge from her life, starting with his belongings.

There wasn't much, despite the fact he spent most of his time in her apartment, given it was closer to all the places they liked to frequent.

There were a few clothes in the closet — all bought by her — a couple of pairs of shoes and some gym gear in a bag. She didn't even bother opening that; she wasn't going to risk getting knocked over by the smell of sweaty laundry. She hoped there was a wet towel in there that would go nice and mouldy.

Quinn called the front desk and informed them that she'd need a new key, and arranged to have the locks changed immediately. No doubt he and Greta would be holed up some place luxurious, gushing over how beautiful they both were. *Ugh. What a pair of arseholes.*

Sitting back down, feeling drained but somewhat empowered by her cleaning spree, Quinn dragged her laptop out of the cupboard and sat down at her dining table. She needed to get her head around her future—this new future without Gran's credit card. She logged in to her bank account and comforted herself with the knowledge that she'd most likely have more than enough sitting in there to figure out a plan of some kind.

Her mouth gaped.

Two hundred and fifty-eight dollars? She searched the screen for her other accounts and found nothing. True to her word, her gran had deactivated every last one. This was her only account—one she had no idea she'd even opened, but which still had a credit balance.

She placed her hands palms down on top of the glass tabletop and closed her eyes, breathing in deeply and trying not to hyperventilate. Everything would be okay, she told herself firmly. There was no need to panic. She slowly opened her eyes and shut the laptop. There was no need to have reality staring at her from the computer screen—that wasn't at all helpful right now. She'd call her parents and they'd sort it out. After all, it was her father's own mother who'd lost her freaking mind and gone on this crazy tirade.

She dialled her parents' number and waited for an answer, but there was none. Frowning, she called her mother's mobile, which rang out and went to voicemail, and the same thing happened with her father's.

She huffily put the phone back on the bench. Where were they? Of course, it wasn't unusual that she couldn't get one of them—they were rarely together anywhere, including home lately—but to not get *either* of them *was* strange.

Chapter 7

Quinn balanced against the hallway wall and slipped on the gold strappy Christian Louboutin stilettos with their signature red sole over her heels. Running her hands down the sides of her sequined gold cocktail dress, she touched up her lipstick and gave a satisfied nod before heading out the door.

What she needed to cure heartache was a night on the town.

Scrolling through her contacts list, she sent a cool nod of greeting to the concierge on duty as he led her out the front of the building to the Uber she'd booked, texting the usual crowd of partygoers to find out where to meet up. She wasn't going to let being dumped by Bryson set her back. She didn't need him to have a good time before, and she sure as hell didn't need him now.

The Uber pulled up in front of Studio Twenty-One and Quinn sashayed her way past the queuing patrons to smile at the big bouncer guarding the front door.

'Hey, Hector,' she crooned, lowering her eyes coyly.

'Ms Appleton,' he greeted with stoic deference, unclipping the roped-off gate to allow her through.

Thank God she hadn't lost her touch completely, she thought, as the room lit up and red and blue lights strobed to the dance music booming through huge speakers.

She headed to the bar and smiled at the bartender, Andrew, whom she'd known semi-well during her particularly wild days before Bryson had come onto the scene.

'Looking fine, Ms Appleton,' he said, leaning across the bar towards her. 'Didn't think we'd be seeing you here tonight.'

'Why not?' she said, accepting the shot he passed her automatically.

'Word around town is the Appletons have fallen from grace.'

'What word around town?' How had any of this had time to do the rounds of the social calendar gossip mill yet?

'Your daddy's been rackin' up big debts all over town.'

Quinn glared at Andrew furiously. 'Who's been saying all this?'

He shrugged and straightened, topping up her glass before looking up at her, wearing a serious expression. 'You didn't hear it from me, but apparently someone in your family did a paid tell-all interview with a major news network. As usual, nothing stays under wraps for too long around here. Just about everyone knows about it.'

If she hadn't been in shock, she'd have noticed the sympathetic glance he sent her, but was too stunned to do more than glare at him.

'Quinn!' a high-pitched voice yelled nearby, and she turned to find Chantelle waving at her as she crossed the dance floor.

'Oh my God! Is it true? Has your gran really cut you all off?'

What the actual hell? She'd barely had time to process it all, and already everyone else knew about it?

'And you poor thing! Bryson and Greta! What a bitch!'

'How'd you hear about that?'

'Greta, of course,' she said, rolling her eyes dramatically. 'She was in here last night and they were all over each other.'

Great.

'I gave them a dirty look. I couldn't believe it. I got your back,' she said, slipping an arm around Quinn's shoulders. 'I don't believe anything she was saying about your dad.'

'What was she saying about my dad?' Quinn asked hesitantly.

'That he's in debt and he's skipped the country. Ran away to leave the rest of the family to clean up his mess.'

'Well, that's ridiculous,' Quinn scoffed, but swallowed hard. He hadn't been answering his phone, sure, but he wouldn't have fled the country. Her mother would have told her by now if that had happened. Right?

'Come on, let's just forget about all this and have fun,' Chantelle said, plastering a bright, if somewhat glassy-eyed smile on her face. Apparently, the partying had started earlier and they'd already broken out the hard stuff. 'You need to catch up,' she said, and Quinn held up her hand to catch the other bartender's eye.

'Two shots,' she said, holding up two fingers as she leaned across the bar.

The bartender, a new guy, not too hard on the eye, poured the drinks and Quinn reached to take them, but frowned when he hesitated in handing them over. 'Ah, that'll be twenty-five dollars,' he said, his thousand-watt smile shaking slightly as he took in Quinn's annoyed expression.

'Put it on my tab,' she said, shaking her head. Boy, the pretty ones sure could be dumb sometimes.

'I'm sorry, Ms Appleton, but the boss said we can't.'

Andrew came up behind the new guy and smoothly replaced him with a nod. 'I'm sorry, but the boss just sent down word. The Appleton tab's been cancelled. It's under your father's name and he owes too many people around here.'

Quinn's clenched jaw slackened in shock. Cancelled? She regained her composure and pulled out her credit card. 'Put it on this,' she snapped, irritated that her night was being ruined before it had even started.

Andrew swiped the card, then glanced up at her with a sympathetic wince. 'I'm sorry. It declined.'

'It what?' *Damn it, Gran.* She'd been hoping it might take a few days until her cards stopped working. 'Look, just make a new line of credit in my name. All this mess will be sorted in a couple of days.'

Andrew pursed his lips together in a regretful expression before shaking his head. 'Sorry, he was pretty specific. No Appleton credit, full stop.'

'Are you freakin' kidding me? Do you know how much clientele your boss has pulled from me over the years? Everyone only comes here because I made this place trendy.'

'I'm really sorry, Ms Appleton. If it were up to me...' He held his hands up helplessly.

Quinn narrowed her eyes and glared at the man. 'You tell your boss he just made a huge mistake.'

'Put it on mine,' Chantelle said, stepped up and taking hold of the shots, before tapping her credit card on top of the Eftpos machine. 'See? All good. Come on, Quinn, drink up,' she said, handing her the small glass.

No bar tab? Whoever heard of such a humiliating thing? She couldn't even *remember* a time she'd had to pay for drinks. *What the actual hell?*

'Ah, Chanty,' Quinn asked hesitantly as her slight problem dawned on her. 'Could you maybe cover my drink rounds tonight? Just until I sort out what's happening with my trust fund.'

'Of course,' she said, waving off the awkwardness Quinn was feeling—another experience she couldn't remember ever having before, at least not over something like money for drinks.

Quinn threw back the shot and let the burn of tequila hit her throat, but it felt good. The previous two had begun to numb the sensation. Two more shots and she was ready to face the rest of the crowd.

Quinn tried to shake off the news she'd just received and dragged out her party girl persona. So what if everyone seemed to be talking about the gossip they'd been hearing—these were her true friends, they wouldn't listen to any of that crap. She smiled as they reached the table of familiar faces, but faltered slightly when she realised hardly anyone seemed able to hold her gaze.

'You guys look like someone died,' Quinn said, trying to lighten the mood. 'God, I need a drink after the last few days I've had, who's with me?'

A round of hesitant smiles touched the group's lips, but it was impossible to ignore the slight chill in the air.

'We were about to leave,' Dominic, a tall, lanky, dark-eyed son of a wealthy import businessman, said.

'Leave? I just got here.' It was still early by nightclub standards, too early to move on to somewhere else...although it *would* make an impressive statement for the group to walk out and show the nightclub owner just who he was messing with. He'd be missing out on all his top-shelf beverage sales tonight. 'Okay. Where to next?' Quinn asked, hearing the overenthusiasm in her voice but refusing to give in to the weird vibe surrounding the table.

'Just a party,' Dominic said with a shrug.

'What party?' Quinn asked, looking around the group. She hadn't heard about any party.

'Paris Hentley,' Chloe, an up-and-coming fashion guru to the local rich and famous, informed her, adding rather waspishly, 'invite only.'

Paris Hentley's family had their holiday home in Surfers Paradise, but their main residence was in London, with high-end stores on every famous shopping strip across the globe. The news sent a jolt of surprise through her. It was while visiting Paris, on her father's yacht, that she'd met Bryson. Why hadn't Paris called to say she was here? They always caught up whenever she was in town.

'She's throwing the party...for Greta,' Chloe said, watching closely for some kind of reaction from Quinn at the announcement. Chloe had never forgiven Quinn for refusing to introduce her to Greta last time she was in town, despite the fact Quinn knew Greta had her own team of personal stylists and would have scoffed at some new kid on the block who only dressed local celebs and clients as Chloe did. She'd been trying to save Chloe from the sting of her cousin's rejection. Looking at her smug face now, she should have just gone ahead and introduced her.

Quinn held the other woman's gaze steadily—as steadily as she could with at least three shots under her belt—and managed a cool smile. 'Oh, was that tonight? I got the invite, but I turned it down. I'd forgotten all about it until now.'

Some of the anticipation left Chloe's eyes and a small pout hovered on her filled lips. Quinn hadn't been raised in a viper pit without learning how to mask vulnerability—something this newcomer to the world of the rich and famous had yet to learn.

The group stood as one, exiting their exclusive table. 'I'm sorry,' Chantelle said, with a smile as close as these people got to something genuine and sympathetic. 'But I'll take notes and get back to you with all the juicy gossip. You know I can't stand Greta, right?' She placed a hand on Quinn's arm.

Yeah, but not enough to stay here with your friend instead, Quinn thought snidely. Still, she couldn't really blame her. No one in their right mind turned down an invitation to a Hentley party.

'Oh, and here,' Chantelle said, pressing a fold of fifty-dollar notes into Quinn's limp hand. 'Of course you can get a loan. Use this to have a good night. Stay and have fun.' Her beaming smile barely masked her pity.

The fact she did it in front of the others was like a slap in the face. Quinn was beyond humiliated as the others swapped a mixture of surprised and knowing raised eyebrows—although not humiliated enough to decline the money. She wasn't stupid.

As she watched the group of people she'd always considered friends leave, laughing and full of excitement for the night ahead, she felt an overwhelming sense of vulnerability wash over her. She was alone. Around her, the music pounded and people danced and laughed; friends out having a good time. *Friends*. She bit the inside of her cheek hard to stop the prickle of tears that threatened. There was no way in hell she was going to mortify herself even more tonight by crying.

Picking up her purse, she stood and sauntered towards the exit, head held high. As she passed a security camera, she stuck up her middle finger, hoping the boss—whoever the hell he was—was watching, before getting into the Uber that arrived and giving him her address. She made one stop at the bottle shop closest to home, heading to where the top shelf wine she favoured was displayed, before giving a dismal sigh and moving further down the aisle to a more reasonably priced section. Once home she scrolled Spotify for a suitably morose playlist and cranked it loud as she drank and tried to wipe the whole horrible night from her memory.

Chapter 8

Quinn walked into the high-end boutique and breathed in the sweet scent of new clothes and expensive leather. Madam Duville was one of her favourite stores.

Instantly, her stress levels eased. This felt like home. The comforting ritual of browsing the racks of designer clothing helped lessen the trauma of the last few days.

A floral sundress caught her eye, and she pulled it out and eyed it critically. The bright pink did certainly lift her spirits. She headed across to the tall, willowy salesperson, dressed immaculately in a body-hugging navy dress, who turned and walked towards her. For an instant, the woman's perfectly made-up face froze, before she quickly fixed a cool smile in place and greeted her. 'Ms Appleton. How lovely to see you again.'

'Hello, Leonie. I'd like to take this one, thanks.'

'Certainly. Will that be cash or card today?'

'Card, thank you,' she said, reaching for her purse automatically before remembering her credit card was useless. *Damn it*. 'Actually, I'll just put this one on the account today. Thanks, Leonie.'

'I'm sorry, Ms Appleton, but the store account has been closed. We can only take a cash or card payment at the moment.'

Normally, the woman would be falling over herself to be helpful. Today, though, Quinn detected a somewhat smug look just underneath her coolly polite expression.

Gran had not wasted any time making sure all access to anything remotely pleasant had been severed.

Two women walked into the shop, and Quinn could hear them behind her, laughing and chatting as they selected several outfits to try on.

'Did you want to try a card?' the saleswoman asked without lowering her voice, and the conversation behind her paused.

'I've changed my mind. I think I'll leave it, thank you.'

'Such a shame. It would have looked lovely with your complexion too, Ms Appleton.'

She stared at the woman, who was not even bothering to try to hide her amusement at Quinn's predicament. *What a cow!* After all the money she'd spent in the store over the years. Narrowing her eyes, Quinn glared at the woman then turned away. *She'd better be ready to find a new job once I get this mess sorted.* She avoided eye contact with the two other women as she left and heard the low murmur of voices pick up as the door shut behind her. She'd never felt more humiliated in her life. The *nerve* of that woman! How *dare* she treat her that way? Was there no loyalty anywhere anymore? A small, angry sob hovered behind her Quinn's clenched lips. A shopping spree had always made her feel better, and now she didn't even have that.

***

A loud buzzing awakened Quinn with a start.

For the last three days, she'd been happy here, alone in her apartment, buried under her covers, drinking and sleeping away the horrible threat of reality that was trying to barge its way in.

Until now, it had been working out just fine.

She answered the phone on her bedside table and heard the concierge apologise for the intrusion, but there was a man waiting to see her and he had an appointment.

'What appointment?' she mumbled, realising her tongue felt as though it were stuck to the top of her mouth.

'It's a Mr Coutts from Coutts, Templeton and Moyer real estate,' the concierge informed her.

'I don't know anything about it. I don't need a real estate agent,' she said crossly. *Seriously?* They woke her up for this?

There was another muffled silence before he came back and announced that there had been multiple messages left and that Jethro Appleton had requested the appointment.

At the mention of her father's name, she sat bolt upright, feeling dizzy at the sudden movement. Quinn tossed the bedcovers back and slid her feet to the floor, hurrying to the front door to find a pile of white envelopes slipped under the door.

Shit.

She bent down and scooped them up, tearing them open to find an appointment had been scheduled for the third of January. *The third?* She frowned, turning her Jaeger-LeCoultre watch band around to check the date. *Today.* How could it already be the third of January? Maybe she really had become a recluse, like in those stories in Facebook articles about the little old ladies who remained holed up in their penthouse apartments for fifty years without being seen by anyone.

'Should I send the gentleman up, Ms Appleton?'

'Ah...' Quinn moved back into the bedroom and stuck the phone between her shoulder and ear as she searched for something to wear, 'just give me ten minutes. I'm running a little late.' She disconnected the line before there could be any further consultation. She grabbed the nearest dress off a hanger, a long sundress in shades of brown and cream, pulling on a bra before tugging the dress over her head and heading to the bathroom to run a brush through her hair and wash her face. There was no time to run the straightener through or do her makeup. The best she could do was run a bit of lipstick across her lips and into her cheeks.

She collected the empty wine bottles and used glasses and put them in the sink, frantically hoping she'd get away with the place not looking like a grown woman had been wallowing in self-pity for days, existing on alcohol and potato chips.

The doorbell rang as she was sliding her feet into a pair of leather sandals, and she did a quick check in the hallway mirror before putting on what she hoped was a calm face.

The man who stood in the doorway was dressed in an expensive suit, but even the designer label couldn't mask the rather prominent beer belly that bulged and hung over his trousers. 'Ms Appleton,' he greeted her with a small incline of his bald head. 'Your father asked me to do a valuation on the property.'

'Why?' she asked bluntly.

'People like to know what the market's doing, how their investment properties stack up,' he said. 'Do you mind if I get started?'

Quinn gave a hesitant frown before inviting him in with an offhand shrug. She didn't seem to have much choice in the matter, but alarm bells were beginning to ring. She took her phone from her pocket and located her father's number, listening as it dialled. Still there was no answer. This was ridiculous. Surely he wasn't ignoring her calls? She left a whispered voice message to call her back immediately, before hanging up and trying her mother's phone.

This time, there was an answer. 'Oh hello, darling.'

'Mum? Where have you been? I've been calling you and Dad for days.'

'After the whole ordeal at Christmas, I just needed some time away. I'm sorry I didn't let you know—I didn't know I was going away myself until the last minute.'

'Did Dad go with you?' Quinn asked, confused.

'Don't be ridiculous, darling. Why would your father come away with me? He's too busy wasting all our money.'

'Mum, there's a real estate guy here valuing the apartment.'

'I don't know anything about that.'

'He said Dad asked him to come.'

'Doesn't surprise me,' she said with an irritated sigh. 'Look, Quinn, sweetheart. Everything's up in the air at the moment. Your gran dropping the hammer like that—well, quite frankly, it's put us all in a very uncomfortable position. We're going to have to make some difficult decisions.'

'Like what?' she asked slowly.

'Like selling off whatever assets your father hasn't already got his hands on.'

'Like the apartment?' Quinn asked, her voice raising in alarm.

'I'm afraid so.'

'But...where am I going to live?'

'I'd offer you your old room back,' her mother said, 'but I don't think we'll have it much longer.'

'Sell the house?' *Oh dear God.*

'Sell, repossess. Tomayto, tomarto,' her mother said blithely.

Quinn froze. 'Are things that bad?'

A deep sign came down the phone line. 'I'm afraid so. Your father's been out of control for a while now...I wasn't aware of how bad it was until we sat down with our accountant. While the company money was coming in, we were able to maintain a relatively normal existence. Now that it's gone, well...there's nothing.'

'So what's going to happen?'

'We need to sell off everything we still own and try to pay off some of the debt.'

'Surely you could sell off the holiday apartment first?'

'Your father sold that last year.'

'He what?'

'Apparently he tried to recover some of his losses, but ended up losing most of that too.'

For the first time in...well, pretty much ever, Quinn heard defeat in her mother's voice. She'd had no idea things had gotten so serious. Sure, over the years she'd overheard her parents arguing about his gambling, but she'd had no idea that he owed so much.

'I'm sorry, darling,' her mother said now, and the genuine sorrow in her tone made Quinn clench the phone tighter in her hand. Everything was falling apart around her.

'I have to go,' Quinn said, feeling numb. 'Bye, Mum.'

She was still sitting on the end of her bed when Mr Coutts came to the doorway. 'I'm finished here now. I'll be going.'

She managed a small nod and was able to hold herself together just long enough to hear the door close behind him before the tears began to fall. She was losing everything, and there wasn't a single thing she could do to stop any of it. She was helpless and, for the first time in her life, she felt lost and completely alone.

***

The apartment went up for sale two days later, and Quinn was given two weeks to pack her belongings and vacate the building.

At first, she'd been in denial, convinced this was all some horrible nightmare she'd wake up from, but eventually she had to accept that it was real and it was happening. She stared at the boxes that had been delivered to her and tried to work up the enthusiasm to start packing. Where would she go? Back home to her parents? For how long? They weren't even sure if they would be keeping their house either. She wasn't going to move all her belongings just to repack everything and end up on the street anyway. She might as well get a head start and find a nice park bench with a view now, beat the rush when the rest of her family found themselves homeless.

She'd started scanning the newspaper for rental properties but soon realised how pointless that was when she rang a few and discovered they wanted a bond of four weeks' rent upfront. What a stupid idea that was. She didn't have four weeks' rent; she didn't even have one week's after she bought food. It was her first hard lesson about the outside world, and it sucked.

A knock on her door brought out a frustrated sigh. What now? There was a rustle followed by the sound of footsteps departing, and Quinn dragged herself to her feet to investigate. An envelope sat on the floor. It wasn't the usual small white one the front desk used. This one was bigger. She almost ignored it; pretended she didn't receive it. She wasn't sure if she could handle any more bad news right now, and somehow, she knew that any message left with the concierge to be delivered wasn't going to be *good* news.

She picked up the envelope and bit the inside of her lip tentatively as she opened it.

Dear Quinn, I will be expecting you for afternoon tea today at 3pm. There are matters we urgently need to discuss. Lionel will be out the front. Gran.

A summons. Maybe not the legal type, but the kind you did not ignore just the same. *Great*. Just what she needed. A visit with Gran to rub salt into the wounds. She wouldn't go. What else could she do to her? She'd already cut off her money and now she was being kicked out of her home. Okay, so technically that part wasn't Gran's doing, but it *was* as a result of what she did. Quinn gave a disheartened sigh. Of course she'd be going. Her short spark of rebellion was abruptly snuffed out. No one disregarded an order from Lady Elizabeth.

True to Gran's word, Quinn found Lionel standing patiently beside the impossibly shiny black Rolls-Royce when she walked out into the sunshine that afternoon. She tried not to recoil and hiss at the brightness like the vampirish recluse she'd become.

'Miss Quinn,' he greeted her in that pompous butler tone he used while on duty.

'Lionel,' she said, playing along.

She slipped into the rear seat and settled in for the ride. 'Any heads up for today's inquest, Lionel?' she asked once they were on the freeway.

'I couldn't say, Miss Quinn,' he answered, keeping his eyes firmly on the road. 'But just remember, your grandmother has your best interests at heart.'

'Somehow, it's not quite coming across that way.'

'Life has a strange way of leading you to the right path. You just have to trust that everything will work out the way it's meant to,' he said, and Quinn hauled her gaze from the window to find his old, knowing eyes watching her from the rear-view mirror.

None of this was Lionel's doing, so she refrained from rolling her eyes at his prophetic words, but finding herself out in the cold with barely a cent to her name didn't make her feel very trusting in pretty much anything at the moment. She dug out her AirPods and plugged them into her ears, selecting a meditation podcast to take her mind off the visit and the hour-long car trip to Gran's. She had no idea what this meeting was about, but she took a small amount of comfort in the fact that at least things couldn't get much worse.

Chapter 9

'Hello, Quinn, thank you for coming,' Gran said as Quinn walked into the drawing room. Last time she'd been in this room, Bryson had informed her family how much he loved her. *Bastard.*

'Gran,' Quinn said calmly—far more calmly than she felt.

'How are you?'

'How *am* I?' Quinn asked, surprised by the question. *Seriously?*

'I imagine it's been an adjustment.'

Oh, just a little. 'I've been fine,' she said coolly.

'Really?' Gran said, tilting her head with a curious smile.

Quinn reminded herself not to flinch under her grandmother's obvious disbelief. If she invited her here to get some kind of satisfaction out of Quinn's suffering, well, she could damn well be disappointed. 'Absolutely.'

'I heard about your father listing the apartment for sale,' Gran said, gesturing for Quinn to take a seat at the settee in front of the coffee table set for afternoon tea. 'Where will you be moving to?'

'I haven't decided yet,' she said, taking a seat and hoping her mouth wasn't watering as she stared at the delicious assortment of cakes and sandwiches before her. She wondered if she could sneak a few of the sandwiches into her handbag to have for later, before realising Gran was still talking and reluctantly brought her thoughts away from planning the swipe of tonight's dinner.

'Have you worked out how you're going to support yourself?'

Irritation rose to the surface once more. Was Gran really that hard up for entertainment around here that she needed to revel in other people's misery?

'Why would you even care?' Quinn found herself snapping. 'You didn't have any concerns about how we'd all support ourselves when you cut everyone off.'

'You're my granddaughter,' she said simply. 'Of course I care. I'm not concerned for any of the others—they know how to take care of themselves. It's you I'm worried about.'

'Well, clearly not too worried, or you wouldn't have frozen my credit cards.'

'Your parents' indulging ways—and mine to a certain degree—haven't been doing you any favours,' she acknowledged gracefully. 'This will be the best thing that ever happened to you, Quinn.'

'Somehow, I'm not quite seeing it that way,' Quinn said dryly.

'I've asked you to come here today because I want to offer you a compromise of sorts.'

Quinn eyed her gran suspiciously. 'What kind of compromise?'

'A job.'

'What job?'

'With the company.'

Quinn's first reaction was to dismiss the idea—after all, she'd never worked in the business before and had no practical experience that could benefit it. But then, the memory of walking into Madam Duville, knowing she could never show her face in there again until she had some money coming in, made her reconsider a hasty no. Maybe she could try working for the business. After all, how hard could it be? She'd have an office like her father, and if her father had done it once, then surely she could too?

'I'm prepared to arrange a position for you,' she said, steepling her fingers together under her chin, 'on the condition that you will not be given any privileges.'

'What's that supposed to mean?'

'It means that you'll work for the company, but no one is to know who you are.'

'I don't understand.'

'I want you to be treated just like any other employee. That means you can't tell anyone you're an Appleton.'

'Can't tell anyone I'm a...' Quinn stared at her grandmother. 'Don't you think that's going to be a bit difficult?' Not to boast or anything, but she was pretty sure most people would recognise her, if not from the local club scene, then definitely from the most unflattering write-ups in the latest gossip magazines.

'I'll take care of that. Fleur, my personal hairdresser, can do something to make you a little less conspicuous,' Gran said, eyeing Quinn's false lashes and hair extensions. 'If you manage to work for six months, and show real effort, I will reinstate your trust fund.'

'Six months?' she gaped.

'Six months,' her gran nodded. 'But if you reveal who you are, or try to use your name to get out of doing something, the deal's off. You have to prove you can earn a living just like anyone else would have to—by working hard and doing your job. This family has lacked a work ethic for far too long.'

'Why am I the one being singled out here?'

'The fact that you see it as some kind of punishment rather than a lifeline tells me you're the one who needs this chance more than anyone else.'

Well, this was bullshit. No one was making Felix or Greta change their identity, like in some warped B-grade spy thriller, and slave away. As far as she knew, Greta had gone back to New York and was still living in her expensive apartment and going to all her exclusive parties. It wasn't fair that her life wasn't being impacted at all by Gran's sudden late-life crisis.

And yet, what choice did Quinn have? She was soon to be homeless and had no idea what she was going to do. She refused to go crawling back to her parents; after all, they were the ones who'd gotten them into this mess in the first place. Not to mention the way things were going, they could very well be homeless soon enough too. Also, she still hadn't been able to get hold of her father, so even if she *wanted* to, she couldn't. No, that wasn't an option. *Damn it.* 'Fine,' she said, closing her eyes in despair. 'I'll work for six months at the company.'

'Lovely. Fleur is expecting you,' she said, handing her a business card with an address on it. 'Lionel will take you.'

It annoyed her even more that Gran knew she had no other choice but to accept. She almost wished she could change her mind and tell Gran where to stick her offer, but she wouldn't. She had no real say in the matter. If she didn't find a job, she would end up having to beg Gran to take her in, and she'd rather live in a cardboard box than do that.

Quinn accepted the card and slipped it into her pocket, standing with as much decorum as she could muster. One thing she had learned was how to not show weakness in front of an enemy.

For an instant, she was sad. How had her gran become the enemy? Sure, she'd never been the kind of gran who'd instigated hide and seek or sat down and played tea parties on the floor, but she'd never been truly cold either. She was just always preoccupied with business and keeping up appearances. Then Quinn remembered the humiliation at Madam Duville, and her heart hardened against any quiver of regret she'd been feeling as she lifted her chin and composed her poker face.

'Take this seriously, Quinn,' Gran said, as Quinn reached the doorway and paused. 'I meant it when I said I was through funding everyone in this family. I would rather sell this business with its reputation intact than let it rot away from the inside. Prove to me this company is worth fighting for.'

The news of Gran selling shocked her, but she pushed that aside to think about later—right now, she was still stinging over being backed into this ridiculous undercover gig her grandmother was forcing on her.

This office of hers had better have a decent view.

Chapter 10

Fleur was not what Quinn had been expecting when she'd pictured her grandmother's personal hairdresser. She'd been expecting someone older, for starters, maybe with an outdated hairdo and wearing sensible shoes. Certainly not the stunning thirtysomething woman with the flame-red hair done up like a nineteen forties pin-up model. She was retro vintage personified.

'You must be Quinn,' Fleur said as she walked inside through a side alley entrance off George Street in the centre of the Brisbane CBD. There was nothing remotely hairdresser-like about the front of the store. In fact, if she hadn't known she was coming here for a makeover, she'd have thought she was in the wrong place. It looked more like a high-end boutique showroom, with clothing sparsely displayed and elegant seating scattered about the room. 'If you follow me, we can get started,' Fleur said, her blood-red lips lifting in a reserved kind of smile.

They walked through a door that led to a corridor with several rooms opening off it, and Fleur stood to one side when she reached the third door down, gesturing for Quinn to enter ahead of her. Inside was a luxurious-looking recliner that faced a mirror, lit up like a backstage Broadway production makeup room.

'Your grandmother has given me a rundown, so all you need to do is sit and relax,' Fleur said, as another woman came in carrying a fabric cape, which she draped over Quinn and fastened around her neck, before exiting wordlessly.

'I have a few ideas,' Quinn started, but was cut off by the tightening of those red lips.

'Your grandmother has already briefed me.'

Briefed her? What the hell did that mean?

Yet another woman wheeled in a trolley, again without a word, and deftly arranged an assortment of scissors and clips, while another brought in premixed bowls of hair colour with brushes.

'What's all this? I haven't chosen a colour or style yet.'

'It's been taken care of,' Fleur insisted.

'I don't care. I'm not going to just sit here and let you do God only knows what to my hair.'

Without comment, Fleur took out a phone from her pocket and pressed a button, her eyes holding Quinn's with a dull, unimpressed expression. 'Yes. She's here.'

She handed the phone over, wiggling it at Quinn impatiently when she didn't immediately take it.

'Hello?' Quinn asked hesitantly.

'Quinn. Fleur has been briefed as to what I require. I trust her judgement impeccably.'

'Gran. I'm not just going to sit here and let some stranger—' she lowered her tone, albeit ineffectively '—do whatever the hell they want to my hair!'

'Our deal was you were not to be Quinn Appleton. Darling, I appreciate this is unorthodox, but for the conditions of this agreement to work, you need a complete makeover. I promise it will be worth it. Think of it as a new beginning. A new you.'

The call disconnected and Quinn numbly handed the phone back to Fleur, who stood waiting with obvious irritation, cocking one sculptured black eyebrow impertinently. 'If you're ready, can I get started?'

Quinn quietly fumed. She had no option but to trust that this woman wasn't going to do something crazy, like shave her head and give her a face tattoo. Although judging by her snooty attitude, Quinn suspected she'd probably like to do just that.

With one last reluctant glance at the trolley of equipment, Quinn leaned back and let out a slow, calming breath. It would be okay. How much could they really change her appearance anyway?

***

Six hours later, Fleur eyed Quinn like a proud artist viewing their masterpiece. While she'd been cut, coloured and bleached to within an inch of her life, another assistant had come in and started on her face. Her eyebrows were waxed, her eyelashes—or rather, implants she'd spent a fortune on— were removed, and a manicure, which resulted in the removal of her beautiful acrylic nails, had all happened in a whirlwind of activity.

It was the most bizarre experience Quinn had ever endured; it was a makeover in reverse...a makeunder, if you will. Instead of enhancing her, they removed everything that made her special and restored her to factory settings.

'Okay. You may look now,' Fleur said graciously, stepping aside to allow Quinn to see herself in the mirror for the first time.

Quinn stared, completely dumfounded. This had to be some kind of trick mirror...that was not her reflection looking back at her. It couldn't be. The woman in the mirror had dark hair—like rich dark chocolate, not the frosty ash-blonde balayage, with highlights, her stylist had spent eons perfecting—and instead of silky long tresses, it was cut into a short, somewhat edgy style.

'You see, I have created a sassy, tousled look, with an undercut at the back and longer, asymmetrical choppy pieces to give the more traditional pixie cut a bit of oomph,' Fleur said, lightly touching her creation as though it were a fragile piece of glasswork.

Her once lush, full eyelashes were now...normal, and her luscious brows, inspired by Emilia Clarke from *Game of Thrones*, had been thinned out and reshaped, giving her eyes a whole different shape.

The face before her was almost unrecognisable.

'Well, I think I managed to fulfil your grandmother's brief,' Fleur said. 'You're a new woman. Congratulations.'

Quinn didn't recall walking from the salon back to the car, or much of the drive back to the Gold Coast for that matter. It had to be shock, she thought later, as she sat on her balcony taking in the ocean far below and watching the waves roll onto the beach. A storm was brewing far out to sea; streaks of lightning were beginning to flash across the sky in the distance.

Quinn had always loved the smell of an approaching summer storm. There was electricity in the air, and the unmistakable feel of change loomed above her like a dark, threatening cloud.

***

As she'd exited the car the afternoon before, Lionel had handed her an envelope and given her a gentle smile. 'I think the new look suits you, Miss Quinn,' he'd said, before giving her a wink and closing the door behind her.

She'd thrown the thick envelope on the table as she'd walked past without bothering to open it. She'd had just about enough of her grandmother's crazy demands for one day, but now, as she sipped her first cup of coffee for the morning, her eyes fell upon the envelope and curiosity got the better of her.

She picked at the flap of the envelope and hooked a finger beneath it, tearing it open, uncaring that it ripped rather untidily down the centre. That would have sent her OCD gran over the edge, she thought with a malicious grin. It was a pity she hadn't been able to open it yesterday during her visit.

Inside she found a Medicare card, an ATM card and paperwork with various identification. She gave a small, incredulous chuckle. The name written on the card was Amy Sinclair. *Amy. Sinclair.* That was her new name. She didn't even get to come up with her own new identity? Typical.

This was past the point of ridiculous, it was now treading closer to insanity. Why was it so important to keep who she was a secret? She did concede that *possibly,* if the chance arose, she *might* have thought about pulling rank on whatever poor assistant was appointed to her, to take over any menial tasks she couldn't be bothered doing...possibly. Okay, so it was more than likely she would palm off boring jobs using the "I'm the granddaughter of the owner" card, but she'd find a way of saying it a bit nicer—after all, she wasn't a complete bitch. But was there really a need for so much cloak-and-dagger stuff? How did Gran even manage to get hold of fake IDs anyway? It was a little disconcerting to think her gran, of all people, might actually have contacts in disreputable, not to mention illegal, practices.

She shoved the envelope into her handbag to deal with later and headed to the bathroom for a shower. She paused in front of the mirror, still stunned by her transformation. She wanted to despise it—she was still indignant about the whole process—but as annoyed as she'd been, she couldn't bring herself to actually hate her new look.

It was weird to see her eyebrows reshaped, and she'd never have chosen this shade of dark brown, almost black, despite it being closer to what her natural hair colour would be—not that she'd seen that since she was about twelve. She'd never had a colour put through her hair without some kind of highlights; she felt a little...naked. But the cut had so much texture and, dare she say it, sassiness, that it didn't look dull and unappealing in the least.

Chapter 11

Quinn realised after a while that she was rather hungry. She hadn't eaten since the day before and suddenly had a craving for sushi from her favourite Japanese restaurant. She always felt better when she had sushi. Her spirits lifted, before quickly sinking back down as she remembered her dismal bank account balance. Quality sushi didn't come cheap around here. Could she get used to having to buy cheaper food court sushi? She gave a small shudder and realised she would have to. Just when she thought her day couldn't get any more depressing.

After a half-hearted glance at the pantry, finding nothing but the bare essentials, Quinn realised she'd need to go shopping. She had never been much of a cook. It wasn't something that she'd grown up around; her parents ate out a lot. Her father *had* mastered the art of the barbecue, although his state-of-the-art outdoor kitchen was more suited to a restaurant than a weekend get-together, and she was fairly sure nothing as simple as a humble sausage had ever graced the hot plate of his pride and joy. He liked to do pork belly and legs of lambs, although Quinn couldn't actually recall the last time her parents had entertained.

She herself preferred to go out and let those with a lot more skill do the work. Besides, who wanted to clean up all that mess?

She decided to go for a walk. The fresh air would do her good, and she hadn't just *walked* for the sake of it in who knew how long. She crossed the road and headed down to the beach, taking off her shoes. The sand was cool under her feet now that the heat of the day had faded, and she wiggled her toes deep into the darker wet sand closer to the water's edge. Quinn took a slow breath and allowed the salty scent to fill her lungs, closing her eyes and tipping her head back. She listened to the soothing rhythm of the waves gently washing up on the shore. Here it was calm and peaceful, but further up, along the points, the waves crashed and smashed against the rocks, the sound more of a roar than the gentle, soothing meditational soundtrack she needed right now.

She took her time walking, inspecting the footprints in the sand made by people who'd walked here earlier. She moved closer to the water, so her feet made deep prints before the next wave rolled in and washed them away, leaving behind a blank canvas. If only life did the same, she thought wistfully. She'd give anything to have a clear slate and start over again, without the memory of Bryson and everything else that had been going so wrong lately.

Her gran wanted to punish them—wake them up and remind them of their obligations—and yet, out of the grandkids, it was only her who was being punished. Greta had her own money and career and didn't need Gran or the company. Even Felix had his own life—despite the fact Appleton's was his major sponsor, the money had already been allocated and he was famous in his own right. He didn't need the company anymore either, he had sponsors lining up to back him.

It was just her. Quinn, the useless one.

It had never occurred to her that being a socialite wasn't an actual career. From the outside, maybe it looked like a life of privilege and excess—and okay, it mostly was—but there was more to it than just going to garden parties and polo matches, high teas and nightclub openings. They raised money for a lot of charities; places that depended on their contributions for funding. Quinn was instrumental in organising the majority of the company-sponsored charities. It was practically a full-time job pulling together a gala or a ball; *and,* she might add, she did it without being paid. She'd always considered her trust fund money to be her payment for all the selfless hours she invested (well, maybe not the nightclub openings, they were her way off blowing off steam and having fun).

And now look at me. No boyfriend, no car, no money. Quinn felt the squeeze of pressure tightening around her chest once more as the gravity of her situation set in. Her parents weren't returning her calls, and she only had a couple hundred dollars left in her account. *A couple hundred!* She couldn't even think what that might pay for. It was maybe a quarter of one shoe…just. She had food to buy; she remembered the bare cupboards at her apartment. She wouldn't be needing petrol, she thought, and gave a rude snort; it was a good thing Gran had taken her car—one less expense. No, it was still too soon to joke about that.

How could her father have given her a gift that he'd known wasn't really hers at all? That was another worry she knew she'd have to face soon. Her father's gambling problem. Everyone knew about it—kind of. Of course, no one ever dared address it as a *gambling problem* though. 'The Appletons don't have problems,' she could hear her mother say pompously.

Maybe if her mother had been paying more attention, instead of leading her own separate life, she'd have seen some of this problem coming and stepped in.

Her parents' relationship had always been unconventional. She'd never thought anything of it until she'd heard her friends talking about how their family dynamics worked. There was a mum and a dad and they shared the same bedroom and talked over the dinner table and went away on holidays together.

Her parents had always had separate bedrooms for as long as she could remember. Up opposite ends of the house. Mum liked nice things and needed lots of wardrobe space; it hadn't seemed like a strange thing to Quinn growing up. After all, *she* had her own room.

After all these years, Quinn couldn't figure out why they just didn't go their separate ways. She'd thought maybe they'd stayed together because of her and Felix, but she and her brother had been old enough to handle a break-up for a long time now and still their parents remained together. She put it down to the fact they were both comfortable with the arrangement. It gave them a safety net, she supposed. It was familiar in a weird kind of way.

One thing Quinn had taken from her parents' marriage was that she was never going to settle for safe or familiar. She wanted excitement and mystery. Although, in hindsight, perhaps not quite as much mystery as Bryson had brought along. *Arsehole.*

She was over the shock and denial, so she figured she was at stage two now—anger. Depression had been mixed in there a bit lately, but Quinn drew the line at the bargaining stage—she didn't ever want to see that creep again. Maybe she'd skipped ahead and already reached stage five, acceptance. *No,* she thought, she liked the anger stage. It was rather liberating and much better than crying.

Her stomach rumbled, and she remembered she'd been on her way to find something to eat.

Her spirits momentarily lifted as she remembered the ID her grandmother had sent. There'd been an ATM card in there. She'd shoved the envelope into her bag earlier, and was glad she had now. She'd check it and see how much was on it. Relief flooded through her. Thank goodness for Gran. She wouldn't go hungry.

She headed up from the beach to climb the stairs back up to the esplanade and found herself mingling with the tourists. She didn't often come this far up to do any grocery shopping—in fact, she really only ventured into a supermarket to buy mixers for her drinks and the occasional dip and biscuits for entertaining if she didn't have it catered.

Stopping at the first ATM she came across, she dug out the card with a triumphant smile, then looked for the instructions on how to activate it. So far, so good, she thought as she keyed in the digits.

Once she'd set her password, it allowed her to select her account and Quinn hit the button, waiting expectantly as the balance came up on the screen before her. Slowly, her smile drooped. *Bal: Nil.*

What. The. Actual. Fu—

'Excuse me? Have you finished with the ATM? I'm in a hurry,' a whiny teenaged voice said from behind her. Quinn turned to find a skinny, acne- speckled boy of about fifteen standing with a girl of similar age, staring at her impatiently.

'Oh, I'm sorry, *you're in a hurry?*' she said, raising her voice. 'Well, pardon me. I'm having a crisis of my own right now, kid, so no, I'm not finished with the ATM. In fact, I might be here all night, so why don't you bugger off and find another one to use.'

The boy shrank back in alarm, but the girl, with her ripped jeans, crop top and nose piercing, glared at her, before sticking up her middle finger and dragging her boyfriend away.

Shit, shit, shit, shit, shit. Goddamn it, Gran! Thanks for nothing, she snarled under her breath. What was the point of giving her a debit card if there was nothing on the stupid thing?

Quinn walked into the supermarket and scanned the refrigerated shelves for something simple to have for dinner. She'd lost her appetite for sushi and moved on to the ready-to-eat meal section, but everything looked as inviting as the cardboard boxes they came in.

'Don't try the bolognaise, even my dog wouldn't eat it. The carbonara isn't too bad though.'

Quinn glanced sideways in the direction of the deep voice and looked its owner briefly up and down. He was tall, lean and tanned, complete with the stereotypical longish dirty-blond-brown hair of a surfer. He wore board shorts and a pair of Surfer Joe thongs, the wide kind designed for walking through sand easier. She sent him a brief, awkward kind of smile, before hesitantly reaching for the frozen meal-for-one box of carbonara.

'Do you live around here? I feel like I know you from somewhere?' he said, watching her place the box in her basket.

'Not too far from here.'

He nodded, as though confirming something to himself. She didn't know him from a bar of soap. 'I've probably seen you at the beach.'

'Maybe,' she agreed offhandedly, before making to move around him.

'I'm Hugo,' he said, stepping back in front of her.

'I'm *not interested*,' she replied firmly, stepping around him once more.

'Ouch. Okay. I thought saving you from having to eat that bolognaise might have at least got me an introduction.' He grinned, falling into step beside her.

Was this guy serious? 'Look, maybe this is your weekly pick-up place or something, but I'm really only here to buy dinner, not find a date.'

'Hey, I hate to break it to you, but I wasn't trying to pick you up. It's called being friendly.'

'Oh. Okay,' she said, rolling her eyes.

His bemused chuckle annoyed her. 'Wow. The jaded kind,' he murmured.

'I'm not jaded. For your information, I'm usually very nice. I just don't appreciate being hit on in the supermarket.'

'Again with the jumping to conclusions. Okay, sorry,' he said, his hands held up in front of him in surrender. 'Obviously I'm rusty at this whole social interacting thing. I'm sorry.'

Quinn sighed. 'Look, I'm sure you're a nice guy,' she said, then gave his tattooed arms a cursory glance and wondered if *nice guy* was the correct description to use here. She gave herself a mental shake to get back on track. 'The fact is, I've had a particularly crap day. I'm hungry and I'm tired and I'm fairly sure I'm still hungover, not to mention I'm broke and all I can afford is this pathetic excuse for a carbonara when, usually, I'd just walk down to the Italian place and buy the real thing, only now I can't, so I'm stuck with this.' Her eyes were beginning to sting once more. 'So you'll have to excuse me if I don't feel very interested in interacting with anyone at the moment—socially or otherwise.' Mortification coursed through her as the tears began to fall without her consent.

'Hey,' he said, stopping to look at her. 'Whoa. I'm sorry, I didn't mean to upset you.'

Quinn wiped her eyes and gave a frustrated groan as she looked up at his concerned face. 'You didn't. I'm just having a bad day.'

'Yeah, well, the last thing you needed was some dickhead making it worse. Look, you're right—that stuff tastes like shit too,' he said, nodding down at her basket. 'Let me shout you some real carbonara. Seriously, there's no ulterior motive. I'm not hitting on you.' He turned his palms upwards. 'I just can't stand seeing women cry and I hate that I was the one who did it.'

'No, you weren't. I told you, I'm just having...'

'A bad day, yeah, I know. But I'm going to feel bad for the rest of the night if you don't let me make sure you're okay. Come on,' he urged, lowering his voice in a cajoling way, 'I'm really fangin' for some Italian now, and I don't want to sit at a table all by myself. Please?'

She knew the correct answer was no. She didn't know this guy, and, okay, she wasn't exactly a stranger to the odd one-night stand in the past, but the combination of hunger, fatigue and, quite frankly, zero willpower, suddenly made the offer of sitting at a restaurant table and eating *real, honest-to-God Italian carbs* completely irresistible.

'Yes?' he prompted with hopeful eyes.

'Okay,' she said.

'Great. Put this back,' he said, diving into her basket to return the package to the freezer. 'Did you need anything else?' he asked, then took the basket from her limp hand when she shook her head. 'Awesome. Then let's go. I know a great little Italian place.'

Quinn found herself following obediently behind this tall, board-short-clad stranger, out of the fluorescent-lit supermarket and into the balmy early evening. The sun had not long gone down, and lights shone from shop windows that lined the footpath.

Delicious smells floated through the air, escaping from the multitude of restaurants nearby, mixing to create a heady scent of multicultural feasts. They passed by Greek, Mexican, Japanese and seafood places, and Quinn's stomach rumbled embarrassingly loudly.

She found herself distracted by the man beside her and wondered why she'd agreed to this impromptu dinner date. He could be a serial killer, for all she knew. But there was something about him that put her at ease (though maybe that's what made serial killers so good at their work). But they were going to a crowded restaurant—surely it was safe to assume that, even if he was some psycho, he wouldn't kill her in public? She just wouldn't go home with him and she'd be fine.

Her stomach growled again and she knew that, potential murderer or not, there was no way in hell she was going back to buy a supermarket frozen meal tonight.

Chapter 12

They walked in silence, but it wasn't awkward. All around them was chatter and music and conversations coming from the seated diners on the footpaths, so there was no need to make small talk, and the restaurant he had in mind was only a short stroll from the supermarket. They walked inside and instantly he was greeted by a very Italian-looking man, who opened his arms wide and smiled. 'My old friend, welcome,' he said in a singsong accent.

'G'day, George, any chance of a table without a booking?'

'For you, always, my friend. Come this way,' he said, gesturing extravagantly and leading the way to the rear of the restaurant.

Quinn stopped abruptly as she looked around at the décor, then down at her faded jeans and loose-fitting off-the-shoulder top. It had a coffee stain where she'd spilled some earlier, and her sandshoes were hardly fine dining attire.

'What's wrong?' he asked, looking concerned.

'I'm not dressed for this kind of place,' she murmured under her breath.

'Nah, you look fine. George isn't hung up on appearances,' he assured her as they walked past a table where a woman was wearing a pair of Jimmy Choos, dark blush suede mules with a crystal and pearl strap, which cost a cool fifteen hundred bucks. If Quinn knew anything, she knew her shoes. She had two pairs, in caramel and red, at home.

She was relieved when their host seated them at a corner table somewhat away from the other diners. This guy might think his friend didn't care about a dress code, but Quinn suspected otherwise. Clearly, these men must have a strong friendship if he hadn't been automatically booted out of the place for dressing in a T-shirt and board shorts.

'George, can we get two of the carbonaras please and a bottle of...' He glanced across at Quinn for a wine suggestion, but she quickly shook her head. *Oh God no.* She couldn't stomach any more wine just yet. 'Ah, make that a beer and a Moscow mule, but hold the Moscow,' he said with a wink. George nodded and walked away. 'I think you'll like it,' he said when she asked what a Moscow mule was. 'It usually has vodka, ginger beer, lime juice, a slice of lime and mint. I figured it might be good on a post-hangover stomach...without the vodka, of course.'

It did sound pretty good, she had to admit. The ginger might just do the trick.

'I haven't been here before,' she said, wondering why she hadn't. It was certainly swanky enough, although she couldn't recall noticing it. Then again, it was a distance from where she usually dined when she ate local. She had her favourite places and usually stuck to them.

'It's only fairly new. George is an old family friend. He's just started the place up.'

Well, that explains a lot. Family friends would allow you to get away with stuff normal people wouldn't. Still, why would this guy put his friend in such an awkward position? Surely, he could tell this was not the sort of place you just dropped in to for a meal on your way home from the beach?

She took a moment to look at him from across the table. Now that there was a little more distance between them, she felt a lot less crowded.

He had a broad face and a strong-looking chin, although he wasn't what she'd call attractive, at least not in the fashionable sense of the word. He was too rough around the edges to be the kind of playboy attractive she usually found herself drawn to. His eyebrows had that manly kind of unkempt look, not the salon-styled kind most men in her circle of friends had. The lower portion of his face was covered in a dark five o'clock shadow, which looked a little closer to maybe seven o'clock, like he'd simply let it grow a little too long and slightly uneven, or had maybe forgotten to shave for a few days, instead of grooming it that way intentionally, as was currently the trend.

He had nice eyes though. They were blue, a deep denim blue, the way the ocean looked on a clear sunny day. And his mouth was...she paused, feeling the oddest kind of reaction as she stared at his lips. They weren't full, but they weren't thin either—they were *strong.* Could lips be strong? She was drawn to his mouth for some inexplicable reason. It seemed the perfect way to describe them.

Somehow, she knew that being kissed by those lips would never be some fleeting, unmemorable event. They'd be forceful yet not rough. Demanding but never cruel. They were lips that knew how to kiss.

Suddenly remembering where they were, Quinn ripped her somewhat gawking gaze away and, to her horror, found him watching her rather intently, his eyes slightly hooded, as though enjoying the fact she'd just been ogling him from across the table like some sex-crazed weirdo.

She was *not* sex-crazed, she reminded herself firmly. She was *so off sex* it wasn't funny. Bryson's cold dismissal still stung, and the reminder of the two-faced creep was like a bucket of cold water over her head—shocking her from her moment of...whatever the hell that just was.

This was a mistake.

'Your carbonara is ready.' George miraculously appeared with two huge bowls piled high with the devilishly creamy pasta.

Quinn's tastebuds went into overdrive, and she prayed she wasn't actually drooling as she stared at the enormous meal before her.

'Oh my God, this smells amazing,' she whispered reverently.

'Wait until you taste it,' he said.

And he hadn't exaggerated. *Oh. My. Effing. God.* She closed her eyes and allowed the buttery, garlicky, creamy flavour to move across her tongue. It was *so good.* A tiny moan escaped from her between forkfuls and she looked up when she felt his eyes glued to her mouth.

'What?' she asked nervously, wiping at her mouth, fearing she had sauce all over her face. 'Did I get it all?'

'No, I mean, you didn't have anything on there,' he said, clearing his throat abruptly. 'I just—' he shifted in his seat a little '—ah, haven't seen anyone enjoy food as much as that before.'

'Oh. I guess I was a lot hungrier than I thought. Sorry.' *Great.* Not only was she dressed like a slob, but here she was, acting like some starving prisoner eating their last meal in front of...*crap*. She couldn't remember what he said his name was.

'No, don't apologise,' he said quickly. 'It's not often dates...allow themselves to enjoy a meal.'

'Dates?' she asked, making an attempt to restrain herself from scoffing the remainder of her meal. 'Is that what this is?'

'I asked you out to dinner, and you said yes, so...' he said, leaving the sentence hanging.

'This is *not* a date.'

'Okay, if you say so.'

'I do,' she said firmly. 'Dating is the last thing I want to be doing right now.'

'So, what happened to make your day so bad?'

Quinn gave an unamused grunt. 'It's more like a bad few weeks.'

'Sometimes talking about it helps put things into perspective,' he suggested helpfully as he continued eating.

'You wouldn't believe it if I told you. My life is a total disaster at the moment.'

'Try me,' he said.

Quinn was tempted, just to see what a normal person's reaction would be to the shitshow her life had become, but then she remembered her gran's threat. What if this guy was sent by Gran to test her? Maybe she was being paranoid—okay, it was likely that she was being more than paranoid—but could she really risk losing her only chance at gaining back her inheritance? Gran's threat of selling the company scared her more than she cared to admit. If she sold, then the money would truly be gone, or at least until Gran died, and who knew how long that could be? She hated thinking that clinically; she didn't hate her gran. She'd always loved her, but she'd known from an early age that maternal affection was not abundant in their family. Elizabeth Appleton was a hard-nosed businesswoman, and she ran her family like the commander of a ship.

'It's just my family,' she finally said. Surely, she could vent a little to a stranger without risk of being kicked to the gutter. *Harry?* she thought absently as she tried to remember his name. *No. That's not it.*

'Oh. I see. Enough said.' He nodded sympathetically. 'I had a falling out with mine a few years ago when I left school and decided to wander the world for a while.'

'Really? What did you do? Where did you go?'

'All over the place. I'd been studying business at uni—my dad wanted me to join the family business. He's an electrician.'

'You didn't want to be an electrician, I take it?'

'Nope, which is why the old man suggested getting a business degree. My brothers are both electricians and work for Dad and it was always his dream to expand the business. He figured if I wasn't going to learn the trade, I could at least get a degree in business so I could run the business as it grew.'

Maybe they weren't so different after all.

'I woke up one day and just saw my whole life mapped out before me. I'd only just discovered surfing when I moved here to go to uni. I'd lived my whole life in a small town out west and, all of a sudden, I discovered the ocean. I took up surfing and that was the end of life as I knew it. I couldn't go back home and give up surfing, so I left university and decided to backpack and surf around the globe for a couple of years. My parents stopped talking to me for about twelve months.'

'Wow. So what did you do for money? How did you fund your travels?'

'I worked,' he said simply. 'I followed the surf and picked up whatever work I could find. Sometimes I did bar work, other times I picked fruit or washed dishes. I taught surfing for a while in Hawaii, and volunteered teaching English in Bali and India.'

Quinn felt a little light-headed at the thought of roaming the world without any idea where your next meal or pay check would be coming from. But then again, if this guy had done it, maybe she'd be okay after all? She wondered if she could wash dishes somewhere, and almost ruled the idea out because, hello? Her nails. But then she glanced down at her ugly, soft, nubby excuses for fingernails exposed after Fleur's brutal overhaul the day before and realised that would no longer be an issue.

'I guess what I was trying to say is, parents might lose their shit now and again over the stupid stuff we pull, but they always forgive us eventually. Maybe just send them a text and say hi. You'll see, it'll break the ice and they'll be back to normal in no time.'

Quinn gave a half-hearted smile at his optimism. *Back to normal* would never be an option for her family. Even if Gran did reinstate her father's inheritance along with her own, the debts that had apparently forced his hand to sell everything they owned would mean life as they once knew it would never be the same again.

But maybe he was right about one thing—reaching out to her parents might at least stop her feeling as though she was completely alone. As furious as she was at them both for not telling her how bad things were, they were still her parents, and maybe together they could work out a plan to make things better. If nothing else, she might at least have a place to stay until she could find something of her own.

After their meal, Quinn walked outside and waited as her knight in shining boardies tucked his wallet into his back pocket and stepped out onto the footpath beside her. Her plan to sneak a glance at his credit card to find out his name failed. It was too dark inside to see.

'I'm sorry...this is a bit embarrassing, but I don't remember your name. I know you mentioned it earlier, but I honestly wasn't paying much attention.'

'Hugo,' he said with a charming smile. 'In all fairness, I had just made you cry, and my name was probably the last thing you cared about.' He grinned. 'And yours?' he prompted.

'Oh, sorry,' she said, shaking her head, 'Qu—' She paused, remembering the deal with the devil she'd made. Crap, what was the stupid name on the cards she'd looked at earlier? 'Er, just a moment.' She dug through her bag and slid out the card she'd tried in the ATM. 'Amy Sinclair,' she said, summoning a bright smile, as though saying her new name was completely normal.

'Oh, okay. I see.'

'What?'

'The old "give a fake name so the strange guy won't track you down on social media and stalk you" trick.'

'Fake name?' she said, forcing a chuckle that she hoped sounded off the cuff. 'No, that's my name. Plain old boring Amy Sinclair. I just had a terrible feeling I'd left my ATM card in the machine earlier and had to check.' She shrugged. 'How annoying would that be, to find yourself without any money, ha,' she added, now feeling like she should stop talking before she did sound like a crazy person.

'Oh. Yeah, I hate when that happens. Like trying to remember if you turned the oven off when you go away for the weekend,' he said.

'Yeah. Totally,' she agreed faintly. *Forget to turn the oven off?* She didn't even know where hers switched *on*.

'Well, I better let you go, I guess,' he said, looking down at his feet.

'Yeah, I should get home.'

'I can walk you, if you like?'

'Ah, no thanks. I'll be fine. I actually still need to do some groceries before I head back. But thanks anyway.'

'Well, can I get your number? What if we don't bump into each other again?' he asked.

'Then it wasn't meant to be,' she blurted, instantly feeling stupid. God, the last thing she needed was to start something with a guy when she was about to become homeless.

'So, if we do see each other again, it's destiny, is that what you're saying?' He grinned, seemingly unwilling to let her shrug him off too easily.

'Yeah, sure,' she agreed. *Corny, but whatever floats your boat, bud.* There'd be no chance he'd be bumping into her around here for much longer. Soon she'd be out on her ear and who knew where she'd end up.

'Well, I guess I'll see you around.'

'Bye.' She waved and turned away, unsure why she suddenly felt so awkward. He was just a guy, and she brushed off men all the time, but somehow this guy was...different. Silently, she scoffed. *Yeah, right*. Had she learned nothing from recent events? Men were all the same. She'd completely missed Bryson's agenda, and she'd thought *he'd* been in love with her. Life was way too complicated to add some guy into the mix at the moment.

Chapter 13

Later, as Quinn came out of the supermarket after buying enough basics to get her through the next couple of days, her gaze fell on a noticeboard. Pinned among the brightly coloured paper signs for lost cats and missing garden gnomes was a purple scrap of paper that looked as though it had been torn out of a notebook; Wanted: flatmate to share costs was scribbled across it, along with a phone number.

She knew she couldn't put off working out her accommodation situation much longer, but the thought of going from her penthouse to a shared flat was such a huge leap that she felt ill thinking about it. Deciding she needed to suck it up, she ripped the note from the board and shoved it in her pocket. She'd deal with it, but not just yet. She wanted to savour her full belly and the nice non-date she'd just had before she dealt with reality.

***

Quinn checked the address once more on the note in her hand and eyed the building before her dubiously. *This can't be the right place.*

The old two-storey house seemed to lean slightly sideways. Maybe it was her imagination; it was hard to tell. An overgrown bush seemed to be the only thing holding it up. The white paint had been peeling for decades by the looks of it. Bare boards underneath were pretty much all exposed, with only the occasional panel of white to be seen.

On either side of the old house stood huge new apartment blocks, making it look out of place. Clearly, whoever owned the land had been resisting property developers for quite some time; this parcel of land would be worth a small fortune in the current market. It sat on prime real estate, being close to the beach, and there was something about the way it struggled to stand upright, in the shadows of these resort-like buildings next door, that screamed rebellion.

Quinn took a fortifying breath, set her shoulders, and headed for a set of rickety steps that went up the side of the house to a door. From inside, reggae music played and chimes tinkled in the gentle breeze through an open window.

Quinn tapped on the door and waited.

When there was no answer, she tried again, knocking harder. This time, after a few moments, she heard the shuffle of footsteps on the other side of the door seconds before it opened, and she came face to face with a man in his early twenties with frizzy black hair.

'Hi. I called earlier about renting a room?'

'Ah! You must be Amy,' he said in a heavy Jamaican accent, flashing a wide, white smile.

'Yes. That's me,' she said cheerily.

'Come in, come in,' he said, stepping back and waving a hand wide to allow her to pass by.

Quinn looked around the small lounge room, taking in the mismatched, mustard-coloured corduroy lounge chair and the green shag-pile carpet. A tall lamp sat in the corner, its gaudy, faded floral shade tilted unevenly, missing chunks of its gold fringe. There was a semi-familiar smell in the air, and she spotted a plastic bottle with a suspicious piece of hose sticking out the side sitting on the coffee table.

'I'm Atticus. Take a seat,' he said, before turning to yell through a doorway, 'Vivian! Get up here.' He turned back and smiled once more. 'Vivian's an artist. She spends most of her time downstairs in her studio.'

Quinn gave a weak smile in return. She was slightly distracted by his accent and kept picturing Sebastian, the red Jamaican crab from *The Little Mermaid,* which she used to be obsessed with as a kid. *Ar-ee-elle!*

A young woman trudged up the staircase just outside the lounge room.

'This is Amy,' Atticus said. 'She's come about the room.'

Vivian stopped at the top of the staircase, where she rested one paint-splattered arm along the top of the railing. 'Hi,' she said, smiling. She had brown dreadlocked hair that hung to her shoulders, tied with woven bits of fabric, and wore a baggy pair of overalls, also covered in paint. 'Have you seen the room yet?' she asked, glancing at Atticus.

'I was just about to show her. Come this way,' he said, waving her forward.

Quinn followed him down a narrow, pale green hallway and opened a door. Inside there was a double bed and an old dark timber wardrobe that looked like it had been left over from *The Lion, the Witch and the Wardrobe* set. The floorboards were bare, as though someone had decided to renovate at one stage and removed the carpet but hadn't gotten any further. A round, faded pink rug did its best to cover the worst of it.

It was depressing. She hated it. But she had no other option. Turning to the two expectant faces in the doorway, she tried for a smile, but felt it was little more than a grimace. 'I'll take it,' she said.

'Yay!' Vivian smiled, clapping her hands. 'Another female in the house! I'm always getting outvoted on movie night by the boys.'

'Boys?' she asked, realising she'd only suspected there would be the three of them living here.

'There's only ever been male roommates in this place,' she said, rolling her eyes. 'There's two bedrooms up here and two downstairs. Craig, had to move out in a bit of a hurry a few days ago, so you'll have this whole floor to yourself until we manage to rent out his old room.'

'There's another room?' she asked, hope flaring instantly. Maybe she wouldn't have to be in this one after all.

'Yeah, but you wouldn't want that one. It's only got a single bed, and it's smaller than this one,' Vivian said with a grimace. 'Feel free to repaint or fix it up if you like. The landlord's pretty cool with everything.'

Damn it. She was stuck with the crap room. They took her out to the kitchen and showed her *her* shelf, where she'd be able to keep *her* food in the fridge and *her* space in the pantry, and when Quinn asked about rent in advance, they simply waved her away. 'Just pay when you move in.'

'Really?'

'Sure. We're pretty casual around here.' Vivian shrugged, then stretched her hands over her head, like some exotic-looking cat. 'So I'll see you when you move in, then.' She waved and headed back towards the staircase.

'So that's it? You don't need references?' Quinn asked Atticus.

'Nah, you got an honest face.' He chuckled, and Quinn once more had to restrain herself from asking him if he could please sing a line from "Under the Sea". She was a little bit smitten with Atticus and his accent.

'Well, okay then. Thanks. I guess I'll start moving my stuff in over the weekend?'

'That'd be fine, man. We'll be around.'

She left the same way she'd come in, down the rickety stairs and across the dry, unkempt grass onto the footpath. She sighed at what would be her new reality. No more manicured lawns and tropical gardens. No pool or gym room. No penthouse apartment all to herself.

Surely this was what hell was like. If in hell you still had to come up with two weeks' rent in advance by the weekend.

***

'Amy!' She heard a voice call out but didn't bother to turn around until she heard it again and suddenly remembered that *she* was Amy. She swivelled to see Hugo walking towards her, carrying a surfboard under one arm and wearing a wetsuit, unzipped to the waist. Quinn found her gaze following the light dusting of hair across his chest that travelled down towards his belly button before disappearing below the zip fastening, which was almost level with his hips.

'Oh. Hi,' she stammered, feeling a little flustered as she realised she'd, once again, been blatantly ogling the man, and dragged her gaze back up to eye level.

'I was calling out for ages,' he said, coming to a stop. 'I was worried it wasn't you.'

'Sorry, I was off in my own little world, I guess.'

'So it must be destiny, then?'

'Sorry?' she asked with a frown.

'Last time we were together, you said destiny would decide…and here we are,' he said, spreading his free arm out and planting himself firmly in front of her.

'I guess it must be,' she said weakly, and couldn't help but notice how blue his eyes were. He looked like the quintessential surfer with his sun-bleached shaggy hair, slightly longer at the back than his collar, and tanned skin.

'You know, I almost didn't come down for a surf, but changed my mind,' he said, lifting an eyebrow. 'If that doesn't scream destiny, then I don't know what does.'

'Do you often surf in the middle of the day?'

'Nope.' He grinned. 'But today I just needed to get out of the office.'

'You must have a very understanding boss,' she said, as she turned and they headed down the steps towards the beach.

'Yeah, he's pretty good about stuff like that.' He waited while she slipped off her sandals, holding out an arm for her to balance on.

'Thanks,' she muttered as she straightened, hooking her fingers through her sandals and enjoying the warm, soft sand between her toes.

She'd been heading back along the esplanade, planning to walk along the beach below, hoping the ocean would do the trick and lift her spirits, and they did. At least she'd managed to sort out housing for the moment, and she would still be close enough to walk to the beach.

'So, what have you been up to today?'

'House hunting—well, share house hunting,' she amended with a small grimace.

'Oh yeah? Did you have any luck?'

'Yeah. I found a place. It's nothing fancy, but beggars can't be choosers,' she said, forcing a smile. Damn it, it was hard work trying to be upbeat. She wasn't even sure why she felt a need to be—usually she wouldn't if she didn't feel like it—but somehow, being around this guy made her feel like she should try harder. Which was confusing—that had never happened before.

'Everyone has to start somewhere, right?'

'Yeah, I guess.' They'd reached the end of the dry sand and stood where the tide had begun to recede, leaving a wet strip of sand just before the water's edge. 'Well, it was good to see you again. I better let you get to your surf.'

'It's a pretty crap time to be surfing anyway—hardly any swell at all, really.'

'So why did you bother coming down then?'

'Sometimes I just need to be out there, you know?' he said, looking from the horizon back down to her.

She didn't really. She'd never been a fan of the deeper water. Once she'd gone a bit too far out on a boogie board with a group of friends and had drifted away from the group. She could still recall how the laughter and chatter had suddenly become muted, and the steady thump of waves hitting the underside of her board was all she could hear as she was dragged out further and further by a rip. Even now, the panic of that moment made her heart race. It had been both the single most humiliating and grateful moment of her life when the surf lifeguard had arrived next to her on a jet ski and brought her back in to safety. That was the last time she'd ever gone deeper than her knees into the ocean.

'Sometimes I like to just paddle out when it's flat and take it all in. There's a peace out there that's like nowhere else.'

Had she not experienced her own terrifying encounter with the ocean, she may have allowed his calm, soothing words to sweep her away. 'It was good to see you, Hugo,' she said, smiling gently.

'I'd like to see you again,' he said simply, his words stopping her from turning away.

'When?' she asked. There was no point in fighting it. Her life was a mess—she had no idea what she was doing, but this man seemed to make things feel a little less shitty when she was around him, so why the hell not? She wasn't going to do anything stupid, like fall in love with him.

'Tomorrow. Give me your address and I'll pick you up.'

Yeah, nah, that wasn't going to work. 'I'm moving house over the next few days. I'll just meet you somewhere.'

'I can give you a hand, if you like?'

'Thanks, but I'll be fine.' There wasn't any easy way to explain why she'd be moving from a penthouse apartment to a run-down share house—at least, not without launching into a very long, drawn-out story, which she was not about to do.

'Okay, well. I'll meet you for dinner. Back at George's at seven?'

Awesome. This time, she'd be able to dress a little more appropriately. 'Okay. I'll see you there.'

She could feel his eyes on her as she headed back up the beach and away from him, and she wasn't going to lie, it gave her a morale boost. For the first time since Bryson had dumped her, she felt a little like her old self again.

Whether that was a good thing or not, she supposed she'd have to find out.

Chapter 14

All the furniture was being sold with the apartment, and she almost cried at the thought of leaving her imported Swedish mattress and custom designed dining suite. An image of her new sparse bedroom with its charity store bed and ugly old wardrobe flashed through her mind, and she once again felt herself approaching the edge of that deep dark pit that loomed before her. Sometimes lately, she felt as though she should just take that step and plunge herself into the darkness. She didn't know where it would end, or even if it *would* end. Maybe she'd just fall forever. Faced with this new life, she wasn't altogether sure that it might not be the better option right now.

Reaching for another sheet of newspaper to wrap her jewellery and keepsakes in, she stopped, her mouth dropping open at the photo staring back at her. It was Bryson, grinning at the camera like the proverbial cat who stole the cream. She unfolded the paper and felt the colour drain from her face as the person his arm was wrapped around was revealed. Greta.

Millionaire heiress turns her back on family fortune and marries her Prince Charming.

Quinn threw the newspaper on the floor and stood up, pacing, placing her quivering fingers across her lips. *They got married?* It didn't make any sense. Why? She knew Greta had jumped at the chance to rub it in at Christmas lunch, but to *marry* him? A surge of fury and hurt exploded inside her chest. How could Greta *do* such a hurtful thing?

***

Quinn listened to the dial tone and relief rushed through her at the sound of her uncle's familiar, if not grumpy, voice on the other end of the line.

'Have you seen the paper?' Quinn demanded without greeting.

'What time is it?' Tobias muttered, followed by rustling and a spluttered expletive. 'What the hell are you calling at this hour for?'

'It's barely lunchtime,' she said, checking her watch.

'Not over here, it isn't,' he snapped.

'Over where?'

'I'm in London. With Claude.'

'London?' Had *everyone* abandoned her?

'Well, it's not like there was anything left back home for me, was there?'

She supposed he had a point, but it still felt like they'd all fled and she was the only one left to deal with the fallout.

'Do you know where Dad is?' she asked, suddenly feeling more inclined to believe some of those rumours after all.

'No. I haven't spoken to anyone since the great Christmas fiasco. What's got you so worked up that you've woken your dear old uncle up at this ungodly hour?'

'Greta and Bryson got married,' she said. Her voice, much to her shame, began to quiver.

'Oh, sweet pea.' Her uncle's tone lost its earlier sarcasm and her throat tightened as unexpected emotion forced its way out. 'I'm truly sorry.'

'I mean, I know she hates me...but how could she stoop that low?'

'Because she's inherited her dear mother's cold dead heart. I know you don't want to hear this right now, but you really are better off without that little creep. He's an opportunist and thinks he's climbed his way to the top with Greta. But you and I both know she's going to eat that kid alive, then spit him out once he's served whatever purpose she wants him for. He'll soon be wishing he'd never laid eyes on her.'

She knew Tobias was right and, briefly, the thought of Bryson suffering cheered her up a little. But the feeling faded just as fast as it came and she was once more left with the knowledge that everyone she knew would know about how her beautiful, rich cousin had stolen her boyfriend from her, while Quinn was left here, penniless, humiliated and pathetic.

'Look, kiddo, I know you must be going through hell right now, but your father always manages to land on his feet. This thing will blow over. He'll get back into Mummy's good books and everything will go back to normal. She always did think the sun shone out of his arse. She won't be able to turn her back on her precious Jethro for long,' he spat bitterly.

'I don't know, Tobias. She seems pretty determined.'

'Hang in there, kid. You'll see. Everything's going to be fine. We all just have to ride out the storm. On the upside, I can now do whatever the hell I like, and I personally have never been happier.'

'I'm glad,' she said, managing a small smile. 'Give my love to Claude,' she added before disconnecting the call. Usually, she'd believe her uncle in matters of anything family related—he'd been playing the game a lot longer than she had—but this time it felt different. Somehow, she couldn't see how her father was going to ever get back everything they'd lost. It was just too much.

She tried his number again and listened to it ring out before the option to leave a message played. *Where the hell are you, Dad?*

***

The very last thing she felt like doing tonight was going out to dinner, but faced with an empty fridge and a lack of care factor to work up the enthusiasm to cook something, she decided it was worthwhile making the effort.

When she arrived at the restaurant, Hugo was already there, and he stood to greet her when she approached the table.

'Wow, you look...stunning,' he said, his eyes slowly roaming her from head to toe. Had anyone else done it, she'd have felt violated, but Hugo made it feel as though he were almost drinking her in, appreciating every minute detail about her. As ridiculous as it sounded, somehow, he just made her feel...alive. She was glad she'd decided on her skinny jeans, gold top and Jimmy Choo heels.

He looked different tonight. There were no board shorts or wetsuits; tonight, he wore a white button-up shirt, the top two buttons left undone to reveal a tanned chest beneath, and a pair of dressy, fitted cargo pants.

He looked a little less like a beach bum, and yet she could tell smart casual would probably be the only other kind of clothing the man had in his wardrobe.

'So let me get this straight,' Quinn said after they'd finished their first wine and she'd asked about his job. 'The company you work for does volunteer work in third world countries?'

For a moment, she thought she saw him hesitate before answering, 'Yep. We donate money, time and staff to projects worldwide.'

'What kind of projects?'

'All kinds. We help build houses, sometimes schools in communities in the Philippines and Africa. We do surf schools and help with clean water strategies, assisting in digging wells, building dams and installing pipes to transport water to isolated communities. There are lots of ways we try to assist.'

'And the staff are okay with this? Donating their time?'

'It's one of the things that makes the company special. We're a philanthropist-based organisation.'

'So you joined the company because of what they do?' she asked slowly.

For a minute, he seemed to study her before a slow smile touched his lips. '*I* started the company,' he said. 'Hugo Cannon is *my* business.'

Hugo *Cannon?* Quinn's mouth opened slightly. *He* owned Hugo Cannon? The largest surfing chain in the country? He was *that* Hugo?

'I thought you might have figured it out,' he said with a small chuckle as she continued to stare at him, completely shocked by the revelation.

'No. I had no idea,' she said, feeling more than a little bit stupid that she hadn't realised earlier.

A passing waitress had to stop abruptly when a customer pushed their chair back to stand and almost bumped into her. The tray she was carrying wobbled, and the drinks toppled, one spilling next to Hugo, splashing wine on his leg as it landed on the floor.

'Oh my God, I'm so sorry,' the girl gasped, mortified.

'It's all good,' Hugo told her, dropping to one knee to help pick up the fallen glass and clean up.

'No. Please, I can clean it up,' she said, reaching for the glass.

Another older waitress came over, fussing about and snapping at the younger woman, but Hugo intervened quickly, smoothing over the incident and explaining what had happened in defence of the other waitress.

Quinn stared on in silence, watching him take control of the situation without fuss or vitriol. She'd seen her aunt have a waitress fired for spilling a drink on her, and often among her friend group, clumsy waitstaff had received a scornful remark or the odd dirty look. She'd never seen anyone take something like this in their stride before.

Their dinner had come out not long after and conversation continued without missing a beat.

'Enough about me,' he said, pouring more wine. 'What's your story, Amy Sinclair?'

His smile was like a hot knife melting through ice. 'I don't really have a story.' Which was true. Amy Sinclair had only existed for a few days. Quinn wasn't sure what Amy's story would be yet. So far, it seemed horrible. No money. No car. No apartment. As far as stories went, it actually sucked.

Chapter 15

'Everyone has a story. Although, at a guess, I think yours is a sad one at the moment?' Hugo asked, tilting his head slightly as he studied her.

Quinn dropped his probing look. It was a little unnerving, to say the least. 'It's just been a rough Christmas. Family stuff...and, well, actually, I'm just coming out of a break-up.'

'Ah,' he said with a nod, then cringed in sympathy. 'Yeah, I've been there recently too. It sucks.'

'Yeah. It kinda does.'

'If it's any comfort, the guy must be a complete tool.'

A small grin tugged at her mouth at his words. 'I think so too.' She paused. 'How long ago was your break-up?'

'A year ago,' he said, putting his glass down. 'I thought we were going to get married and settle down, but apparently she had other plans.'

'I'm sorry,' Quinn said, understanding completely. 'I think I was thinking the same thing with my ex. But it turned out he was just using me to—' She stopped. *To get to my family's fortune* sounded melodramatic and dumb now. 'Well, he was just using me, apparently.'

'Sounds a bit like my ex,' he said. 'But it taught me a good lesson. From now on I stay away from high-maintenance, spoilt little rich girls.' He glanced over in alarm as Quinn spluttered her wine across the table. 'Are you okay?' he asked, jumping to his feet.

Quinn waved him back into his seat as she tried to stop coughing, quickly mopping up the spilled wine with her napkin. 'Went down the wrong way,' she said weakly, when he continued to eye her worriedly. 'Sorry.'

'That's okay, as long as you're all right.'

'I'm fine.' She hadn't been expecting that.

'So, yeah,' he continued, obviously trying to ease her embarrassment by brushing over her choking incident, 'I can't stand liars and people with no social conscience. Never again,' he vowed. 'What about you? What are *you* thankful for learning from your ex?'

What *had* she learned from Bryson? That she shouldn't trust any smooth-talking charmers ever again? Well, that wasn't working out too well, considering she was sitting across the table from one right now. Then again, that wasn't entirely true either. Even in the short time she'd known Hugo, she'd already seen something she'd never seen in Bryson—kindness and an easy-going, honest nature. In fact, no one she'd normally spend time with had that. 'I guess I'm grateful that he showed his true colours before it was too late and made me realise how naïve I really was.'

He raised a glass to tap hers. 'Here's to dodging bullets!' He grinned. 'Took me a long time to get through it, but I'm on the other side now. All I can offer in the way of advice is to just keep putting one foot in front of the other.'

It was all right for Mr Philanthropist of the Year to say that, when you had enough money not to worry about anything but putting one foot in front of the other, and you owned the company you worked for and could take off to the beach whenever you felt like it. It was a little different when you had no money and no idea how you were going to survive.

It was a shame she'd found out who Hugo really was. Quinn was enjoying getting to know this man. But that was before she found out he was a gazillionaire. She liked him more when she thought he was just some beach bum with even less to his name than she had. There was no way she would be able to spend time with him now, even if the advantages of fine dining and nice dates would ultimately be on the table. Once he found out who *she* really was, he'd be horrified. He'd just said he couldn't stand liars and spoilt little rich girls, and she was both. Although maybe not so much the rich part anymore. Still, she could imagine he wouldn't find it very amusing if she told him she was an Appleton.

Outside the restaurant, Quinn stopped him from offering her a lift home in his modest four-wheel drive. No extravagance there either. This guy was a bloody saint.

'I can't let you walk home alone,' he protested.

'No, really. It's fine. It's not far from here.'

'Amy. I'm not going to let any date of mine walk home in the dark. That's just not who I am.'

Oh, for goodness' sake. 'Okay. Thanks.' The stubborn look in his eye warned her he wasn't going to give up on this, so she gave him the address as he started the car. 'I've just been staying there until I move into my new place,' she added feebly.

When they pulled up, he made to get out of the car and walk her inside, but she stopped him quickly. 'Thank you for tonight, Hugo. I really enjoyed it.'

'I did too, Amy. I knew there was something special about you and fate confirmed it.' He grinned.

'Yeah, well, I'm not sure about fate, but it was nice seeing you again. I've got a big few days ahead of me. I better get inside.'

He stopped her as she went to move. 'Amy, have I done something wrong?' he asked quietly.

His question surprised her. 'Of course not.'

'It's just that, I thought there was a connection here…at least, I know there's one for me.'

A car drove past, its headlights lighting up the interior of the car briefly and catching the confused look on his handsome face. 'Hugo, I'm sorry. You're a great guy. You're kind and, well, let's face it, pretty amazing, but it's like I told you. I've just come out of a relationship and my whole life is one huge disaster right now…I just don't have the time or the energy to start something new.'

He gave a resigned, deflated kind of nod, and for a moment she wished she could just forget everything and let this guy sweep her off her feet. All her problems might even go away if he fell head over heels in love with her.

He was loaded. Although he didn't come from any old family lines and Gran would most likely turn her nose up at that. The sudden thought of Gran's disapproval almost made her change her mind. What she wouldn't give to drag Hugo before her gran and declare that she didn't need her grandmother's blessing *or* her money. The idea sent a rush of rebellion and satisfaction through her veins—until she remembered that Hugo had sworn off liars. He thought her name was Amy.

'Thanks again, Hugo,' she said and leaned across to kiss him. She'd meant the kiss to be a goodbye kiss, but as her mouth touched his, it deepened, and she found herself caught up in a wave of unexpected desire. When he pulled away slightly to catch his breath, she immediately forgot any of the good intentions she'd just had.

'I don't want the night to end yet,' he said in a low voice that tugged at a place deep inside her.

She didn't want it to end either. She was with a man who liked her and wanted her—for *herself*. After the humiliation of Bryson and Greta running away together, it was a soothing balm to her smarting pride.

'Can we go inside?' he suggested, and she realised she was staring at him, her breathing still a little heavy. He kissed her once more and Quinn gave up even trying to fight it.

She nodded quickly at the concierge, and was grateful the elevator door was open as it deposited its load of holidaymakers onto the ground floor and they were able to walk straight inside. As the doors closed, Hugo pulled her against him, and once more she was lost in his heady kisses. The ding announced their arrival far too soon.

'I'm sorry about the mess,' she said as they walked through a stack of boxes.

'I have to be honest,' he said with a grin, 'I couldn't care less right now.'

Thank goodness for men and their ability to only concentrate on one thing at a time. They wasted no time on any further small talk; Hugo wrapped his arms around her waist from behind and nuzzled her neck as she led him to her bedroom.

It felt so good to be desired. Ever since Christmas Day, her ego had been taking hit after hit. From Bryson. From Gran. From everything she once found familiar. To have this man wanting her right here and now went a small way to restoring her confidence.

He was gentle and thoughtful, so different to Bryson. She hadn't even really noticed before, the difference. Bryson was like a tornado that swept you up and took you for a wild, crazy ride. It was fun, exciting—even bordering on a little dangerous on occasion—but gentle was never a word she'd have used when it came to Bryson.

She had always assumed gentle meant boring, but it wasn't. It was...nice. Quinn gave a rueful smile at that. Nice was not a word you should use when talking about sex. No, this was definitely more than just nice, but it was refreshing to experience sex with a man who didn't seem to think there was something to prove, some personal best to beat. A man who seemed content to explore her body like it was a sacred temple. Hugo did not disappoint. At all.

Later, as they lay side by side, Quinn knew this could never happen again. God, she'd tried to be so strong earlier, and all it had taken was Hugo to kiss her to change her mind and weaken her resolve.

She was not going to lead this guy on. He was a good guy. He didn't deserve to be caught up in her family's messy drama. She tried to imagine what it would have been like if Hugo had been at the Christmas lunch, what he would have made of the whole thing. She shuddered. He'd have been appalled. There was no way a man like Hugo, with all his good intentions and generous spirit, would understand the greed and excess her family thrived on. The thought of his disappointment made her feel immediately ashamed.

There wasn't any point in throwing her family under the bus. She was just as bad. What was the last completely selfless thing she'd done, the kind Hugo did on a daily basis?

Sure, she hosted charity events all the time, but there wasn't any that she'd ever personally gotten involved with, or spent the time getting to know so she knew what the money they were raising would do for them. In all honesty, she didn't really care. Her life wasn't affected by any of the things these charities had been created for — poverty, domestic abuse, illiteracy, the list went on. She *should* have shown more interest.

Maybe in a normal family these things would be important, like they were to Hugo, and she would have been brought up to take an active interest in helping people. In her family, you helped by inviting other rich people to parties and donating *their* money — anything that didn't involve actually getting your hands dirty.

Hugo could never know who she really was. She couldn't bear the look on his face if he ever found out.

'What are you thinking about?' he surprised her by asking.

'I was thinking how busy tomorrow's going to be and that I probably should have an early night,' she said, staring up at the ceiling and praying her voice sounded convincing.

'Yeah. I'm sorry about that. I know you said that before and I kind of overrode your protest.'

'I'm glad you did,' she said gently. 'But nothing's changed. I'm not ready for this to be anything serious — it can't even be casual — I just don't have room in my life right now to worry about hurting someone.'

'I'm a big boy. You won't hurt me,' he said, turning his head to smile at her.

'I will. I always do. I'm sorry, Hugo, but this can't happen again. I need to concentrate on getting my life sorted out.'

He sighed as he sat up and swung his legs to the ground. 'I won't pretend to understand,' he said softly, 'but I will respect that's what you want. Although,' he added, and Quinn's heart stopped momentarily, 'if we meet up again, I'm going to take that as fate stepping in.'

They wouldn't be meeting up, she was a little sad to realise. Not after she moved out of here. Honestly, of all the times to suddenly develop a conscience, or whatever this annoyingly goody-goody thing was that was happening to her. She really liked this guy.

'I'll see you around, Amy,' he said, leaning over to kiss her. It was a slow, searching kiss—unhurried, yet still as potent as the kiss they'd shared earlier. Then he was walking to the door and gone.

FML, she thought bitterly.

Chapter 16

For someone who spent a considerable amount of time at the gym, Quinn found herself questioning her level of fitness as she made the eleven millionth trip up the dodgy staircase at her new flat.

Thank God it was her last trip. As she dumped the last box on top of the others, she put her hands on her hips and tried to catch her breath. She looked around; boxes took up most of the room.

She hadn't realised quite how much her wardrobe would take up in box space once she'd started packing. She'd tried to divide her clothes into a giveaway and keep pile, but each time she held up a dress, she'd remembered how many good times she'd had and couldn't bring herself to throw it away.

Then she remembered a conversation she'd had with Chloe and Chantelle about buying second-hand designer wear online. Actually, it was more like they'd been looking down on people who bought said second-hand designer wear online, but remembering it now, she forced herself to do a search just to see what was out there. She found a Zimmermann evening dress that had retailed for three and a half thousand dollars selling for two thousand eight hundred, and bit her lip, as her mind went through the inventory of her old walk-in wardrobe and its financial possibilities.

She knew the sensible thing to do was to sell some of it—it was worth a small fortune, and she could certainly use the money right now—but she could only imagine the humiliation of having people recognise her name and laugh at how she'd resorted to selling her outfits in order to eat.

Then she remembered—she wasn't Quinn Appleton anymore. Amy Sinclair could list whatever she wanted and no one would bat an eyelid.

She still needed to pay her rent in advance and eat. It couldn't be put off any longer; her room looked like she'd been hoarding for twenty years, with only a narrow path from the door to the bed. It was ridiculous. With a heartbroken sigh that ended on a small sob, she opened the first box and pulled out a red Zimmermann halter-neck gown and hung it on the wardrobe door to take a photo. She loved that dress. She'd worn it to a Gold Coast fundraising ball the year before.

She moved it to one side and pulled out another one. Over and over again, until she reached the last one in the box, uploaded the photos and posted them for sale.

She sighed as she counted out the last of her cash to give to Vivian and Atticus. Eating was overrated anyway.

Her phone pinged with a notification, and she opened the message to discover someone had just bought her Collette Dinnigan cocktail dress for four hundred dollars. Another ping sounded, and the red Zimmermann dress had sold for eight hundred. Quinn stared at the phone in disbelief. She'd just made twelve hundred dollars in less than twenty minutes. Okay, so she'd technically lost about twice as much as that from the original price she'd paid, but right now, she didn't care—twelve hundred dollars would come in very handy.

She looked at a second box filled with shoes and quickly started pulling them out to take photos. It hurt a little less this time. She wasn't going to go too crazy, but if she had to make some room, she might as well make some cash out of it.

***

A gentle tap sounded on the door. Quinn opened it to find Vivian standing outside, smiling. 'Sorry I wasn't here earlier, I just wanted to say welcome. Are you getting settled in?'

Quinn glanced over her shoulder and tried not to grimace as she turned back. 'Getting there.'

'Well, I'll leave you to it. We're heading out for an art show in a few minutes, if you want to tag along?'

'Oh, no thanks. I better stay and try to get unpacked.'

'No worries, maybe next time,' Vivian said with a friendly wave before turning away. 'This is your place now, so make yourself at home.'

Quinn shut the door and surveyed the mess she'd just made photographing all her pieces, before setting about organising the chaos that was now her life.

Later, she took a towel and her toiletry bag and walked down the hallway to the bathroom.

Judging by the state of the sink, she guessed Craig, the previous roommate, didn't like to wash out the basin after he shaved. Clearly no one had checked to see if he'd bothered to clean before he left either. She stared in horror at the ring in the bathtub, which she discovered was also the shower. What kind of fresh hell was this? She'd never seen a shower in a bathtub before.

The whole bathroom would have fitted inside her walk-in wardrobe back in her old apartment. The pink and grey floor tiles looked like they were the original tiles from the 1950s, judging by the number that were cracked or missing, and the black tiles around the shower wall at the end of the bathtub had definitely seen better days.

She gingerly opened the vanity cabinet above the sink and found it almost empty except for a small can of shaving cream and a disposable razor. Clearly Craig *had* left in a hurry and hadn't packed his toiletries. She eyed the small cupboard under the sink doubtfully—it had two doors but was half the size of her old one. If they got another tenant in, how on earth were two people supposed to share this? Upon inspection, she was relieved to find it empty, and she quickly unpacked her belongings.

Once her bed had been made up with her favourite sheets and she'd spruced it up with her quilt and decorative pillows, she felt a little better. She'd need curtains to replace the hideous orange material that currently hung over the window and, as she'd unpacked, she'd been thinking about the ugly old wardrobe. Maybe a coat of paint would fix the problem short term? She'd have to make a note to ask Vivian if it would be all right.

She'd fashioned herself a bedside table out of a stack of empty suitcases and arranged her night and hand creams on top, along with some pretty candles and an alarm clock. She wasn't even sure where she'd gotten an alarm clock from—she couldn't recall ever using one—but if it had come with the apartment and she was supposed to have left it there, then they could bloody well come and get it.

She'd stacked the rest of her boxes along the side of her room and covered them with a spare sheet for now. Later she'd see if there was somewhere she could store them until her (hopefully) timely exit from this place.

Climbing into bed, she laid down and closed her eyes. Downstairs, she could hear Vivian and Atticus talking. Not their words, just Atticus's low, rich tone followed by a slightly higher one that rose and fell in a melodic murmur. A few moments later there was a ticking noise, followed by a creak up in the roof. She wasn't used to noises in the night—her air conditioner usually drowned everything else out. She kicked her foot out from under the sheet with a disgruntled huff. It was hot. She missed her air con.

Eventually, she must have fallen asleep. When she awoke, it was to the sound of birds chirping outside her window and traffic driving past.

Quinn selected her outfit carefully. She needed to dress the part of her new job, but not look like Quinn Appleton. That seemed simple enough, seeing as Quinn Appleton had never dressed to work at Appleton's, yet because she'd never *had* to dress to work in an office, she also didn't have any idea what she should wear. *What would Quinn wear?* she asked herself. She'd probably go completely over the top and wear something like a leather skirt and an off-the-shoulder top with her tallest pair of stilettos, to make a grand entrance.

So, she needed to do the *opposite* as Amy Sinclair.

She settled on a straight linen skirt, a tailored top and a pair of not-*too*-high heels.

Gran had texted her the instructions for her first day. She was to report to the office and tell them her name. *Amy Sinclair* had been written in bold type, and Quinn rolled her eyes. As if she'd forgotten the ridiculous terms of earning back her inheritance.

Quinn sent a message back asking what time Lionel would be out the front to pick her up, and stared in horror when Gran replied that he wouldn't be.

Quinn hit call and waited for her grandmother to pick up.

'What do you mean Lionel isn't coming? I don't have a car, remember?'

'You're just any other employee. No special treatment, remember?' Was that *sassiness* in her gran's tone she detected?

'Then how am I supposed to get to work?'

'I suggest you look up a bus timetable, darling.'

A bus? Was she serious?

'You can do this, Quinn. You're an Appleton. Remember that.'

Angry tears pricked the back of her eyelids. 'Apparently I'm supposed to forget it,' she snapped and disconnected the call.

This was utter bullshit.

***

Quinn walked up the street to the closest bus stop and waited. Sitting on the bench was an older lady, a wheeled, long-handled shopping cart by her side, and a young girl, dressed in jeans and a ripped T-shirt, head bent over her phone with earphones stuck in her ears, blocking out everything around her.

Quinn gave a vague smile to the older lady and chose to stand, keeping her eye out for the bus number she needed. She'd had to leave extra early to buy a stupid transport card from the supermarket down the road to use for getting to and from work. Somehow, she vowed, she was going to find a way out of this.

As the bus pulled in, she waited for the woman with the trolley to make her way up the stairs before taking out her own card, tapping it and scouring the aisle for a spare seat. A boy up ahead sat on the aisle seat, the window seat beside him empty save for his scruffy backpack. His head was bent over his phone as he frantically pressed buttons, probably playing a game of some kind. The older lady was still standing in the aisle and a quick glance around showed Quinn there were no other spare seats. The bus lurched forward as it took off and Quinn grabbed hold of the lady's arm as she almost toppled forward with the sudden movement.

'Thank you, dear,' the woman muttered quietly, rearranging her grip on the trolley.

Quinn stared at the boy with the spare seat, but he refused to glance up. Everyone else around them seemed equally as absorbed in whatever they were looking at on their phones and tablets. What was wrong with people?

'Excuse me,' Quinn said, and waited for the boy to respond. When he didn't, she leaned closer and raised her voice. 'Excuse me.'

He looked up, and Quinn eyed him expectantly, looking across at the older lady beside her. 'Can you move over, please?'

To her utter amazement, the kid simply looked back down at his phone and ignored her. *You have got to be kidding me.*

'Hey! You!' she said, ignoring the fact several people were now looking up from their zombie-like existence. 'Move over and let this lady sit down right now.'

'Rack off,' he muttered, sending her a scowl before dropping his gaze once more.

'It's all right, dear,' the lady said quickly. 'I'm used to standing.'

'Well, you shouldn't be. That's not right.'

'It's a different world now,' the woman agreed sadly.

Quinn was furious at the woman's ready acceptance of this mannerless society. She leaned across the boy and snagged his backpack from the seat beside him and dumped it on the floor. The look of shock on the kid's face would have been hilarious if she'd been in the right frame of mind to appreciate it, but she wasn't. He flew up with an outraged, 'Hey!' and squeezed past her to retrieve his bag that had rolled towards the front of the bus, and Quinn ushered the older lady into the two spare seats, taking the seat on the aisle beside her just as the teen came storming back.

'You can't do that!' he yelled.

'I just did,' Quinn said calmly. 'Next time, if someone asks you nicely to move over, I'd suggest you do it. Then you won't lose your own seat.'

'Bitch,' he spat, just as the driver touched the brakes, sending him sideways back down the aisle. As the bus pulled over, he stormed to the front and got off, gesturing madly at the window as they pulled back into traffic. She glanced up and caught the bus driver's eye in the mirror; he gave a small smirk.

'Thank you, dear, but you didn't have to go to all that trouble. I don't know what's happening to kids today.' The woman shook her head.

Were kids all like this now? She hadn't been on a public bus in years, so she had no idea if this behaviour was considered normal or not. Surely not. If it was, clearly she'd been living way out of touch with the world. God, give her a private car any day. It smelled a lot more pleasant, for one thing. How did this many complete strangers sit so close together and endure those who chose not to wear deodorant? Who the hell *didn't* wear deodorant?

The trip to the factory seemed to take forever, and she was relieved when she finally spotted her stop up ahead.

Three other people exited at the same stop, and Quinn briefly wondered if they'd be her employees. Chances were she'd never set eyes on them again once inside. Although she wondered how it was going to go over once people knew the new girl in the office caught a bus to work each day? Heels were not the best footwear for public transport. Gran didn't think that one through too well. Her hopes lifted. Maybe she'd *have* to get Quinn a car to use— after all, it was *her* idea for Quinn to fit in without drawing too much attention to herself.

She headed along the path towards the office. The large white building loomed ahead. She hadn't been here in years, but it still looked much the same. Someone had tried to revamp it at some point with the introduction of a garden out the front—like the building it was simple and functional. Inside, she let the door close slowly behind her as she looked around the bustling foyer. On the walls were old black-and-white photos of the company as it grew. She recognised many of them; she'd seen them in photo albums in her grandfather's office at home. It was strange to see how much had changed since the original Appleton brothers had started out in the very first factory, a small stone building somewhere near the docks area. Now there were factories all across the country and some overseas. Appleton's was a household name. It was wild when she actually stopped to think about it. Maybe Gran was right. Maybe they *had* been taking the company for granted all this time. She rarely spent time like this thinking about her heritage. Sure, she thought about her name—it came with a lot of clout—but she rarely thought about it in terms of how much history was attached to it.

A woman behind the desk cleared her throat and Quinn gave a small start before turning to smile at her. 'Hello, I'm—' she paused, distracted by the photos she'd been looking at '—Amy Sinclair. I'm starting work here today.'

The woman consulted a large book on her desk and ran a finger down the lines. 'Oh. Yes. There you are. Welcome to Appleton's, Amy. I'll just call up your supervisor. If you'd like to take a seat, he won't be long,' she said, giving a friendly smile.

After a few minutes, a tall, lanky man came in through a set of doors to the left and glanced into the waiting area. 'Are you Sinclair?' he asked briskly.

'Ahh...yes,' she answered slowly, getting to her feet.

'Follow me,' he commanded, and left her staring at the closed doors. Well, that was a bit rude, she thought, but took off after him.

She hurried to catch up, swearing a little as her heels and straight skirt made it difficult to move too fast. He was waiting with an irritated frown beside a door that read

Employees only. His frown deepened as he looked her up and down disapprovingly. 'The staff lockers are inside. I've told Maureen to get you set up with a uniform, so go see her, then meet me out on the floor once you've changed.'

'On the...? I think there's been some kind of mistake,' she said, stopping him as he went to leave.

'A mistake?' he quipped.

'Well, yes. I'm clearly in the wrong place. I should be up in the offices.'

'Your name's Amy Sinclair?' he said, looking down at his clipboard.

'Yes.'

'Then you're in the right place. Factory floor. That's the position you've been hired for.'

What the hell?

Chapter 17

'But I don't know anything about working in a factory.'

'I'm sure they told you there would be on-the-job training at the interview?' the man said, eyeing her weirdly.

The interview with her gran? Strangely, no, there hadn't been any mention of on-the-job training to work on the *factory floor!*

What the hell kind of game was Gran playing here? Wasn't it bad enough she'd had to agree to this ridiculous plan in the first place? At no point did Gran mention anything about working in the *actual* factory. This was stupid. She was supposed to have some cruisy job in an office, for Christ's sake! *With* an office!

'Get a move on,' the man snapped, leaving her outside the door.

Quinn dug out her phone and brought up her grandmother's number.

'Hello, dear,' Gran greeted her smoothly.

'This was not part of the deal.'

'What wasn't?'

'Working in the factory,' Quinn hissed into the mouthpiece, as a woman walked past and glanced at her strangely before opening the door. The deafening noise of the factory floor momentarily flooded in, until the door eased shut and muffled the sound once more.

'You agreed to work for the company.'

'I thought you meant in an office—like Dad and the others.'

'I don't believe I ever gave you that impression, darling. I never specified this would be an office job.'

'Of course you wouldn't, would you? Otherwise I wouldn't have agreed.'

'Herbert and Jonas Appleton started at the bottom. In the beginning, they had to do everything. Think of it as learning the trade from the bottom up.'

'I don't want to learn the trade—you said six months.'

'There's no harm in working your way up to an office job. There's nothing stopping you from getting there.'

'Gran, I don't know how to do any of this,' she said, hating that she sounded so desperate and scared.

'You can do anything you set your mind to, Quinn. All you have to do is listen and learn. I believe in you. Now, off you go and get started.'

Quinn listened to the silence on the other end of the phone and felt abandoned. She really didn't have an option. If she walked away now, she'd never get her inheritance back. She'd have to find another job—probably just as dismal as this one—somewhere else, and that would be her life forever. Or she could just accept that she had to work here and make the best of it for six months.

Six months sounded as far away as six years right now, but at least she knew that one day it would be over. She could last six months. She had to. The alternative was too horrible to imagine.

Inside, a woman named Maureen, who'd been working for the company for close to thirty years, introduced herself, handed Quinn a pair of trousers, a shirt with the company logo on it, a pair of particularly unattractive work boots and a very unflattering hair net, and pointed her in the direction of the staff toilets to get changed.

When she came out, she was given a locker to store her clothes and handbag in, and was sent out to find Darrell, the man who had delivered her earlier.

Quinn took a deep breath and pushed through the doors to the factory. It was huge, like walking into the belly of the Titanic, with massive machines everywhere, connected by huge conveyor belts.

'Right,' Darrell said once she found him. 'I'll give you a brief tour, then set you up at your station.'

Quinn walked at a trot to keep up with the man, and wondered if she was supposed to be taking notes or something as he rattled off statistics.

'This is where the biscuit dough is mixed. It's then transferred to the moulding area, where it's cut into the shape of a biscuit...'

Quinn watched the huge stamp-like machine press out round biscuit dough before setting them on the conveyor belt to head off on their journey through an oversized oven.

'They cook for six and a half minutes, and the oven cooks fourteen thousand biscuits at a time.'

'That's a lot of biscuits,' she said, suitably impressed by the sheer enormity of the factory output as they followed the biscuits along the conveyor belt.

'The biscuits come out through here and are cooled.'

She heard the blast of giant fans blowing onto the freshly baked biscuits as they passed through another tunnel.

'After they've cooled down, we add the caramel, then they drop down onto another conveyor belt, where chocolate is added.'

Quinn watched the biscuits flip over as they dropped onto another conveyor level, applying melted chocolate to cover the other side.

'After the chocolate is added, they're flipped again, then they pass through another cooling machine and, once cool, they're ready for packing.' Darrell sounded like he'd given this tour way too many times.

'Is there a job licking the chocolate conveyor belt clean?' she asked hopefully, but sighed at the unamused expression on Darrell's face. *Okay, clearly he doesn't have a sense of humour.*

Her eyes followed the wide, orderly queue of biscuits being channelled into a narrow shoot, where they were organised into four lanes. It reminded Quinn of rush-hour traffic converging off the bridge to go through the toll booth lanes.

'I'll get Maureen to continue the tour and show you where you'll be working,' Mr Chuckles said, nodding briskly to the woman she'd met earlier who had come across to join them, before bustling off.

'The biscuits go through these guides,' Maureen said, as the biscuits were shaken and pushed into some semblance of order. 'They get divided into groups of sixteen to form a packet.' Each group passed below a machine that rolled the packaging down and over them, cutting and sealing each packet with precision.

'From here, they are put into cartons,' she continued, as they followed the packets' progress through a door and out into a large packing area, where groups of workers moved with swift care to grab the packets and drop them into cardboard boxes, which were then sent out another set of doors into the warehouse, where more workers took them off, two at a time, and stacked them onto a crate, to be wrapped in plastic ready for dispatch and delivery.

Quinn shook her head. 'It all just flows,' she said. She remembered watching the process as a kid with her grandfather, but there was so much more done by machinery now.

'It does. Until it doesn't,' Maureen said drolly.

'Do things go wrong often?'

'Not so much anymore. You just have to put a lot of faith in computers, don't you? Once, all of this was done by hand.'

'There must have been a lot more people employed back then?'

'We had over three hundred people working here when I first started—a long time ago,' she said with a dry smile. 'So this is where you'll be working.' Maureen stopped in front of a station where the recently packed boxes were coming down the conveyor belt to be stacked on a pallet. 'But before you do that, you'll have to go through a workplace health and safety training induction, which we'll start after morning tea.'

At morning tea break, Quinn followed Maureen into the staff tearoom and obediently took a mug from the shelf as directed and moved along the bench to make herself a cup of coffee. She hesitated briefly as she clocked the stained ring inside the mug, but with others coming in behind her, there wasn't time to search for another one, so she gritted her teeth and tried her best to ignore it.

Maureen introduced her to two other women seated at the table. 'This is Tara and Janelle,' she said, pulling out a chair and sitting down. 'This is Amy. She's just starting today.'

'Hi, Amy. What do you think of the place so far?' Tara asked in a broad New Zealand accent.

'It's very...noisy,' she said, deciding against mentioning how much she truly disliked the whole thing. She didn't think it wise to alienate the people she had to work alongside for the next six months.

'You get used to it,' Janelle assured her, as she reached for a biscuit from the plate in the middle of the table. Appleton's, of course.

'How long have you all been working here?' Quinn ventured as she sipped at the hot coffee and tried not to grimace at the cheap instant blandness. Oh, she'd kill for a real coffee right now.

'I've been here about fifteen years now,' Janelle said. 'Maureen's been here, what, twenty-five?' she asked the older woman across the table.

'Twenty-seven this year,' Maureen corrected, reaching for another biscuit.

'I've only been here five,' Tara said ruefully.

'That seems like a long time to be working for the one company,' Quinn said, wondering how on earth someone worked close to thirty years in the same job.

'Wouldn't want to work anywhere else,' Janelle put in, dunking a cream-filled chocolate biscuit into her coffee.

'Why not?' Quinn couldn't help the undisguised disbelief.

'Not often you find a company that treats its workers like family. Even in one as big as this.'

Trust me, Quinn thought, *if you knew how they treated their real family, you might not be so damn cheerful.*

'This place has been a godsend,' Janelle said. 'It's allowed me to raise three kids without having to be on government handouts. Around here, that's pretty rare. My kids wouldn't have had the life they have if it wasn't for this company.'

'What about you?' Tara asked. 'What made you get a job here?'

'I kinda had to. I need to pay rent and buy food,' Quinn said dryly.

'I'm hearin' ya,' Tara grimaced. 'With four kids and a husband, I'm fairly sure most of my wage goes on grocery bills and day care.'

'Four kids, wow.'

'Yeah, my husband and I come from big families.' She grinned, taking out her phone and bringing up some photos of four beautiful, smiling children.

'They're gorgeous,' Quinn said.

The round-faced woman broke out in a wide smile and bobbed her head shyly. 'Thanks. I think so too. That's my husband, Terry. He works here too.'

'Do you have any kids, Amy?' Janelle asked.

'Oh God no,' she answered quickly. 'I can barely take care of myself. I don't even have house plants.'

The women chuckled, most likely thinking she was joking, but she wasn't. She sucked at any kind of responsibility. If she couldn't remember to water a useless indoor plant, how on earth was she supposed to keep a child alive?

With the break over, people rose from their seats, washed up their cups, and headed back out to the floor. Quinn stifled a groan as she walked through the set of doors, following Maureen like a lost puppy.

Chapter 18

'Mum! I've been trying to call you for days. Where are you?'

'I'm sorry, darling. I've been...busy.'

Quinn didn't have the patience to listen to how busy her mother had been. She'd needed her parents over the last few days like she'd never needed them before, and neither of them was anywhere to be found.

'Where's Dad?'

'Darling, I don't know,' she said impatiently.

'How can you not know? He's your husband. I'm really worried, Mum.'

'Your father can take care of himself—it's what he does best,' she added snidely. 'Anyway, I have news.'

'What news?' The announcement momentarily sidetracked her.

'This is going to come as a bit of a shock, I'm afraid, but there's no easy way to tell you...I've left your father.'

What? Quinn wasn't sure she'd heard her correctly. 'You've...left Dad?'

'I know it's not the best timing, but this situation has forced my hand. I can't live my life the way I was anymore.'

'Because there's no money?' Quinn supplied.

'Well, of course there's that,' her mother snapped, 'but come on, Quinn, you're not a child anymore—you know your father and I haven't had a proper marriage for years. I'm not going to be dragged down with him now.'

'So you're just abandoning him?'

'He abandoned us, Quinn,' she wailed. 'Surely you understand that? He's gone. He left us here to face the fallout of his mess.'

'Gone where though?' Why couldn't she understand that was still a problem? No one knew where he was. Her mother and her uncle both assumed he'd fled the country, but neither of them actually knew that's what he'd done. He could be missing. Something could be very wrong and no one but her seemed to care.

'Honestly, Quinn, I don't care where he is. I'm actually relieved I was forced to make the jump. I should have done it years ago.'

It shouldn't have surprised her and, to some extent, it didn't, but she'd gotten used to their kind of normal for so long that part of her felt like a little kid, hearing that her parents were splitting their family in half and she was staring down a very long, scary tunnel she was supposed to walk through alone.

'Does Felix know?'

'You know your brother. He can't focus on trivial matters when he's racing.'

'His parents divorcing isn't exactly trivial.'

'He's got enough on his plate to deal with at the moment.'

And I haven't, Quinn filled in sarcastically. 'Well, we wouldn't want to inconvenience him.'

'Don't be bitter, Quinn. It'll age you.'

'Have you even bothered to wonder what's been happening to me?'

'What do you mean?'

'The apartment was put up for sale and I had to move out.'

'Oh. So soon?'

Quinn clenched her jaw tightly. 'And Greta and Bryson are married,' she added, hating that it still hurt so much.

'Really?' That did seem to pique her interest. 'Why would Greta be interested in a nobody like Bryson, I wonder?' she mused, much to Quinn's disbelief.

Stillness descended upon her. 'Are you kidding me right now?' she asked quietly.

'What?' her mother asked.

'I'm telling you, my boyfriend of only a few short weeks ago has dumped me to marry my *cousin*, and that's all you have to say?'

'Well, it is strange...he's not Greta's type at all,' she pointed out.

'What about me?' Quinn said, raising her voice slightly despite her best attempts to stay calm. 'What about the fact he broke my heart?'

'You were lucky he showed his true colours before you'd gotten too serious. Greta did you a favour.'

'Is it too much to ask for just a little bit of sympathy?' Quinn snapped. 'Could you pretend for one minute to be a mother and remember I actually have feelings?'

'I hate to point this out, Quinn, but you weren't the only one affected that day at your grandmother's. We all lost something. I've been going through my own hell.'

'Really? And where are you sitting out this hell, exactly?' Because it sure hadn't been around here.

'I'm in Bali.'

'Bali?'

'Yes, I've…met someone. I'll fill you in later, darling, once things settle down a bit. Look, why don't you come up here? I can organise a plane ticket.'

She might be desperate, but she was not desperate enough to land on the doorstep of her mother's love nest with some new boyfriend. 'I'll be fine, Mum,' she bit out.

'Of course you will. You're the strong one. You're like your gran—a survivor.'

'I'm nothing like Gran,' she scoffed. The idea was ridiculous.

'You are, you know.' Her mother's tone lowered slightly. 'Anyway, I have to go. I'll send you my address in case you change your mind. Bye, darling.'

It took a minute for Quinn to realise she was still holding the phone to her ear as she struggled to untangle all the emotions the conversation had revealed. Anger seemed to be the loudest. She was angry at her mother. She was angry at her father. She was angry at everyone. When the going got tough in the Appleton family, apparently the tough abandoned ship and it was every man for himself.

Felix had his career to think about and was clearly too wrapped up in his own world to give the whole thing any thought; but then, he didn't have to, did he? He'd used his family name and contacts to launch his own career independently of the company, and washed his hands of them. Greta had done the same. She'd spent her career distancing herself from the wholesome, family-oriented image of Appleton's Biscuits, even though, again, it was the family's influence and contacts that had handed her a modelling contract on a silver platter.

And that just left her. Here. Sinking with the ship.

***

Quinn waited in the drawing room, ignoring the lavish furnishings around her. Lionel had been surprised when she'd knocked on the door a few minutes ago—not that his face had actually shown it—but she'd heard the slight hesitation in his welcome. 'Miss Appleton. Lady Elizabeth wasn't expecting you today.'

In his defence, it had been more of a question, but she was fairly sure most other people surprising their Gran with a visit wouldn't have to go through a butler and get a slight rebuke for not having made an appointment beforehand.

Well, tough. Quinn's life had been turned upside down lately—Lady Elizabeth would have to cope with an unexpected visit.

'Quinn, this is a surprise,' Gran said, entering the room with her usual grace, taking a seat across from her.

'Hi, Gran. I need to talk to you about—'

Lionel, right on cue, came in carrying a tray and placed it on the coffee table between them, and Gran leaned forward in her seat to pour two cups of tea.

'I trust you're settling in well at Appleton's?' Gran asked, handing Quinn a delicate bone china teacup and saucer.

'I trust you've been well informed about my every move at Appleton's, Gran,' Quinn countered dryly.

'Not much happens that I'm not aware of,' she said, tilting her head slightly as she studied her. 'Things seem to be working out.'

Quinn dismissed her observation; even though it had been a week, she was still smarting about the job criteria misconception she'd been under on day one. 'I'm here about Dad.'

Gran hesitated briefly before taking a sip of her tea, then placing the cup back in its saucer where it balanced delicately on her lap. 'What about your father?'

'I'm worried,' Quinn said, not bothering to hide her frustration. 'I haven't heard from him, despite leaving messages. No one's heard from him. Mum doesn't seem to care,' she started, and was cut off by her gran's harsh and somewhat un-Gran-like snarl.

'Your mother, as I'm sure she's already informed you, has finally come clean about her long-term lover and moved in with him.'

'Long term?'

'Yes, dear. She and Marcus Lovette have been having an affair for the past twelve months.'

Her yoga teacher? 'How do you know that?'

'Darling, I know everything,' she said with a wave of her elegant hand.

'Did Dad know?'

'Yes.'

'For how long?'

'For as long as I've known, of course.' She eyed Quinn as though she were stupid. 'I informed him of his wife's infidelity as soon as I became aware of it. He's my son.'

'Dad's known that Mum was having a serious relationship with another man and he didn't say anything?'

'I warned him he couldn't trust her. He was convinced she'd never leave. At least, not while there was still money,' she added bitterly.

Quinn goggled at her gran as a thought occurred to her. 'Is that what this whole thing was about?' she demanded. 'Did you cut everyone off to force my mother to leave?'

'I didn't force anyone to do anything.'

'You've turned everyone's life upside down just to get rid of my mother?'

'Don't be so dramatic, Quinn. That was just a happy bonus.'

Quinn was stunned. She'd been sure nothing her gran could say or do would be able to surprise her anymore, and yet, here she was, surprising the shit out of her yet again!

'Your father is his own man. He's also a fool. Your mother, unfortunately, has always been his weakness—he loves her and not even the humiliation of discovering that she'd been having an affair with another man would change his mind. No,' she said, placing her cup on the coffee table and leaning back, 'I'd given up trying to make him see sense where Lyla was concerned. I did what I did because I'd finally realised I was becoming exactly like your father. I'd been turning a blind eye to this family's selfishness and overindulgences for too long and I did what had to be done to save the company.'

'You disowned your family,' Quinn said bitterly.

'I didn't disown my family,' Gran said, shaking her head with a sad smile. 'You are all still welcome here. Interesting, though, don't you think, that once the money was gone, so too was the family?'

'What did you honestly expect?'

'Obviously too much,' she said, and for a moment, Quinn felt a tug of sympathy for Gran. She understood abandonment. But then remembered the reason she came here.

'I think we need to call the police about Dad,' she said, forcing the conversation away from messy emotional topics.

The abrupt change also seemed to catch Gran unaware. 'Why would we do that?'

'Do you know where he is?' Quinn asked pointedly, holding the woman's gaze.

'No, I don't,' she said quietly.

'You just said yourself he knew about Mum's affair. Add that to the rumour about all the debt he owes around here and the fact he's had to sell everything we owned.

What if he's...done something?' Quinn dropped her eyes to her fingers twisting together anxiously in her lap. 'What if, while everyone's been talking crap about him and blaming him for all the debt and things we've lost and saying he's run away...' She stopped and swallowed, trying to compose herself. 'What if something terrible's happened? What if he's...' *Dead.* She couldn't bring herself to say the word out loud.

'I don't think your father's capable of harming himself,' Gran said, and surprised Quinn by leaning across to touch her arm. 'I really don't.'

'But what if...' A thousand thoughts raced through her mind.

'Your father is more resourceful than we give him credit for,' Gran said reluctantly. 'He's a fool where his gambling and your mother are concerned—and I've always thought the two things were connected. He's always felt a need to prove himself to her, buy her more. She was never satisfied with what they had. However,' she said, realising she'd revealed more than she'd probably intended, 'he's always had the uncanny knack of falling on his feet.'

'But how can we be sure he's safe when he won't call? And why won't he call just to let me know he's okay?'

'He's a man. He's most likely hiding away to lick his wounds for a while before he works out how to deal with everything. But if it makes you feel better, I'll look into it some more.'

'You will?'

'I don't think we need to involve the police in this. There's no point risking a scandal breaking out—*another* scandal,' she added pointedly. 'I can have someone dig around to see if we can locate him.'

For the first time in days, Quinn felt like a small amount of the weight she'd been carrying had been lifted from her shoulders. 'Thank you,' she said with honest gratitude. Somehow, she knew something wasn't right with the whole situation, and the sooner they figured out where her father was, the better.

'All right now,' Gran said, sitting back in her chair. 'You just remember our arrangement.'

Like she could ever forget it. 'Yes, Gran,' she parroted obediently. She could play along with Gran's little control game for now. It wasn't like she had much choice, but at least she'd managed to get someone to take her concerns about her father seriously.

'How did you get here today?' Gran asked as Quinn rose to leave.

'I caught the bus,' she said, unwilling to show how much she hated losing the independence of having her own car.

'I'll have Lionel take you home.'

'No thanks. I'll manage on my own,' she said coolly. She wasn't sure where the streak of rebellion was coming from, especially when it came to accepting something that would make life a lot easier. All she knew was she wasn't going to be a victim any longer. She'd managed to survive everything they'd thrown at her so far, and even if she hated every moment of it, she felt a weird feeling growing inside her that felt a lot like...pride. She'd been doing things she'd never imagined herself doing before. That, and she was still incredibly pissed off at her grandmother, so refusing her offer was more out of spite than anything else. But it felt good.

She walked along the busy tree-lined street and enjoyed the cool respite the shady trees offered. She ignored the first two bus stops, choosing instead to continue walking. She'd been doing a lot of that lately, and although she'd never admit it out loud, she hadn't actually missed not having her car the *whole* time. Walking to the shops gave her time to process things, and the exercise seemed to help keep her dark mood at bay.

Brisbane was so different to the more laid-back holiday feel of Surfers Paradise, and where once she'd craved the nightlife and lifestyle of the hectic inner city, now she wondered what she'd ever seen in it. These days, she craved the sound of the ocean and the salty smell of the sand.

Once on the bus, Quinn settled into her seat and took out her phone, noticing with a pleasant surprise two more of her dresses had sold, as well as a pair of Prada leather pumps. She'd hovered over the box full of shoes the night before; making the decision to sell some was a lot harder than selling the clothes—shoes were her kryptonite. However, the pull of a steadily growing bank account was proving to be a satisfying pastime as well.

It had been the most bizarre thing; she'd never batted an eye at the cost of things before—it had never been an issue. Most likely because she'd never had to think about where the money came from. There was something very different about money you'd earned. She felt a little stupid that it had taken until now to realise what most people probably figured out before they'd even left school.

Chapter 19

After yet another seemingly endless long day, Quinn kicked off her heels and sank to her bed, massaging her aching feet one at a time. She was desperate for a bath, but an image of the scum rings around the tub at the end of the hall sent a shudder through her. 'Looks like a hot shower it'll be,' she muttered despondently, dragging herself back upright to find her comfiest lounging clothes before heading to the bathroom.

She opened the bathroom door and a wave of steam poured out to greet her. As it cleared, she found herself staring open-mouthed at a man who was shaving, standing naked except for a fluffy white towel wrapped around his hips. She did a double-take—*her* fluffy white towel!

'Hi,' he said, far more calmly than the situation warranted.

'That's my towel!' she shrieked.

He slowly looked down to the towel in question, which was tucked, somewhat haphazardly, around his lean hips, before glancing back up at her.

'Yeah, sorry. I forgot to grab mine.'

'Well, take it off!'

He kinked a lazy eyebrow and gave a slow smile that momentarily distracted her outrage.

'Well, okay, if that's what you want,' he shrugged, putting down the razor and moving his fingers to the corner of the towel, holding it gingerly across his hips.

'What the hell are you doing?' she gasped, coming to her senses.

'Giving your towel back.'

'Oh my God. You're naked. I don't want to see you naked!' she snapped, then swallowed nervously. *I mean, it wouldn't be the absolute worst view in town,* a little voice inside reasoned, before she shook her head swiftly to dislodge the wayward thought. 'What's wrong with you?'

'Just trying to keep you happy.'

She stared at this man before her, half his face freshly shaved, the other half still covered in shaving cream, watching her through slightly amused dark-blue eyes, and found herself close to tears. It really was too much. All she'd wanted was to take a hot shower to try and wash away the frustration of another day working in a stupid job she hated, and now she was standing here, being laughed at by some half-naked stranger wearing her Abyss and Habidecor one hundred percent Egyptian cotton towel!

'Hey, I'm sorry,' the stranger said, his demeanour changing instantly. 'Seriously, I jumped in the shower and forgot my towel. I saw this one and figured I'd be able to duck back to my room and get dressed and replace it before anyone knew it was missing.'

'Are you freaking crazy? You were going to use my towel—a complete stranger—and then just put it back?' It was beyond gross.

'I was planning on washing it first,' he said, sounding insulted she'd even consider him doing anything less.

'Oh, well, that's big of you,' she snapped, wiping her eyes before sniffing and searching for the box of tissues she'd put in here that morning.

'We were out of toilet paper,' he said sheepishly, looking across the room where the tissues sat on the floor beside the toilet.

Quinn's shoulders slumped in defeat. Just when she figured this day couldn't get any worse, it just kept proving her wrong.

Without a word, she turned on her heel and walked out of the bathroom.

She sank down on her bed and let the tears fall freely. She hated this house. She hated her job. She hated what her life had become. She had no family, no friends, and she was sick to death of living in a room of boxes.

A soft tap on her door was followed by a male voice. 'I've just put your towel on to wash. I'll bring it back after I've put it in the dryer.'

'I don't want it back,' she yelled, jumping to her feet with renewed energy. Who the hell did this guy think he was?

She reefed open the door, and he took a tentative step backwards, watching her warily. 'Keep it. I don't want it back after you've just wiped all your...*bits*...over it. No amount of washing is ever going to remove that from my mind!'

'Okay,' he said, biting back a grin, which only served to infuriate her more. 'I'll buy you a new towel to replace it.' He sobered as she narrowed her glare. 'You can use mine tonight if you want,' he said, handing her a hideous brown and orange striped miniscule cloth that had frayed edges and a hole at one end. 'It's clean—I haven't used it.'

'Thanks, but I've got another one,' she bit out, trying not to recoil at the sorry excuse for a towel.

'Okay, well, sorry again. I'm Scott, by the way,' he said, pointing at the bedroom door next to hers. 'I'm your new flatmate.'

Quinn followed his gaze to the door and frowned.

'I just got into town. Here to start a brand-new chapter,' he said with a hopeful grin.

'I don't care,' she said almost desperately. 'Just don't touch my stuff.'

'Okay, fair call after today—not my finest moment,' he apologised. 'I'll, ah, leave you to it then.' He stepped back and returned to his room.

Letting out a frustrated sigh, she gathered a new towel from the bottom of her wardrobe and her change of clothes and headed back to the bathroom. Closing the door behind her, she eyed the lack of lock and vowed to bring it up with Vivian next time she saw her. After undressing, she stepped into the bathtub and reached out to turn on the tap, stepping beneath the disappointing trickle of water. She felt new tears beginning to form. This sucked so bad. She missed her old shower. If ever she'd needed a dose of chromotherapy to renew her emotional, spiritual and mental energies, it was now.

She reached for her shampoo and recoiled in horror at what had been a practically brand-new bottle of Oribe shampoo, with its delicate scent of watermelon and lychee, that was now well below half. This was her last bottle! She'd been rationing it religiously, knowing full well she wouldn't be able to afford another one until her grandmother reinstated her inheritance. *This has to last six mother-effing months!*

Fury, the likes of which she'd never known before, reared up inside her, but just then the water went from hot to arctic and the shock momentarily took her breath away.

She let out an outraged scream. Turning the taps off with a force that should have snapped the handles off, she grabbed her towel and wrapped it around her, threw open the door and marched down the hallway to the room at the end. She banged her fist against the door, wishing it was actually the face she was picturing.

'Whoa. Hey. What's wrong?' Scott said, staring at her furious expression.

'What's *wrong?*' she snarled. 'You used all the bloody hot water *and* my shampoo is missing!'

'Oh. Yeah, the shampoo. I accidentally knocked it over, and the lid wasn't on properly so it leaked everywhere, but I managed to scoop as much of it back in as I could. And I'm sorry about the hot water...the shower took longer than it usually takes on account of trying to clean up the shampoo...' His voice trailed off, and he winced as he took in her dishevelled, incensed state. 'Sorry.'

Quinn let out a furious, almost silent scream before returning to the bathroom and slamming the door. Clenching her fists at her side, she stood before the basin and closed her eyes, fighting for her murderous rage to subside before drying herself and getting dressed to return to her bedroom.

She pulled back her bed covers and climbed in, dragging them up over her damp unwashed hair, and gave into her misery, crying herself to sleep.

***

Quinn opened her eyes early the next morning, noting it was still dark outside, and realised she'd had her first solid sleep in weeks. She'd missed dinner and was still dressed in the track pants and loose top she'd pulled on after her disastrous day yesterday.

Quinn climbed out of bed and walked to the window, looking out at the predawn glow that was just starting to lighten the sky. She couldn't see the beach from her room, thanks to the high-rise apartments on the main beach strip two streets over, but she could hear the ocean through her window at this early hour, before the rush of traffic and daily life drowned it out. The unremitting rumble of distant waves calmed her mind, which had been far too overactive of late.

She made a spur-of-the-moment decision. She turned away from the window and dug out her joggers, pulling them on. She felt like going for a run. She grabbed for her hair to pull it back, before realising she no longer *had* long hair, and stopped to look at her reflection in the long mirror on the wardrobe door. She didn't know this woman staring back at her. She was a stranger. There was nothing of the high-maintenance Quinn Appleton in this new version— no expensive hair to upkeep, no nails to get constantly refilled and manicured, no fake lashes to be maintained. And now, thanks to her *not* office job, she didn't have any kind of makeup routine to go through each day; new identity aside, there was little point, working on the floor, as it would have melted off her face by lunchtime. It felt so strange to find herself stripped back to some bare canvas version of Quinn.

She picked up her phone from the bedside table before quietly letting herself out of her room and making her way through the silent house.

Outside, the morning air felt cool against her skin, chasing away the remaining remnants of sleep as she set off at a gentle pace, her feet making a light *slap, slap, slap* as they hit the bitumen beneath her. She increased her speed, picking up the pace gradually until, by the time she reached the promenade, she was pushing herself harder than she'd ever done before. As she reached the sand, she bent over, hands braced on her knees as she took in long, deep gulps of air. Once she had her breathing under control, she walked towards the water, shaking out her arms and cooling down after her run.

The gentle break of the waves on the sand soothed her—they always had, even as a small child. Her dad would often take her to the beach when she was little. It was one of the few times she could remember they'd spent time alone. Her mother refused to do the beach—she didn't do much outdoor activity at all, terrified of the damage the sun would do to her skin—but her dad had loved it. Quinn frowned as she looked out over the vast ocean before her. It'd been a long time since she'd remembered any of that. When had their family life started falling apart? Not that it had ever been like the shows you saw on television where the parents kissed in the kitchen and everyone sat around the breakfast table smiling and eating together.

Her parents had never been the touchy-feely kind. They were always off doing dinner and socialising, and she and Felix would be left at home with the live-in housekeeper. But occasionally they'd have a happy time together. Usually when they went overseas, away from everything else that always seemed to be a distraction— away from the extended family and the business.

Her father had once been at the heart of the company. He'd been his father's right-hand man and had always worked hard—too hard sometimes. She recalled many a childhood fight between her parents when her mother would accuse him of wanting to be at work more than he wanted to be at home.

It was only after her grandfather died that everything changed. Her father had shouldered a lot of the business, although it had been her grandmother who called the shots, and gradually, as the years wore on and her father wore down, he seemed to lose interest in the company.

Quinn suspected it had a lot to do with Gran's inability to hand over the reins completely to either of her children after Grandfather died. Often Quinn heard her mother taunt her father in the heat of an argument that he needed to grow some balls and stand up to his mother, but for whatever reasons, he never had.

And now, with no interest in the company from any of her children or grandchildren, Gran was facing the prospect, for the first time in five generations or more, that no Appleton would be heading the company after she stepped down.

Thoughts of her upcoming day at the factory threatened to ruin her new-found serenity the beach had almost restored.

Despite the early hour, it was surprising how many other people were out getting their morning exercise. As Quinn turned to walk back to the esplanade, she spotted another jogger heading towards her and groaned as he grew closer.

'Hey, roomie,' Scott said cheerfully.

'Morning,' she muttered, stepping around him.

'Look, I know yesterday was…well,' he chuckled dryly, 'it was a disaster. Can we start again?'

'There's really no point,' she said, tilting her head, irritated when he fell into step with her.

'Why?'

'Because it's not like we're going to be seeing much of each other.'

'We share a bathroom and a wall,' he added.

'And that's pretty much the extent of it. Now if you'll excuse me, I've got a job to get ready for.'

'I'll walk back with you,' he said, ignoring the less-than-thrilled look she sent him. *What part of 'I'm not interested in being sociable' doesn't this guy get?*

'So you're into jogging?' he asked after they'd walked in silence for close to a block.

'Not really. I just had an urge to do it today.'

'Yeah, it's great for blowin' off steam. I guess I probably had something to do with that after yesterday.'

'It wasn't all you,' she finally said. 'It's just been a rough few weeks.'

'Well, if you want a running partner, I'm up for it.'

'It probably won't become a habit. I rarely stick to anything for long,' she said dryly.

'It's pretty addictive. You might be surprised.'

They arrived back at the house and Quinn returned to her room to get ready. She wondered if it was going to drag on as long as yesterday had. She still couldn't fathom why anyone would want to work so long in the one job as Maureen had. She pondered the thought. It wasn't as though it was anything exciting. Sure, she could understand if your job was doing something you loved; your passion. But this was a factory making biscuits, for goodness' sake. She just didn't get it. She was grateful she only had to last for six months. Although right now, *that* felt like thirty years.

Chapter 20

Quinn closed her locker and took a deep breath before heading out of the staffroom and onto the factory floor. She was getting used to the noise and the smells now. She looked for Maureen and smiled as the older woman waved to her.

'Morning, love, ready for a big day?' she asked in her usual jolly tone. It still mystified Quinn how anyone could be this happy when this was their life. You expected people who'd won the lottery or just retired to be happy all the time, not everyday people who had to come to a job like this just to pay the bills. What made people like Maureen so damn happy?

'A big day?' Quinn asked, suddenly nervous as Maureen's words registered.

'Boss man said you're on your own today,' she said, lifting an eyebrow, which was the closest thing to *not* happy Quinn had yet seen Maureen express.

'On my own? But…I'm not sure I'm ready.' Panic began to swell at the thought of not having Maureen by her side.

'We'll all be right here; if you have any trouble, you just let me or the girls know and someone'll be there in a jiffy,' she said with a reassuring pat on Quinn's arm, before adding with a serious look, 'Don't know why, but you rub old Darrell the wrong way and he seems to have it in for ya. He's never been the easiest man to get along with, but he seems to be extra dickheadish lately.' She sent the man in question a dark glare across the room. 'Nothing would ruin his miserable day more than if you did really well on your own today,' she chuckled, giving her a wink. 'You'll be right, love. We'll all be here keepin' an eye on ya.'

Quinn looked over her shoulder and saw the three other women nearby, smiling. For the first time in...well, she couldn't actually remember when she'd ever had people behind her, believing in her, and she suddenly felt teary at the thought. Thankfully, she caught herself before the moment got too embarrassing, and she straightened her shoulders and walked across to her station.

She could do this. She *would* do this. She was not going to let a weasel like Darrell ruin her only chance at getting her old life back. She looked across at the lanky man in question and narrowed her eyes. She was Elizabeth Appleton's granddaughter. She could squash Dickhead Darrell under one Louis Vuitton heel. The thought gave her a renewed determination.

Darrell turned around and noticed her, and Quinn held his eye for a moment before dismissing him and concentrating on the job at hand. She'd show him. He might think Amy Sinclair was some kind of pushover, but he was yet to meet Quinn Appleton.

***

'Told you you'd be fine,' Maureen said cheerfully as Quinn sat down at morning tea. 'Did you see our girl out there on her own, ladies?' she announced as Tara and Janelle sat down.

'You go girl,' Tara cheered, holding her hand up for a high five across the table. Quinn wanted to scoff at how absurd this whole thing was, only to find...it actually wasn't. Instead, she found she was wearing a stupid grin and then went and ruined it by clumsily sloshing her coffee over the side of her mug and spilling it all over a stack of magazines on the table.

'Crap,' she gasped, searching for something to wipe up the mess.

'All good, it was only some old issues,' Janelle said, waving off Quinn's attempt to help clean up as she carried the top magazine to the kitchen and tipped the spilt coffee into the sink, wiping it over with paper towel. 'Good as new,' she said, holding it up, and Quinn felt the colour drain from her face as she saw her cousin on the front cover staring back at her.

'Ha,' Tara said with a smirk, 'wouldn't be the worst thing Greta Appleton had spilled on her face, I'm willing to bet.'

'Tara!' Janelle chortled as Quinn let out a strangled laugh.

'Oh, come on, she doesn't even make a secret of how she made her way to the top,' Tara scoffed.

'Poor Lady Appleton,' Maureen said, shaking her head. 'I can't imagine how embarrassed she must be, reading about all the terrible things her grandchildren get up to. I tell you, if my grandkids ever did half the things these little wretches have done, I'd skin them alive.'

Quinn swallowed back a rush of shame and lowered her eyes.

'Oh, come on, Maureen, your grandkids probably do plenty of crazy shit—you just don't get to read about it,' Tara pointed out.

'Maybe. And for that, I'm glad. I don't know how she puts up with it,' the older woman said with a disapproving shake of her head, gawking at the tabloid on the table.

Quinn pressed her lips together tightly. These people didn't know them. It shouldn't matter what any of them thought of her family. But it did, and she didn't like the way it made her feel.

'You know, *you* could almost pass as a lookalike for one of this lot,' Janelle said, tilting her head slightly as she studied Quinn thoughtfully. 'Maybe you're a distant relative,' she said, suddenly grinning.

'Or a secret baby? Wouldn't put it past that lot,' Tara added.

Her dad might be a lot of things, but he wasn't the kind of man who'd be careless enough to leave a string of illegitimate children across the countryside.

'I wish,' Quinn said, giving a somewhat forced laugh. 'If I was, I wouldn't have to work here,' she added for good measure.

'Good point.' Maureen nodded sagely. 'None of that lot would lower themselves to work like the rest of us.'

A chorus of grunts circled the table and Quinn swallowed nervously, getting up from her seat quickly. 'I'm going to head back out there and get a head start,' she muttered, eager to leave before anyone else started making comparisons. That had been a little too close for comfort.

'See! That proves she isn't one of them—work ethic!' Janelle called out after her. Quinn didn't stop, but waved a hand in the air and quickened her step.

***

When Quinn got home that afternoon, she found a plastic shopping bag propped up against her bedroom door. Cautiously, she picked it up and looked inside, finding a fluffy white Abyss and Habidecor towel. A reluctant smile tugged at her lips, and she sent a quick glance at the door beside hers. She knocked, but there was no response.

A few minutes later came a knock on Quinn's door, and she groaned as she'd just laid down and had to drag her aching body up to answer it.

She'd expected to find Scott on the other side, but was surprised when she came face to face with Vivian instead.

'Hey. Just letting you know we're having a round table at seven tonight.'

'A what?'

'A round table. It's a thing we do here every now and again to touch base with everyone and meet with new flatmates. It's pretty chill. We order takeaway and have a few drinks. So, I'll see you at seven, out the back.'

Quinn didn't have time to reply before Vivian waved and walked away.

Out the back? She didn't even know the house *had* an *out the back*.

At seven, Quinn finished giving herself a pep talk and stood up, taking a deep breath. *I can do this.* She walked across her room dressed in a pair of ripped jeans and an oversized grey T-shirt knotted at the waist, and hesitated as she reached for the door handle. *What am I doing? I don't know these people.* Why was she bothering to socialise with a bunch of strangers? She was only renting a room off them. She frowned at the little voice. It sounded so—she mentally squirmed—snobbish. Quinn Appleton might not have had time for touching base and having a few drinks with a bunch of people she had nothing in common with, but she wasn't Quinn, she was Amy. Amy Sinclair would absolutely drink with strangers and try her best to fit in. She was a factory worker, and she had no inheritance to dip into to buy luxuries like food...and shelter...

She followed the music as she reached the bottom of the steps outside and gasped as she rounded the corner of the house. A paved courtyard was lit up with fairy lights, and a round fire pit sat in the centre surrounded by a curved bench.

'Grab a drink and come over and join us,' Vivian called as she walked towards the three people already seated.

Quinn stopped by the table with a large punch bowl, filling a ladle with peach-coloured liquid with fruit bits and pouring it into a glass before taking a seat.

'I hear you've already met Scott, your new next-door neighbour.'

Quinn gave a tight smile, wondering what the hell he'd told them about their first meeting.

'It's nice having all the rooms full again,' Vivian said with a smile.

'You don't get many people wanting to rent here?' Quinn asked, thinking there mustn't be as many desperate people—like her—around as she'd thought.

'Oh, it's not that. The owner moved back in, so we were the only tenants for a while. He's only not long moved out again.'

'Where does he live when he's not here?' And, more to the point, when would he be moving back and kicking her out?

'He travels,' Vivian supplied, moving one long, graceful hand holding her glass. 'Sometimes he's gone for years before we hear from him again.'

'So you manage the place for him,' Quinn said, nodding, finally understanding their role here a little clearer.

'More or less.' Vivian shrugged. 'We don't like to label things.' Tonight, she was wearing a long, flowing kimono in shades of jade and purple over a pair of baggy pants and a shirt, with a purple scarf tied around her head.

Quinn took a sip of the punch and froze as she tried to figure out what the hell she'd just ingested. It was the weirdest taste she'd ever experienced. Slightly fizzy but with a warm, tangy, herbal kind of flavour.

'What do you think of the kombucha? Atticus makes it. Isn't it divine? This one's mixed with water kefir, ginger and turmeric.'

'It's really...'

'Refreshing,' Vivian said enthusiastically.

'Yes, and...different.'

'Help yourself, there's plenty there.' She smiled, and Quinn bravely put on a smile of her own and hoped it passed as polite. 'Scott was telling us you two went for a run this morning?'

Quinn glanced over at the man in question and found him sitting slightly sideways, resting an arm casually on the back of the bench.

'We bumped into each other on the beach.'

'I prefer yoga as my exercise,' Vivian said sagely. 'It's a far gentler way to nourish the body. Anyway,' she said, clapping her hands, 'round table time! This is something we used to do, so we can air any issues before they become problems. I find if we communicate and have open channels, everything just seems to flow better.' Quinn found herself nodding along. 'Amy? Do you have anything to bring up?'

'Oh. Me?' Quinn said, a little uncomfortable to have everyone's attention suddenly on her. 'Um, nope. I'm good.'

'Nothing?' Vivian seemed disappointed. 'Scott?' she asked, turning her wide-eyed gaze on the other man. 'This is our chance to connect with each other and build trust through open communication,' she said, sending her glance around the small group.

'Ah, no. I think Amy and I have managed to communicate pretty well so far,' he said, and Quinn looked swiftly across at him to check if he was being sarcastic or not. She couldn't actually tell. His face gave away nothing.

'We can always enhance our communication though,' Vivian added, and for a moment Quinn was concerned it was going to turn into some kind of group therapy session.

'Baby, I think it might be a bit early for anyone to have any issues,' Atticus cut in, and Quinn had almost forgotten about that smooth Caribbean accent. 'I'm starving. Let's eat.'

'Well, we'll have another one next week then,' Vivian said with a determined nod of her head.

'Awesome.' Quinn tried for her best non-sarcastic tone.

'We'll be right back—you two stay and get to know each other.'

Silence followed the couple's departure as they went inside through a screen door and the sounds of the oven door opening and closing echoed out into the courtyard.

Quinn glanced over at Scott's soft chuckle and found him watching her. 'Thanks for not dropping me in it about the bathroom fiasco.'

'Thank you for the towel.'

'Yeah—I kinda wished I'd known how much they were gonna cost before I went in the store. I had no idea a towel could cost a hundred and sixty bucks. I should have known they weren't going to be cheap when I had to track down a place that stocked them.'

Next time, you might think twice about using a stranger's towel. 'Thank you for going to all that trouble.'

'Least I could do,' Scott said, then took a sip of his drink.

'How the hell are you drinking that stuff?' Quinn asked, barely containing a grimace.

'Here.' He took a flask out of his pocket and tipped some of the contents into her glass. 'Still tastes like shit, but at least the alcohol takes some of the edge off.'

Quinn took a tentative sip and gagged. 'Oh God, that's horrible.'

'Why do people drink all this health nut stuff? You can't tell me they like the taste?'

'I don't know. They've got stronger willpower than me. Maybe after a while your tastebuds die and you can't taste it anymore?'

'Could be something in that theory.'

The squeak of the screen door opening alerted them to their hosts' return, and Quinn's stomach grumbled. She was so hungry, she seriously couldn't have cared what she was about to eat right now, but when the plate of tofu and bean sprouts was presented, her heart sank a little.

While it didn't taste as horrible as she was expecting, it didn't go far in taking the edge off her hunger either, and she mentally went through her handbag to see if she had any food stashed in there to eat later in her room.

When Atticus and Vivian eventually wandered off to bed, Quinn made to stand, but stopped when Scott asked her if she wanted a real drink and something to eat.

'I know I do,' he added dryly, grimacing down at the remaining third of the now-lukewarm, tea-like drink they'd both been sipping all night.

'Actually, I would,' she surprised herself by saying. What the hell—she'd endured a lot so far this week, and she felt like doing something to celebrate.

'It's still early. We can go to the pizza place. I don't know about you, but I'm craving a feed of pepperoni.'

The mention of pizza suddenly had her mouth watering. 'Absolutely. Let's do it.'

Chapter 21

They walked towards a rather nondescript-looking sedan and Scott dug in his pocket to retrieve his keys.

'Would you mind if we walked?' Quinn asked. 'It's a really nice night out.'

'Sure,' he said amicably, pocketing his keys once more.

'I just need to run upstairs and grab my wallet,' she said, turning away as they approached the front staircase.

'No, it's on me,' he said. 'I still feel bad about the shampoo and I haven't been able to find anywhere that sells that brand.'

Quinn couldn't help the wry smile that touched her lips. 'No, you probably won't find it here,' she said wistfully.

'Then the least I can do is pay for the pizza and drinks,' he reasoned as they fell into an easy step next to each other.

'You said the lid wasn't on properly, so technically, it wasn't your fault,' Quinn pointed out, recalling she *had* been in a hurry that morning—and nervous. It was quite possible she'd been the one at fault.

'Yeah, but it was a pretty ordinary first impression.'

'Actually,' she corrected lightly, 'it was one of the most memorable first impressions I can honestly say I've ever had.'

'For all the wrong reasons.'

She liked his voice; it was deep, but not the seductive, hypnotic type of deep like that of Atticus. Scott's was rougher, much like himself—rough around the edges. His clean-shaven jaw of the day before had already grown into a shadow of stubble, and he wore his whisky-coloured hair shaved short—typical of a man who had no time to waste on barbers and probably did it himself with a set of clippers.

'So, what's this job you head off to every day?'

Quinn bit back a groan. That was the last thing she felt like talking about. 'It's nothing exciting. I work in a local factory.' Nope, even saying it out loud didn't make it seem any less surreal.

'What kind of factory—what does it make?'

'Biscuits.'

'What kind?'

She glanced across at him, trying to work out if he was simply humouring her, but was surprised to find he looked genuinely interested. 'Chocolate Heavens.'

'No way.'

She sent him a slight smile.

'I love those things. Do you get to eat them whenever you want?'

'Not whenever you want, but there's the imperfections—the ones that get pulled out if they don't look right,' she added.

'So, Appleton's? That's the factory?' He waited while she nodded. 'Do they make the others there too? Or just the Heavens?'

'They make quite a few of the other biscuits too.'

'Takes me back to being a kid. I grew up on those things. My mum didn't really do much cooking, but we had those.'

'Mine didn't cook much either,' she said with a smile, somehow finding it fun that they had something in common. Even if that one thing was a biscuit.

'So did you grow up around here?'

Her smile faded a little. 'On and off.' She shrugged. 'How about you? Where did you come here from...to start your new chapter?' she added, recalling his introduction.

'Oh yeah. The new chapter.' He chuckled. 'I came from Sydney. I wanted a change of scenery.'

'It's certainly that. What kind of work do you do?'

'I've done a bit of everything. What's that saying—jack of all trades, master of none? That's pretty much me.' He flashed her a grin, and she swallowed hard and quickly dragged her eyes away.

She hadn't expected to find him attractive. He wasn't really, not in the same way most of the men she knew were. She couldn't imagine Scott wearing a tuxedo or an Italian cotton shirt and loafers. She *could,* however, imagine him walking around on a yacht, wearing cut-off shorts and an open shirt blowing in a soft Mediterranean breeze as he hoisted sails and tied off ropes, barefooted on deck. Her heart rate kicked up a notch or two as an image of his toned torso in the bathroom the other day instantly came to mind, and the two nicely pronounced obliques that formed a V shape that pointed towards...

'Amy?'

With a start, Quinn realised she'd been daydreaming. 'Sorry?'

'You okay?' he asked, ducking his head to get a better look at her.

'I'm fine, I was just thinking about...' She swallowed quickly, searching for something to change the subject with. Thankfully, the pizza place was in sight. 'Oh good, we're here. I'm starving,' she said, picking up her pace to find a table.

What was wrong with her?

They ordered their pizza and found a table; it was still relatively busy, despite the hour, but the crowds were beginning to thin out. Scott went to order drinks and came back with two beers. 'Hope these are okay? They don't have much of a selection, I'm afraid.'

'That'll be fine,' she said and smiled, accepting the icy cold bottle. She couldn't say she drank much beer, but she didn't mind the taste. It reminded her of her dad. For a man of expensive and somewhat highbrow tastes, he'd always enjoyed a simple beer, and she remembered him telling her about the time his grandfather had shared his first beer with him. *'I remember him saying, "Jethro, there are only a few things in life a man truly needs: the love of a good woman; a job that earns you an honest living; a family you can be proud of; and a cold beer at the end of a long day."'* Her father had shaken his head sadly. *'I failed him, Quinn. If he were alive today, he'd shake his head and turn his back on the man I've become.'*

Quinn had always wondered about that conversation. She'd come across her dad sitting in the backyard after she'd come home from a friend's house.

She'd only been maybe fourteen at the time, but the sadness in her father's eyes had stayed with her.

She took a sip and let the yeasty brew settle on her tongue as it filled her with memories.

'You seem pretty far away tonight,' Scott observed, leaning back in his chair as he watched her.

'Sorry. I don't know what's come over me lately,' she said, feeling slightly embarrassed and more than a little vulnerable. Once, she would have been able to keep her defensive shield up around her without a problem. She'd have been able to put on her party girl face and dance the night away, no matter how miserable she was feeling. It's what they did.

'If you need someone to talk to, I'm apparently a great listener,' he said.

'Apparently?' she asked, lifting an eyebrow.

'Well, so I've been told,' he added modestly. 'But seriously. I'm here.'

'Why would you want to listen to some stranger's problems?' she asked, only half-joking as she took another sip of her beer.

'I don't know. Maybe because we both seem lost and in need of a friend?'

'How do you know I don't already have a heap of friends I can go to?'

''Cause if you did, you wouldn't be here with me right now.'

Fair point, she supposed, although it hurt more than she'd expected when she realised the truth of it. She'd always thought she had lots of friends. She knew so many people—she'd hung out with the same group for the last three years, for goodness' sake—and yet...where were they now?

She couldn't call Chantelle and cry over the phone about her situation—she might as well do an interview with the bloody *Women's Weekly,* it'd be all over town the next day. Which didn't say much for their friendship, despite the fact they'd travelled together and partied, spent pretty much every day with each other, and had always assumed they'd been best friends...clearly that wasn't the case.

'You don't have any friends up here?' she asked, turning the conversation away from herself.

'Nope. I've got a few mates I've grown up with, but they all live back in Sydney and have families. We don't catch up too often anymore.'

'What about your family?'

He moved a shoulder disinterestedly. 'My old man shot through before I was born—never knew him—and my mum passed away years ago. After I left home.'

'I'm sorry about your mum,' she said gently. As distant as she and her mother were at the moment, she would be heartbroken if anything happened to her. Lyla hadn't always been the ice queen she'd become lately; admittedly, she'd never been the kind to read Quinn bedtime stories or cook her a meal before a big exam at school to make sure she ate right, but she *had* made sure they spent mother–daughter time together growing up, going to spas and beauty salons and on shopping trips. They might have been materialistic things, but her mum had always made them special events.

'She wasn't a happy woman,' he said, dropping his eyes to the bottle he cradled in his hand.

'Is anyone really?' Quinn asked with a slight scoff. *She* certainly didn't know any truly happy people. Well, there *was* Maureen, she supposed.

'I reckon Vivian and Atticus are,' he said, smiling, lifting his gaze lazily to hers.

There it was again. With one smile, he'd managed to make her go all jittery and stupid.

She swallowed and cleared her throat quickly. 'Yeah, those two do always seem unnaturally cheerful.'

He chuckled. 'Unnaturally.'

'Well, seriously, who can be that bloody jovial first thing in the morning? I swear to God, if that woman sings "Have a good dayyyyyyyyy" one more time as I'm leaving for work, I won't be responsible for my actions.'

His deep laugh drew a reluctant smile, and she gave up trying to figure out why she reacted the way she did around him as their sizzling pizza was delivered to the table and Scott ordered two more beers.

'Oh. Dear. God,' she groaned as she took her first bite of the cheesy, meat-loaded slice of deliciousness.

'Now that's what I'm talkin' about,' Scott said, already reaching for his second piece.

'So why here in particular for a new start?' she asked, wrapping her tongue around a wayward strand of mozzarella.

'Why not here?' he countered. 'Sun, sand, surf?'

'Do you?' she asked.

'Do I what?' He paused, eyeing her over his next bite.

'Surf?'

'No. But who knows? Maybe a new chapter includes learning how to surf?'

'New chapters aren't always everything they're cracked up to be,' she said, wiping her hands on a serviette and picking up her beer.

'Sounds like the voice of experience?'

'Voluntary new chapters are probably different from forced ones.'

'Is that what yours is?'

She gave a bitter laugh. 'You could say that.'

'It can't be that bad?'

'You have no idea,' she said, shaking her head and taking another long swig of beer.

'So tell me,' he invited, watching her as he bit into his pizza.

God, how she wanted to. She wanted to blurt out the whole sorry, pathetic story to anyone who was stupid enough to want to listen, just to vent and get it off her chest, but she didn't trust herself not to withhold any of the vital things she wasn't supposed to talk about to anyone once she was on a roll.

'You wouldn't believe it if I told you.'

'It can't be worse than what was my final straw,' he said.

'You think?'

'I came home from a big night out and found my flatmate had changed the locks on the house and all my stuff was out on the front lawn.'

Quinn gave him a dubious look. 'Is "flatmate" code for ex-girlfriend, by any chance?'

His grin widened. 'No. It was a guy. But looking back, it was kinda creepy, ex-girlfriend-like behaviour.'

'What did you do to the poor fella?'

'Apparently, my excess drinking was causing too many problems,' he said dryly. 'I will point out, though, that the guy was a born-again Christian and had a strict no drinking policy around him.'

'Why were you living with him in the first place?'

He shrugged. 'It was a company shared apartment type thing.'

'As heartbroken as I am over your flatmate fallout, that's not even in the same league as mine.'

'So you keep saying,' he said, hinting that he still wasn't convinced she had anything to be complaining about.

She leaned towards him. 'Okay. My boyfriend, who broke up with me on *Christmas Day,*' she said with emphasis, 'just married my cousin.' She toasted the air, feeling a little light-headed from the two beers she'd downed in fairly quick succession.

'Okay, that sucks,' he said, after considering her quietly for a few moments. He nodded and clinked her bottle. 'Okay, you win.'

'Oh,' she added, putting up a finger in warning, 'not only that, he married her *after* telling me my family was too crazy to marry into!'

'The bastard,' Scott said sympathetically.

'He really is,' she said.

'Is it too soon for the "you're better off without him" speech?'

Quinn grimaced. 'I'm still at the pissed off stage, I think.'

'Understandable. What about your family? Your parents? Do they still live around here?'

All thoughts of Bryson and Greta instantly faded. 'In Brisbane.' At least they *did,* she thought, before everything was put on the market.

'So you're close, then?'

She'd never really given much thought about her family being close. She was dependent on her family; they were all ruled by Gran and her purse strings, and once, she would have said that yes, her family was close. They gathered when Gran called. They accepted one another despite the many flaws they had. And yet, surely in a crisis such as the one they'd just experienced, a family would pull together? Instead, hers had scattered. Even her parents had gone their own ways. 'Not really.'

'Yeah, I'm not close with mine either.'

The ambient restaurant sounds lulled them into a comfortable silence. 'I'm really glad you suggested this,' Quinn finally said, wiping her hands on the serviette. 'I didn't realise how hungry I was.'

'I'm glad you said you'd come.' He held her eyes a little longer as they exchanged a smile, before he lowered his and finished off the last piece in only a few bites.

Quinn's phone sounded, and she dug through her bag to locate it. Seeing the name on the screen, she answered it quickly. 'Hello? Dad?'

There was only silence on the other end of the line.

Chapter 22

The soft click sounded in her ear and she pulled the phone away to look at the screen, huffing with frustration.

'Everything okay?' Scott asked, watching her.

'I'm not sure. I've been trying to call my dad for ages and that was the first time he's called back. Something must have happened though, it cut off.' She pressed call back and then gave a click of her tongue. 'Straight to voicemail.'

Damn it. Why wouldn't he answer? 'I just need to call my grandmother,' she said, glancing at Scott in apology. 'Sorry, I won't be long.'

'Is it maybe a bit late to be calling your grandmother?' he asked, looking down at his watch.

Quinn checked the time and was surprised to see how late it actually was. He was right. Gran would no doubt be in bed by now, and not be too pleased by being woken up. Quinn would call first thing in the morning and see if she'd had any luck in her search. Maybe this call could shed some light on where her dad was.

'Yeah, you're right. I'd better get back though.'

'I didn't mean to keep you out this late,' he apologised. 'It's been a while since I had a night out that went by so fast.'

'Yeah, me too.' It *had* been nice. Scott was easy to talk to, and it seemed they had quite a lot in common. However, her father's phone call had put an end to the brief moment of carefree fun. Now she was back to feeling anxious again. Where the hell was he?

'I'm sure your dad's okay,' he said, breaking the silence they'd fallen into as they left the pizza shop and began walking home.

She glanced over at him, surprised.

'You seemed worried about the call back there.'

'Oh. Yeah, I am. My dad's taken off somewhere. It's not like him to do something like that. I just want to make sure he's okay and I don't know what to make of that call.'

'Where do you think he'd go?' Scott asked.

'I have no idea. I mean, he could be anywhere,' she said, frowning. 'He travels quite a bit.'

'Maybe he's just travelling with work?'

'No,' Quinn said dryly. 'He recently got...put off,' she corrected, remembering she wasn't supposed to get into family business with strangers.

'Well, maybe he was just in some really crappy reception. He'll call again when he finds somewhere better to call from.'

'You think?' she asked, hoping that logic really was what was going on. It stood to reason, she supposed. If he really *had* fled the country, maybe phone reception *was* an issue.

'Yeah. Has to be it.'

When they reached the house and walked inside, Quinn felt a bit guilty and hoped they didn't bump into Atticus and Viv, but the house was silent, save for the low hum of soft music playing downstairs. She breathed a sigh of relief as she reached her bedroom door.

'Thanks for the second dinner,' she said, as Scott walked past.

'I've always thought I might be part Hobbit.' He grinned. 'There are never too many meals in a day.'

'If I ever became a vegan, I'd probably have to turn into a Hobbit too.'

'I'm always available for second breakfast if you're looking for company,' he said with a wave. 'Night.'

'Goodnight,' she said, stepping inside her room and closing the door. She pondered the night's unexpected dinner date and found herself smiling. Scott was somewhat of an enigma. They hadn't started out on the best of terms, but he'd managed to turn things around. Funny—he wasn't someone she would normally give a second glance to; it was doubtful they'd ever have crossed paths, to be honest, let alone share a pizza and beer, yet she'd been pleasantly surprised by his easy company and how much she'd enjoyed herself.

As she climbed into bed, though, her thoughts went back to her father. She felt that pang of uncertainty once again, arriving just in time to rob her of precious sleep.

***

In the tearoom during lunch break, Quinn took out her food and sat down with her cup of instant coffee. Perhaps her tastebuds *had* died and she no longer tasted anything, or she was somehow psychologically conditioning herself to accept that instant coffee was now part of her everyday life. Either way, part of her soul felt as though it was withering away.

'Oh, boohoo,' Janelle was saying across the table from her. Quinn's head snapped up guiltily. *Crap. Did I say that out loud?* But Janelle was looking down at a magazine. 'Have you seen the latest about our ladyship's family troubles?'

'What now?' Maureen asked in a decidedly unimpressed tone, followed by a chorus of groans from a few people around them.

'Who are we talking about?' Quinn asked, confused.

'The Appletons,' Janelle informed her, before going back to the magazine. 'Her granddaughter, the famous model one'—she flipped her hand in the air for added *lah-di-dah* emphasis—'has just separated from the new husband.'

Quinn dropped the spoon she'd been stirring her coffee with, making a loud clatter on the table. She fumbled to pick it up, almost knocking her mug over, and quickly steadied herself, muttering a hasty apology.

Maureen eyed her before switching her gaze back to Janelle. '*S*eparated? Didn't they only just get married? What is it with these celebrities?' The woman clicked her tongue impatiently. 'Why do they go to all the trouble of getting married just to change their mind like they're changing their underwear?'

Quinn gave a small snort at the term 'celebrity'. Greta would love that.

She *knew* it. Greta had been playing her usual games. Why she'd gone to the extreme of getting married, though, was beyond her. In fact, why her cousin, who seemed to have everything, would still be so intent on playing her juvenile games now they were all adults was also a complete mystery. Quinn had posed no threat to her beautiful cousin—even less so now. So why had she tried so hard to hurt her?

'Bored,' Janelle said, tossing the magazine into the centre of the table as she rose from her seat and moved towards the sink. 'Once you've got all that money, there's nothing else to do, is there?'

'I reckon I could think of heaps of things to do if I had that much money,' Tara scoffed. 'At least, I'd give it a good crack.'

'Yeah, it must be nice to have those kinds of problems—bored because they have too much money,' another woman who'd been sitting nearby added.

Quinn bit back the urge to defend herself and her family. It wasn't always a bed of roses coming from a wealthy family. Look at how quickly the tides could turn. But she had to admit, she was feeling exactly like the people around her, wistfully thinking about a life of luxury. That *had* been her life not so long ago, and it felt strange now. *She* felt strange. Quinn sat straighter in her chair. That's not how she was supposed to be feeling. Her life *was* her old life. Or it would be again soon. This was only her *temporary* life. This was just humouring Gran. Wasn't it?

Her gaze fell to the cover of the magazine, which boasted a photo of Greta and Bryson ripped in half and the headline *Supermodel Greta Appleton's new diet: How to lose 90 kilos in less than a month—divorce it!*

Quinn gave an almost silent snort. She didn't feel hurt or angry anymore. She felt…nothing. The realisation surprised her. She felt freer.

***

'Sinclair!' Darrell yelled, and Quinn glanced up, a packet of Chocolate Heavens in each hand, pitying whoever Sinclair was. Wait, *she* was Sinclair. She swore under her breath. *What now?*

'You need to work faster.'

She looked at the box she was packing. She thought she was doing fine. Nothing was backing up anywhere. What was his problem? She took a slow breath and forced a smile. 'Working on it,' she said, without stopping.

'Well, work harder,' he snarled as he stalked past.

'Ignore him,' Tara said quietly, sending a narrowed glare after him. 'You're doing great.'

'Is he always this warm and fuzzy?' Quinn asked dryly.

Tara chuckled and shook her head. 'He's been brought in from the Sydney factory. Everyone suspects this place is about to get a major overhaul. Apparently, that's his specialty—giving a report so management can implement changes.'

'What kind of changes?' Quinn asked suspiciously.

'The last place he went to ended up putting off over two hundred people when they upgraded the factory to pretty much all automotive.'

'That's crazy,' Quinn said, shocked. That seemed like an awful lot of people to be put off.

'Everyone's a bit nervous, to say the least,' Tara muttered, worry tinging her features.

'Still doesn't give him the right to be a dick,' Quinn added pointedly, but the women continued working in silence, Tara seemingly distracted as her practised hands threw in packets of biscuits and closed boxes on autopilot.

Quinn thought about the effect something like that would have on this factory. Surely, they couldn't justify laying off that many people here, in favour of making *everything* electronic? A family like Tara's, with so many small children at home, would feel the impact of this job loss terribly, considering both parents worked in the same factory. What would they do?

How could one man—and such a horrible man at that—hold the futures of so many people in his hands? This wasn't right.

Stepping outside, she called Gran. 'Hi, Gran. Any news on Dad?'

'Good morning to you too, dear,' Gran said calmly.

For goodness' sake, she was a working woman now! She didn't have all day to make conversation. She was on her afternoon break!

'There's been no news as yet. I've got my private investigator looking into it. He'll get back to me as soon as he finds anything.'

'Dad tried to call me last night. But it dropped out.'

'He did?' Gran sounded surprised.

'His number came up on my phone, but I couldn't hear him. So he has his phone with him. Can't your investigator do some kind of location search on the phone?'

'I'm sure he's doing everything he can. I only hire professionals, dear.'

Of course she did. Quinn rolled her eyes.

'I will call you as soon as I have any news,' Gran promised, then said a quick goodbye and hung up, leaving Quinn to give a frustrated sigh before dropping her phone into her bag and heading back to her station. She supposed Gran was right. Anyone she'd hired to look into her father's disappearance would know what they were doing and have thought to check if his mobile could be tracked. But all this waiting around was not putting her mind at ease. Maybe she should do some investigating of her own. The thought kept her busy for the rest of her shift.

Chapter 23

After a longer than intended pit stop waiting in line at the toilets, Quinn re-entered the factory floor and groaned as she spotted Darrell. He seemed busy making someone else's life miserable, and she planned to sneak past and hope he didn't spot her coming back late from afternoon tea, when his voice made her pause.

'I don't know what you people do back home,' he was saying in a particularly grating tone; slow and pronounced, 'but here, we don't live like pigs.'

Quinn took a closer step to get a better view. Darrell was towering over a small Asian woman, her head bowed and shoulders hunched. She'd seen her around the factory a few times but wasn't in the same area so didn't know her name.

'Your work station must be kept spotless. No rubbish on the floor,' he said, raising his voice. 'Understand?'

Quinn saw the woman nod vigorously, but she continued to stare at the ground.

'Is everything okay?' Quinn found herself asking. The minute she opened her mouth, she wished she'd just kept walking. Seriously, what was she thinking? None of this mattered to her.

Darrell turned slowly and stared at her, almost incredulously. Quinn held back the wince she felt coming and switched her attention to the woman, who had finally lifted her head to goggle at her with surprised eyes. 'Are you okay?' Quinn asked.

'What do you think you're doing?' Darrell demanded. 'Get back to your own station.'

Quinn ignored his raised voice, realising but not caring they were drawing some attention from people nearby. Who did this idiot think he was, yelling at everyone? Where was his professionalism? He was supposed to be in a position to direct, not abuse. 'Are you all right?' she asked again of the smaller woman, who was flicking a somewhat unsure glance between Darrell and Quinn.

'Yes. Everything's fine,' she said quietly, her accent heavy.

Darrell moved towards Quinn, bringing him uncomfortably close, and she straightened, sending him a glare that had quelled many a rude shop assistant in her time, but did not take a step back. The old Quinn stirred inside her at his blatant attempt at intimidation, rubbing her hands together gleefully. It had been a while since her confidence had a chance to re-emerge.

'Take yourself back to your station and mind your own business, Sinclair,' he snarled.

'Take *yourself* out of *my* personal space before I make a complaint to Human Resources about inappropriate workplace behaviour.'

For a moment, his face went blank, possibly in shock, before his small beady eyes became hooded once more as he seemed to consider his options. Slowly he stepped back, then around her, his expression furious. He went to speak but thought better of it, and stormed away.

'You shouldn't have done that. Now he will yell at you,' the woman said in almost a whisper.

'He shouldn't be yelling at anyone,' Quinn told her, shaking her head. 'Are you okay to keep working?'

The woman nodded and immediately moved back to her station. 'Please. I need my job. No trouble.'

'What's your name?' Quinn asked.

'Sumiko,' she replied, lowering her eyes.

Quinn studied her calmly. 'You won't lose your job, Sumiko.'

She'd thought Darrell only had an issue with *her*, for whatever reason, but it seemed he had it in for almost everyone. She hadn't really cared much when he'd been giving her a hard time; it was annoying, sure, and yes, she needed this job as part of her gran's probation rules, but she really didn't care if this guy made her life miserable—it wasn't forever and, after her time was up, she wouldn't be giving this place or Dickhead Darrell another thought. But it was starting to matter now that she'd noticed him picking on other people. And these other people always seemed to be women. Did he have a problem with women in particular, or were they just an easier target to take his frustrations out on than men?

Today's incident particularly irritated her because of something in his tone. He wasn't just picking on a female; it seemed more insulting than that. He'd seemed to enjoy making fun of someone who clearly spoke English as a second language, as though talking to a small child or someone less intelligent. That irritated her. A lot. If you were going to pick on someone, make sure it was someone who had the ability to take you on—not someone you could send cowering into submission.

The rest of the afternoon seemed to drag on endlessly, and she was sick of the glares from Darrell he threw her way whenever she made the mistake of looking up and catching his eye.

It was going to be a long six months at this rate, and she reminded herself not to go looking for any more trouble between now and then. She had enough problems of her own.

***

'I just heard what happened,' Maureen said, taking Quinn's arm as they walked outside after their shift. 'Are you okay?'

'I'm fine,' Quinn said, brushing off the woman's concern. 'I wasn't the one getting yelled at. That man needs an attitude adjustment. Big time.'

'You need to watch yourself around him,' Maureen warned, lowering her voice. 'You'll lose your job.'

'How does he get away with treating people like that?'

Maureen let out a frustrated breath and shook her head. 'No one knows much about him. But apparently the big guns bring him in to work out where they can make changes in the company. He's not here by accident.'

'Well, I don't care who he is. He can't treat staff the way he does. Someone needs to say something.'

Maureen shook her head and gave a small grunt. 'No one will. Everyone knows that would be as good as getting yourself fired. Nope. Take my advice. Keep your mouth shut and head down around that fella if you want to keep your job.'

She didn't particularly *want* to keep her job, but she did *need* it...for now. It bugged her more than she thought it would, to admit Maureen might be right. Six months...that's all she needed to hold out for. She could do that. Surely.

***

Quinn sat on the beach and soaked up the last rays of sunshine after work. She'd been waiting to hear back from Gran with news about her father but hadn't heard anything. Something wasn't right about this whole thing. She wasn't sure how she knew it—she just did. It was a feeling deep inside that gnawed at her. The waves crashed, clawing their way higher over the dry sand before being dragged back by some invisible force. Quinn watched on, able to relate to that feeling as though she were scrambling for a hold on something solid, only to be pulled back before she could reach it.

She was tired. Every night she tossed and turned; her mind a muddle of thoughts. Her body ached with the unfamiliar physical labour she was doing, but with her thoughts always racing, she was unable to sleep. She knew it was the nagging sensation that her dad was in trouble that mostly kept her awake. She was tired of waiting. She'd given Gran enough time to look into it and, so far, she'd turned up nothing. If she wanted some answers, she needed to do some digging around herself.

Back at home, Quinn walked past her own room and went straight to the one next door. She knocked and waited, hearing a muffled conversation ending abruptly before the door swung open to reveal a bare-chested Scott.

It shouldn't be such a shock—after all, she'd seen his chest before—but it still made her catch her breath, unable to pull her gaze away. Everything about him was so *masculine,* including the hair on his chest. Not that it was ape-like hairy, but the men she knew were smooth and buff, incorporating gym sessions with a strict waxing routine. There was nothing manicured on Scott. She was surprised to discover this wasn't a complete turnoff.

Realising she hadn't spoken since he'd opened the door, Quinn swallowed quickly and tried to ignore the flustered sensation that threatened to reduce her to a blabbering twit. 'Sorry to interrupt,' she said, managing to sound somewhat normal, to her relief, 'but I need a favour.'

'Sure. What?' He tossed his phone onto the bed, snagged a T-shirt off the floor and turned back to face her, pulling it over his head.

Ignoring the disappointed little sigh in her head, she took a slight step back from his doorway. 'I was wondering if you could lend me your car for a few hours.'

'My car?'

'Yeah. I need to get into the city.'

'I can take you,' he said in that casual, nothing-is-a-worry tone he seemed to use with pretty much everything.

'You don't trust me with your car?' she asked, arching an eyebrow. It wasn't as though the guy owned a Ferrari.

'It's not a matter of trust,' he drawled with a slight grin, 'it's more a matter of your personal safety. My car is not exactly what you'd call legal in a lot of ways...it's taken me a few years to master the skill set needed to drive it.'

'Well, that sounds...dangerous. Why don't you just get it fixed?'

'Would cost more than it was worth to replace it.' He shrugged at her obvious next question. 'It's got sentimental value. I haven't been able to bring myself to get rid of it.'

'Right,' she said. It actually made no sense to her at all, holding on to a death trap, but not her monkey, not her circus. 'If you wouldn't mind, then. I do kind of have to get somewhere tonight. I'm not sure how long it'll take.'

'No problem. I've got nothing better to do anyway.' He leaned sideways to grab his keys off his bedside table, and Quinn gained a narrow view into his room behind him. It was small—even smaller than she remembered—but she noticed he'd replaced the single bed with a double, which was pushed against the wall with barely any room to walk around it, and paperwork was scattered across it.

Quinn moved back as Scott stepped out into the hallway, pulling his door shut behind him. 'Ready then?'

Chapter 24

Quinn gave him directions as they headed onto the motorway and looked out her window. Rush hour was almost done and traffic seemed to be flowing, which was a relief. The trip from the Gold Coast to Brisbane should only take a little over an hour, but only if there wasn't an accident or roadworks or school holidays. Quinn supposed she should have waited until the weekend to do this, but she wasn't going to get any sleep until she had some answers about her father, and now was as good a time as any to start searching.

'So, where are we headed?' he asked.

'I just need to check on something,' she said, glancing at him sideways, 'at my parents' house.'

'Is this about that phone call you got from your dad the other night?'

She was surprised by the genuine concern she detected in his voice and on his face as he sent her a brief look. 'Kind of,' she hedged. 'It's complicated.'

'Sounds like it.' He didn't push, and Quinn was grateful. She liked that about him—he didn't poke and prod about where he wasn't invited. She supposed he had every right to want to know more—after all, he was giving up his evening to drive her to Brisbane with no idea where he was going or what they were doing. She would have asked a lot more questions had the roles been reversed. Then again, she couldn't actually imagine she'd even know someone like Scott if the roles had been reversed—if she wasn't broke and her life hadn't fallen apart. What would she be doing now if the last few months hadn't happened, she wondered.

Would she and Bryson still be together if Christmas hadn't gone completely to shit? Probably not. Greta would still have been there. She would have still tried to steal Bryson away. Quinn turned to look back out the window. Maybe fate had been stepping in to save her; regardless of everything else that happened at Christmas, she was almost certain that Bryson would have broken up with her anyway. So really, Greta did her a favour. She shuddered to think how much worse it could have been had she not seen the real Bryson before she'd done something stupid like marry the guy. Quinn closed her eyes briefly at the thought. She'd have been an even bigger laughing stock had that happened. Having everyone know the man you thought you were in love with was only after you for your family's money would have been beyond humiliating.

Was it her imagination, or was it getting a little less painful each time she tried to remember life before Amy? *Don't be ridiculous,* she snapped silently to herself.

She reached for the radio to play some music in an attempt to distract her thoughts, but Scott shook his head regretfully. 'Radio doesn't work,' he said.

'What do you do for music?' she asked, confused, eyeing his profile curiously.

'I don't mind the quiet.'

'Yeah, but...on a long drive?'

He gave a small shrug. 'Gives you time to think.'

How much thinking could a person do? she wondered. 'Tell me why you haven't gotten rid of this thing again?'

'Sentimental reasons,' he reminded her.

'How sentimental can they be to put your life in danger?' she asked dryly.

'This was the first thing I ever bought with my own money,' he said, a fond, almost wistful smile touching his lips. 'I mowed lawns after school and worked at a servo on weekends for two years.'

'Wow,' she said, frowning when he sent her a quick look.

'What about you? Did you buy your first car? Or were you one of those kids who got one given to them on their birthday?'

Quinn gave a weak smile. When she'd first gotten her licence, she'd been given the keys to a sensible Mercedes-Benz, and not even one of the cool sport models, but a boring sedan. Her parents had wanted safety to be the deciding factor when she was still on her P plates. She'd hated that her friends had all been given much hotter cars—BMWs, Porsches, a few even had Ferraris. She glanced around the modest interior and felt a rush of embarrassment at her past behaviour. Had she really been that much of a spoilt brat? The answer was, ashamedly, yes. While Scott had been working two jobs to save for this crap box—and, let's face it, it wasn't even new when he'd bought it—she'd been pouting because her *brand-new* Mercedes wasn't cool enough. Mentally she inserted a rolling eyes emoji. 'Guilty as charged,' she said, forcing a bright smile.

'Half ya luck.' She noted that he didn't sound bitter in the least, which was interesting.

'I guess I *was* pretty lucky. It's funny—I never realised just how good I had it until lately.'

'We never usually do.'

She gave him more directions as they took an exit and headed towards her family's house in Ascot.

Driving along the manicured, tree-lined streets, Scott let out a low whistle. 'Nice place to slum it,' he said, taking in the sprawling homes they passed. 'Did you grow up here?' he asked.

'Yeah,' she said, shifting in her seat. Why did she feel embarrassed by that? The thought distracted her momentarily. She had nothing to feel ashamed of, just because her family had money, and yet, for some reason now, she did. She'd driven down these streets all her life, but today it was as though she was seeing it for the first time.

The houses were grand and imposing. They screamed privilege, with their six-car garages and luxury cars parked in the driveways; it was a world away from the small box-like houses that made up the housing estates she passed en route to the factory every day.

'This is it,' she said, pointing at the driveway up ahead. 'Just park along here.'

Her parents' house was impressive even for this street. They'd knocked down the original modest Queenslander that had once sat in the centre of the large block and replaced it with a giant, three-storey glass architectural dream. Built in a U-shape design, the main house wrapped itself around a central entertainment area and courtyard with tropical gardens complete with a Bali hut and bridge walkways that wove their way over and around the designer in-ground pool.

Quinn tried to open her door but found it wouldn't budge. Scott hurried around the front of the car to reach for the handle. 'Sorry. It only opens from the outside,' he said, pulling hard, the door giving a protesting groan before reluctantly opening. 'Don't often get passengers.' He shrugged at the doubtful eyebrow she raised at him as she climbed out.

A high security fence blocked the lower part of the house from the street, and Quinn led the way towards the front gate, keying in the security code and pushing it open. A gravelled path wound its way through neatly trimmed hedges ending at two steps that led to a massive timber front door.

Quinn inserted her key and pushed it open, the sound of her low heels echoing loudly on the polished marble floor of the entrance hall.

'So, what exactly are we doing?' Scott asked, as he followed her into the massive open-plan kitchen.

'I'm looking for something,' she said, feeling a little stupid now that she had to say it out loud. What *did* she think she was going to find, exactly?

'Okay,' he said slowly. 'Anything I can help you look for?'

'Not really…I'm not sure what it is yet.' She huffed as she caught his slightly bemused expression. 'I don't know what I'm looking for,' she said, throwing her hands in the air. 'Anything that might explain my father's sudden disappearance. I have no idea if there'll be anything helpful here, but I can't just sit around and wait for answers. My father's missing. I need to *do* something.'

'Okay,' he said, lifting a hand to pacify her. 'Let's just take a look around and see if there's anything obvious.'

'Like what?' she asked, after taking a slow breath and feeling her frustration begin to subside under his calm influence.

His eyes flicked around the room, seemingly dismissing anything of importance. 'Let's start in the bedroom. Check and see if there's any sign of someone packing for a trip. Check if there's any luggage missing.'

That made sense, she thought, and was suddenly glad Scott had come along. She hadn't thought of that.

She led the way to the staircase and up to the second floor, walking along the hallway that was more of a suspension-type walkway connecting the two large suites that dominated the second floor at each end. She never tired of the view from up here, overlooking the lush gardens below. The entire back of the house was constructed of glass panels that connected seamlessly to make a massive glass wall, and with the sun beginning to sink, the garden was coming to life, lit up by the professionally designed outdoor lighting system.

Quinn flicked the light switch on as she entered the room and froze. It was like a bomb had gone off in her father's bedroom. Clothes were strewn across the floor and bed, dresser drawers had seemingly been dug through and left partially open, their contents haphazardly discarded, and the safe inside the walk-in wardrobe was open and empty, paperwork scattered across the floor.

'Jesus,' Scott breathed, reaching out to put a hand on her arm to stop her from entering the room. 'Wait here.' He moved in front of her and carefully stepped through the mess to check the ensuite, coming back a few moments later with a frown on his face.

'You think it was a burglary?' she asked as she glanced around the room.

He re-entered the walk-in wardrobe. 'The safe hasn't been forced open,' he said. 'Can you tell if anything else might be missing?'

'I'm not sure what he kept in there, to be honest,' Quinn said, cautiously bending to inspect the small metal box. 'I'm guessing maybe his passport?'

'Yeah, well, that's not there now.'

She noticed a small silver suitcase standing beneath a neatly hung row of evening suits, and a large space empty where two larger cases would normally have sat. 'Suitcases are missing,' she informed him.

'Was your dad normally a messy person, would you say?' he asked slowly.

Quinn frowned a little as she surveyed the room. 'Not really. Not usually.'

'This looks like someone was in a big hurry to leave.'

Panic was the word that came to mind at the state of the place. Panic and fear. Or maybe that was just what she was feeling, because imagining her father racing through his room like a cyclone, she knew he must have been terrified of something…or someone.

'I'm going to check the other rooms to make sure,' Scott said.

'I'll come with you.'

Quinn followed him into her mother's room and found it untouched. A silk dressing gown draped over the back of the chair near the bed was the only thing out of place in the magazine-spread-worthy bedroom.

Downstairs, the other rooms all looked fine, until they reached her father's office. Once more, there were signs of mayhem. Paperwork seemed to have been dumped onto the desktop and scattered, as though someone had been looking for something and then left. The filing cabinet was left open, with files protruding awkwardly, stopping drawers from shutting properly, and a bin overflowed with shredded paper in the corner.

Her heart sank. She *knew* something was wrong. *She bloody well knew it.*

Chapter 25

'Look, we don't know for certain that your dad's in any trouble, right?' Scott said, breaking the silence on the trip home. 'I mean, he could have got a last-minute deal on a really cheap flight and had to pack in a hurry.'

Quinn sent him a sideways glance and sighed. She knew he was only trying to be helpful, but it didn't matter how much of a positive spin he tried to put on it—none of it sounded likely.

She wanted to ask him to drive her to Gran's so she could confront her with the new information, but how would she explain Appleton House to Scott? Gran would probably declare their whole agreement null and void for bringing in some stranger—besides, what was she going to say to him? Yes, my father *is* Jethro Appleton, which makes me *not* Amy Sinclair. It wouldn't take him long to connect the rumours of gambling debts and scandal and suddenly have some interesting fodder for the gossip magazines. It was bad enough he'd seen the house she'd grown up in, and was more than likely wondering what a girl from a rich family was doing working in a factory and living in shared accommodation in a run-down old house.

She thanked Scott when they got home, eager to get to her room so she could call Gran, but he held her back as she moved towards the front stairs.

'Listen, I know you're worried about your dad,' he said gently, butting into her racing thoughts. 'Just promise me you won't do anything by yourself.'

'What do you mean?' she asked slowly.

'Like I said—I'm sure there's an explanation for everything, but on the off chance there *is* more to all this, I just don't think you should go looking into it on your own.'

Quinn heard the concern in his tone and was strangely touched, but at the same time, disturbed. Oh, there was *definitely* more to all of this, and Scott's words only served to worry her further. Even he'd felt the panic and chaos inside that house tonight and was worried enough to warn her against taking further action alone.

'I won't,' she told him, forcing a brief smile. 'Thank you for your help tonight.'

For a moment he held her gaze, his face a mask of indecision, and Quinn drank in his rugged features. To her surprise, this close, his eyes actually comprised slightly different shades. The outer ring was darker—a deep green—while the inside had flecks of pale blue and brown around the pupils. There were lines around his eyes; not quite wrinkles, more like crease marks born from long hours outdoors, maybe. Somehow, she didn't think they were laugh lines—even though she'd caught him amused a few times—he didn't seem the kind of man who spent a great deal of his time laughing.

Quinn suddenly realised how still they'd been standing, both seemingly caught up in their own observations. His eyes softened slightly and, for the briefest of moments, she thought he was moving towards her, and her breath caught and held before his gaze shut down and he stepped back slightly, his hand dropping from her arm. 'You're welcome. Any time.'

Quinn turned and hurried up the stairs, heading for her room, dialling Gran's number before she'd even shut the door.

It rang out. *Damn it.* She left a message imploring Gran to call her back before going to the bathroom to brush her teeth and get ready for bed. She peeped at Scott's bedroom door as she returned to her room but didn't hear anything, softly closing her own door behind her. There was no returned call from Gran and no messages.

Quinn sat on the edge of her bed and sighed impatiently. They'd have to go to the police with this. There was no other option. The longer they left it unreported, the harder it would be for them to find any leads—right? But what did they have to go off? An untidy bedroom and a messy office? There didn't seem to be anything missing from the house—all the expensive electronics were still there—not to mention the antiques and artwork, so a break-in didn't seem likely. There were, of course, all the other pieces of the puzzle that might help justify some kind of police involvement—her parents' divorce, the debt rumours. She sighed again, this time despondently. There was no way Gran was going to get the police involved in this when there was so much room for scandal to be leaked to the press. But she couldn't just sit around and do nothing either—not when she knew deep down that something was very wrong.

***

The next morning, as Quinn signed in at work, she was handed a message to report to the manager upstairs. Immediately, Maureen and Janelle turned to her with wide, frightened eyes.

'Holy shit,' Janelle whispered. 'The manager? *No one sees the manager.*'

Quinn felt a ripple of unease wash through her. She could not afford to lose this job. She was not going to face a future of working for a living *forever.* Screw that.

As she made her way from the factory to the main office, Quinn gave herself a pep talk, ignoring the fatalistic expressions on her friends' faces she'd just left behind. *Maybe I forgot to fill in some paperwork for my records,* she thought hopefully. Taking a deep breath, she pushed open the door to reception and walked towards the woman with a neat brunette bob in a red blouse and gave her name.

'One moment please, Miss Sinclair,' she said, smiling politely before picking up the phone and pressing a number to inform someone on the other end of the line that she was here. A moment passed; she thanked them and hung up, then looked over at Quinn. 'You can go in now.'

Quinn wanted to say, 'No thanks, it's fine,' and scuttle back to the factory floor, but she bit down on that moment of absurdity and forced herself to walk through the two wooden doors on the other side of the room.

Where the outer office was the front office, full of noise—phones ringing and delivery truck drivers bustling in and out—inside these doors was a more civilised environment, where the executive officers worked, and Quinn felt a threatening uncertainty trying to beat down her resistance.

'Miss Sinclair.' A slim young man dressed in a sharp navy suit came towards her. He looked to be in his early thirties, with a thin moustache that Quinn's fingers itched to rip off like a strip of wax. It looked ridiculous. 'Please follow me,' he said, turning on his heel and gliding off down a hallway.

Quinn glanced at another set of doors at the far end and remembered playing on the floor in there when she came here with her father once, a long time ago. That wasn't their destination though; they veered into a conference room and Quinn seated herself nervously at a long table.

Was this a kind of psychological game? Why was she waiting here like some suspect in a crime TV series? She was not going to let them get to her. Everything was fine.

By the time she heard footsteps approaching outside the room, she had almost managed to quell the sick feeling in her stomach.

'Ms Sinclair,' a man with a deep voice greeted her abruptly as he entered the room and took a seat across the table from her. He appeared to be in his late forties, she supposed, with a stocky build and wearing a very serious expression. 'I'm David Fortescue, personnel manager. I won't keep you long, however I wanted to bring you in today to discuss an issue that was brought to my attention by your supervisor, Darrell Cook.' He consulted notes in front of him, then looked up. 'You've only recently started with the company, I understand?'

'Yes,' she answered warily.

Glancing down again, he continued slowly. 'Ms Sinclair, we pride ourselves on being a family-oriented company—we like to consider everyone who works here as part of one big family,' he said, putting the paper he'd been reading from aside to look her in the eye steadily. 'Mr Cook feels you are not being a team player.'

A team player? She wished this guy would get his metaphors sorted out. Were they a family or were they a sporting team? 'I'm not sure what Mr Cook is referring to,' she finally said.

'Mr Cook feels your attitude has been somewhat…belligerent at times.'

Quinn felt her eyebrow raise slightly at this. What a little snitch Darrell was. Slimy little cry baby. 'I haven't deliberately *tried* to be belligerent. Darr...I mean, Mr Cook and I do clash personality wise, but I don't feel as though this has affected my work.'

'Look, I do understand that starting a new job can be stressful, however Darrell was quite adamant there was an attitude problem, and I'd like to nip whatever this is in the bud before it gets out of hand.'

'My attitude isn't the problem here. I think you need to look at how Mr Cook treats his staff.'

'Darrell Cook has been with this company for a number of years. I admit, he's new to this particular factory, however he's a valuable senior member of our Appleton staff. I certainly haven't had any complaints from the staff here about him.'

'Because they all want to keep their jobs.'

'Ms Sinclair, are you making a complaint against Mr Cook?' David asked pointedly. His serious expression had taken on a decidedly harder edge now.

Quinn suspected if she went ahead with a complaint, she might as well start looking for another job. She wasn't sure that anyone would back her up if she took this any further. Job security was extremely important around here and, for whatever reason, Darrell had considerable sway and was a threat to that. She knew the others would be conscious of the fact Darrell could make their lives incredibly difficult if nothing came of her allegations that he was bullying staff.

She'd dealt with much bigger arseholes than Darrell Cook in her life—she came from a family of them, in fact.

She could see out her six months with him and survive, but she knew everyone else here didn't have that luxury. 'No,' she finally said, deciding for now to mind her own business. She wasn't about to risk her inheritance over a dick like Darrell.

'Then let's just consider this a friendly warning. I'd hate to have to revisit this issue again, Ms Sinclair,' David added sternly.

Feeling oddly as though she was in primary school and being scolded by the headmaster, Quinn headed back to the factory floor and tried to remember she was once a rebel and a bad arse, but couldn't shake the lingering feeling that she wanted to hide away and lick her wounds for a bit. She ignored the concerned glances her friends threw her on her return, and forced herself to concentrate on her job. This was the only thing that mattered. If she could survive this, she could survive anything. Once she had her money back, she was never going to think of this humiliating experience ever again.

'So? What happened?' Janelle demanded, falling into step with her at break time as they headed for the tearoom.

'Darrell put me on report.'

'That bastard,' Maureen growled. 'Did you tell them what happened with Sumiko?'

'Wasn't much point. She's too scared to make any trouble. Without her statement, they won't take it seriously.'

'You need to just keep your head down,' Maureen said.

'It wasn't like I went out looking to make trouble,' Quinn mumbled.

'No, it just seems to find you,' Maureen mused.

'Forget about Darrell,' Tara cut in, and her wide smile eased the mutinous thoughts that had descended upon them following the mention of Darrell's name. 'I'm having a party at my place on Saturday. We all need to blow off some steam after the last few days.'

'I'll have to see what's happening,' Quinn said when Tara continued to stare at her, as though waiting for her answer.

'Attendance is compulsory,' Maureen said briskly. 'It's also a welcome to Appleton's for you.'

Quinn opened her mouth to protest, but Janelle and Tara were already planning, and she couldn't have gotten a word in edgeways even if she *had* a good excuse not to come.

Chapter 26

Quinn pressed the intercom on the front gate and waited for Lionel to buzz her in. She'd been distracted on the bus ride over. Gran's brief summons the next day had been her only reply to Quinn's message, and Quinn hoped she'd finally convince her to call the police in.

One look at her grandmother's face, though, and her optimism took a hasty nose dive.

'I think it must be some kind of record at Appleton's,' Gran started, indicating for Quinn to take a seat. 'The time it's taken for a new employee to be put on a warning.'

Quinn stifled a moan. Of course Gran would have heard about that. 'That wasn't my fault,' she started to protest.

'Oh? You didn't show blatant disrespect to a supervisor?'

'He's a dick, Gran,' she whined.

Her grandmother closed her eyes briefly before resuming in her usual calm, collected tone. 'I thought you understood the terms of our arrangement.'

'I do,' Quinn said, swallowing the remnants of her outrage that the mere thought of Darrell Cook always seemed to ignite. 'It won't happen again.'

Gran seemed to be weighing up something, as she studied her granddaughter silently for a few moments before giving a curt nod.

'The more urgent matter I came here to discuss, though, is Dad,' Quinn continued. 'I went to the house to see if I could find anything that might explain where he was. I'm more convinced than ever that something's wrong.'

Her grandmother watched her closely. 'My investigator's still working on some leads,' she said dismissively.

'Well, they need to work a lot faster. The place is a mess. He wasn't just in a hurry to leave—he was running from someone.'

'There's no point in getting dramatic about it until we have some facts,' Gran said firmly.

'I'm not being dramatic, Gran. Why would he have left like that if there wasn't something he was genuinely afraid of? Was he about to be arrested for something?' Her gaze narrowed on the older woman as the idea suddenly came to her.

'What? Of course not,' Gran snapped.

The way Gran refused to look at her was telling indeed. 'What aren't you telling me, Gran?'

'All you need to worry about is keeping your identity to yourself and doing your job. The rest I will deal with. *If* there's anything to be dealt with. Like I said, I have people working on it and you need to stay out of it.'

'He's my father,' Quinn said, frowning.

'And he's my son,' Gran shot back, but there was a hint of emotion just under the surface of the firm words. 'If the business is caught up in any of this, it's going to get extremely messy. Trust me, Quinn, I want to get to the bottom of all this as much as you do. As soon as we locate your father, we'll both have our answers. Until then, there is nothing more we can do.'

***

The soothing sound of waves washing onto sand was a balm that went a long way to easing the jumble of emotions going on inside Quinn as she sat, arms wrapped tightly around her raised knees, her gran's words from yesterday lingering in her head. They should have comforted her, but they didn't. Gran knew more than she was letting on. Maybe she didn't know a *great deal* more, but certainly more than Quinn did. The momentary shock Quinn had seen on her face when she'd asked if her father was in trouble with the police concerned her the most. Whatever was going on, it seemed that even Elizabeth Appleton couldn't cover it up or make it go away—all the things that usually happened to keep up appearances. And that was what frightened Quinn the most. If Gran couldn't fix it, who could?

Quinn's eyes followed the lone figure of a surfer, far out beyond the breaking waves, sitting on his board, facing the horizon. He bobbed up and down with the swell as it lifted his board and dropped it again, perfectly good waves passing below him. At any time, he could have turned and paddled to catch one of them in, but instead, he ignored them. There was something peaceful about the way he seemed captivated by the endless stretch of ocean before him. She tried to imagine the gentle undulation of the waves, but a chill ran through her at the familiar panic of finding herself out there alone. She was fine right here, watching the waves—far less intimidating in size, inching their way up the beach towards her toes.

She closed her eyes and matched her breathing to the ocean's—in and out, rising and falling in slow, deliberate breaths—and felt calmness seep into her soul.

When she opened them again, the surfer had returned to shore, his board tucked under his arm as he walked from the water up the beach.

As he drew closer, recognition dawned. Surprise crossed his face and a smile tugged at his lips. 'Fate's been playing games again, I see,' he said, stopping before her.

She was glad she'd spotted him first—she'd needed the time to cover up her own surprise at seeing him again. She was beginning to wonder if maybe he was on to something with all this fate business.

Hugo shifted his board under his arm as he watched her get to her feet.

'I didn't know you came here to surf?' she said, trying to ignore the little leap of excitement the memory of their night together sparked.

He shrugged one big shoulder casually. 'I felt like a bit of a change of scenery. So, this is where you moved to?'

'Yeah—well, not this close to the beach, but not too far away.'

'Nice,' he nodded, his gaze moving across her face slowly. Was he also recalling that night?

'Yeah, not that nice actually,' she said dryly, 'but it serves its purpose.'

'What are the odds, huh?' he said, shaking his head.

'Well, technically they're probably not that huge. I mean, it's not like I moved to the other side of the world or something,' she said, deliberately trying to instil some degree of rationality into the situation. This wasn't a fairytale, or some chick flick where the male lead shows up at just the right time to sweep the hapless woman off her feet and fix all her problems. This was real life; and real life, she'd come to realise lately, really could suck most of the time.

'Come on, Amy—we didn't exchange numbers or contact information. In today's terms, that's almost the same as the other side of the world. I might also point out, you don't even have social media of any kind. It's like you don't exist.'

Quinn managed to capture the ironic chuckle that tried to escape at his uncannily accurate words just in time. Quinn Appleton officially didn't exist anymore, and Amy Sinclair didn't have time for Snapchat or Instagram. She was too busy trying to keep her life from falling apart.

'Are you busy right now?' he asked. She wasn't sure if they'd originally been standing this close or if somehow they'd moved, but suddenly the heady scent of salt, sunscreen and warmed skin filled her senses.

'Not really,' she managed to get out, happy to simply stand and breathe him in. She watched the droplets of water beading on his skin and had an insane urge to chase them with her tongue across his bronzed chest.

'I'd like to take you somewhere.'

'Where?' she asked, looking up into his eyes. *Big mistake,* she thought belatedly, as she felt what little restraint she may have had slip away.

'My place,' he said, his gaze focused on her mouth in the most distracting way.

'Okay,' she heard herself agree without much thought. Why not? She had nowhere else to be. There was nothing else she could do about her father. He'd decided, for whatever reason, to leave town, and she'd run out of ideas about how else to find him. She needed a distraction and Hugo would be perfect for the job.

He held out a hand and she slipped her own into it as they walked along the beach towards the car park. They stopped beside a new, fat-tyred, testosterone-overloaded, shiny black Jeep with its top down, and Quinn watched as Hugo retrieved a set of keys from somewhere underneath the car.

'Is that safe?' she asked, eyeing the magnetic case the keys had been stored in.

'It's insured,' he said casually, as he loaded his surfboard into the back and headed around to the driver's side to open the door.

Quinn reached for her own door and, when it opened effortlessly, she smirked ruefully as she thought about Scott and his tragic old shit box. For a moment, something strange flickered. There was no way that had been guilt. Why would it be? She had nothing to feel guilty about going with Hugo. Irritably, she dismissed the thought and settled into the luxurious interior. This was about as far removed from what she'd imagined Hugo driving as you could get. Sure, she *now* knew he was loaded, but there was still something so normal about the guy that it just didn't seem to fit. She'd half expected him to stop beside an old Kombi or retro vintage model from the '50s.

As he drove, Quinn took the time to study him, admiring the ease and confidence he seemed to exude without much effort. He was so at ease in his body, in his surroundings, in life. It seemed impossible to imagine him ever looking stressed or upset. The guy seemed to have an uncanny knack of always looking chilled—except when he was looking at her with those sleepy, hooded eyes. She quickly dragged her gaze away and realised they were headed to the Mermaid Beach area. She hadn't expected that of him either. He was full of surprises.

He turned down a street lined with prestigious real estate and once more found her idea about where he lived in no way matched the reality.

This part of town was locally known as Millionaire's Row, but better known as Hedges Avenue, where the houses were more like mansions and were always featured in the luxury real estate pages. He turned into a driveway and Quinn gaped at the gorgeous Hamptons-style home. In terms of size, it was more modest compared to some if its neighbours, but she knew it was probably worth upwards of nine or ten million in the current market thanks to the absolute beach frontage.

Inside was spacious and airy, the living areas all opening out onto back decks with white and blue sun lounges and alfresco dining areas looking over a strip of emerald grass that dipped down a small bank onto a white sandy beach. The main living area had glass doors that opened to create an outdoor–indoor living space that felt as though the ocean was almost part of the house.

A massive TV screen took pride of place along one inside wall in the living room, while another feature wall clad with rough stones held a giant fireplace. Couches were scattered in a casual, conversational fashion; she could picture the parties he'd hold here, with guests spilling out onto the wide decks and lawn outside.

'You like it?' he asked, watching her face as she took it all in.

'It's gorgeous,' she said, hearing her voice sound more than a little breathless. Clearly, she'd been away from luxury for far too long.

'I fell in love with it the moment I saw it.'

She smiled. 'You'd love the beach being on your doorstep.'

'That was probably the main attraction, but when I saw it, I knew this was where I wanted to stay. It felt like a home. I saw kids here,' he said, glancing around the room before settling back on her and ducking his head in the most adorable, slightly embarrassed kind of expression. 'I mean, one day...it's the kind of place I saw a family living in.'

'It certainly has a home feel about it,' she said, shifting a little awkwardly at the way he seemed to be studying her.

'Want a grand tour?' he asked, back to being the carefree, disarming Hugo she knew.

'Sure,' she said quickly. It'd be fun to remember how the other half lived.

By the time she finished inspecting the eight-car basement garage, gym, five bedrooms with ensuites, wine cellar, observatory and twenty-two-metre lap pool, she almost wished she hadn't. How on earth was she going to go back to her dingy little bedroom after this?

They finished up in the kitchen, with its enormous island bench overlooking the ocean, and Quinn gave a despondent sigh. God, she missed being rich.

She thanked Hugo when he handed her a glass of wine and indicated they should head out onto the deck to sit.

Quinn took a sip and leaned back on the recliner deck chair, contentment seeping into every pore of her body. *This is living.*

'Tell me what you've been up to,' Hugo said from the chair beside her.

'Working,' she said with a drawn-out sigh.

'You were moving last time I saw you,' he reminded her, taking a sip of his wine. The action distracted her slightly. Why could she not let go of this surfer dude image she continued to have of him? He should be drinking beer from a plastic cup, not wine from Waterford crystal.

'Yes. All moved in now.'

'How is it?'

'Horrible,' she said, shaking her head. 'Actually, it's not that bad. The people I live with are nice. It's just different from where I used to live.'

'And your family?' he asked, making Quinn start a little and slosh her drink. 'You mentioned once that you were having trouble with family. Did you sort it out?'

'Oh. That. Not exactly. Things are still…unresolved there.'

'Give it time. It'll work out eventually.'

'How's the business?' she asked, eagerly changing the subject.

'Business is great,' he said with an easy smile. 'I'm actually planning a trip to South America in the next few weeks.'

'Oh wow. Nice. Surfing?' she asked.

'No. Well, yeah, I'm sure I'll be surfing too, but it's a working trip. We're building a new school for a small community that had everything wiped out in a landslide a few months back. I'm heading over to lend a hand.'

'You're going to help actually *build* it?' she asked doubtfully.

'Yep.' His grin widened at her astonished look.

'Do you even know *how* to build something like that?' It sounded a bit dodgy to her.

He chuckled, and she felt her cheeks warm slightly. 'We've got builders *building* it. I'm just going over to be a labourer.'

'Oh.' Of course he was.

'I like to be part of the programs we fund—hands-on. There's something satisfying about knowing you helped physically make some of these things happen, you know?' he asked, looking at her in a way that made her wish to God she really *did* know what he meant. 'I mean, sure, the company's sinking a heap of money into these projects already, but to see the faces of these people...to live and work beside families who have basically nothing, and laugh with them, see the hope coming back in their eyes...' He shook his head wistfully, 'it's unexplainable. It's something you need to experience to actually understand.'

His passion for what he did was infectious, and Quinn could see how this man had become such a huge success. He had a presence about him; something special that radiated from him. He was a complicated mix of working-class millionaire, with a hefty dose of social conscience thrown in. He was a *good guy*. He was the kind of person Gran wanted her family to be.

Quinn's eyes shifted to him as he placed his wine glass on the table beside him and stood up, holding out a hand. She took it without hesitation, slowly rising from her chair, allowing him to tug her gently against him.

They stood out on the deck and kissed. The sound of waves crashing created a bubble of illusion; they could have been the only two people on the face of the earth in this perfect place. Eventually, though, the kiss deepened, and Hugo pulled back slightly to suggest they move indoors.

He led her through the house and up a flight of stairs to the second floor, opening the door to the master suite she'd seen earlier. The rustic beach theme used throughout the rooms below had been carried over in here too, with lots of blue and white striped fabric and nautical themed artwork on the walls. There wasn't time to admire the decorating though, as he began distracting her with his clever hands and mouth.

'I'm really glad you were on the beach today, Amy,' he said afterwards, breaking into her quiet thoughts. 'I've missed you. I was days away from hiring a private investigator to try to find you, if I'm being honest.' He gave a mirthful grimace.

His words brought a sudden splash of cold water to her senses. That was the absolute last thing she needed — someone digging about in her personal information and uncovering the truth.

Chapter 27

'Hey,' he said, propping himself up on one elbow to look down at her. 'I was kidding. I'm not some crazy stalker. I swear.' He caught her look with an uncertain glance.

Quinn forced a smile and tried to shake off the unexpected alarm his announcement had caused. 'Of course not,' she said brightly, but the moment had gone. She sat up, collecting the clothes she could reach to get dressed.

'Amy—'

She smiled and leaned over to kiss his lips quickly. 'It's fine, really, I've just realised how late it is. I should be getting back home.'

'I mean it, I wasn't serious.'

'I know. Honestly, it's nothing to do with that. I have something to go to later this afternoon and I need to get ready.'

'What are you going to?' he asked, seeming to accept that she wasn't freaked out by his earlier remark.

'A work gathering.' She still couldn't believe she was going.

'Do you need company?'

She looked at him doubtfully. 'It's like a backyard barbecue,' she told him.

'Sounds great. I'd love to meet your friends.'

'Why?' she blurted without thought.

'Maybe I want to get to know you beyond the occasional fate-induced hook-up we have going.'

'I'm not sure this is the kind of party you're used to.' She was fairly certain it wasn't going to be *anything* like the ones *she* was used to. However, strangely, she was almost looking forward to it—at least, until now. This was an unexpected complication.

'I can fit in to pretty much most places I go,' he said.

She had no doubt he'd be quite at home and most likely win every single person there over within minutes of meeting them. It was more *who* he was that worried her. Did she really want to draw that much attention to herself by arriving with a gorgeous multimillionaire chain-store magnate?

'I just don't know how I'd explain you,' she said awkwardly.

He gave a small chuckle as he watched her from the bed. 'You know, this isn't the kind of conversation I'm used to having. It's usually…never mind,' he said quickly, shaking his head. 'Okay, so how about I don't mention who I am? We'll just say I work in the surfing industry and I come from Central Queensland. How's that?'

'You don't have to…' She paused. What? Lie? Cover up who he was? It was somewhat ironic that she was already doing exactly that to *him*. 'It's not that I'm ashamed of who you are,' she started again, then realised how stupid that sounded. Ashamed of a self-made millionaire who, on the side, rebuilt third world countries. The man was practically a saint.

'It's okay,' he said, standing up in all his naked glory to wrap his arms around her waist. 'I get it. It's a lot to get used to. Seriously,' he stressed, 'I get it. You don't want to freak your workmates out. I don't want you to feel uncomfortable.'

The idea of going to a normal work function with a normal date was something she could almost imagine if she tried really hard, but she knew hiding Hugo's true identity from her friends had the potential to backfire terribly. They were all surprisingly up to date on the who's who of the social scene, and even though she might not have picked up on who Hugo was initially, she had a feeling *they* would be a lot more on task.

A real friend would probably have no hesitation in introducing a super-rich, handsome boyfriend to her workmates, but Quinn was already hiding one secret from them and adding another one was just too much to juggle.

'Would you be upset if I said no to coming along this time?' She saw a brief flicker of something that looked like disappointment cross his face, but she hardened her heart. She seriously had too much shit of her own to deal with without adding this to it. 'We could do something tomorrow instead?'

'Sure. No problem.' He smiled and, much to her relief, it looked genuine. Clearly, she was used to Bryson pouting when he didn't get his own way. Maybe *this* was how real men acted? 'What would you like to do?'

'Maybe we could go for a drive? Or a walk or something?'

'Sounds good,' he said, kissing her gently and, before she knew it, they'd walked backwards and ended up back on the bed.

***

Quinn ran up the stairs carrying the bottle of wine she'd bought on her way home and headed straight to her bedroom. She was going to be so late. She glanced down at her watch and swore as she pulled open her wardrobe and grabbed something to wear.

Tara had said casual, but what *kind* of casual? Good casual, smart casual? Home casual? She studied the contents of her cupboard and felt panic begin to rise. Taking out a pair of denim shorts and a button-up sleeveless top, she decided on a mix of casual, not-at-work chic and hoped it was a *thing*. She pulled on a pair of low-heeled Jimmy Choos and gave a happy sigh of contentment. She could take on *anything* with the right pair of shoes.

Quinn opened her door and immediately collided with something solid. She grunted loudly as Scott held her steady.

'Sorry,' she snapped, feeling frustrated and slightly flustered.

'My fault.'

'I was in a hurry and didn't think about looking before I walked out.'

'What's the big hurry?'

'I'm running late for a party.'

'Party? What, you've suddenly gone and gotten yourself a social life?'

'It wasn't my idea,' she told him dryly. 'The girls at work pretty much told me they'd come and drag me there if I didn't turn up.'

'Sounds like an interesting bunch.'

'Yeah. They're okay. Anyway, I better get going.'

'How are you getting there?' he asked.

'Bus. If I make it in time,' she muttered, looking down at her watch. She would be cutting it close.

'I'll drive you.'

'What? No. I can't ask you to do that.'

'You didn't ask. I offered. I don't mind.'

'You've already driven me to Brisbane once this week.'

'Come on, you know you can't wait to get back in my beast of a car.' He winked.

'Oh yeah. I really enjoy trusting my life to a death trap.'

'Hey! That's my baby you're talkin' about.' He feigned hurt.

Quinn rolled her eyes but followed him, hiding a smile. She'd miss her bus now anyway. She really needed her own car. This was getting ridiculous. Quinn mentally tallied up what she had in her bank account and searched the car yard signs as they drove, giving a despondent sigh at the prices.

'What's that for?' Scott asked, glancing at her as he drove.

'Why's everything so damn expensive?'

His chuckle did nothing to improve her mood. 'What everything in particular are you talking about?'

'Cars. I really need to buy one, so I don't have to rely on you taking me everywhere.'

'I told you, I don't mind.'

'Well, I do. I'm not used to having my freedom suddenly taken away.'

'I can help you look for something if you like.'

'Do you know much about cars?' she asked, eyeing his car meaningfully.

'I'm going to pretend you didn't just ask that.'

'Sorry, it wasn't an intentional insult,' she said sarcastically.

'I'll have you know, I've managed to keep this beauty running all this time, which would imply I know what I'm doing.'

'That's kind of debatable, actually.'

'You shouldn't judge a book by its cover, you know,' he said. 'Just because on the outside it looks a bit rough, doesn't mean it's not mechanically sound where it counts.'

For a moment she held his gaze, before he turned away to look back out the windscreen. 'Well, I'd appreciate any help I can get,' she said.

'I'll keep my eye out for something,' he promised. 'What's the occasion for this party?'

'I'm not sure there is one. It's been a little stressful lately at work, so I think it's just a blow-off-steam kinda thing.'

'What's been happening at work?'

Quinn turned to look out her window. 'There's a supervisor who's making everyone's life a bit difficult.'

'Have you had a run-in with him?' he asked.

'Yeah,' she said drolly. 'He seems to particularly dislike me.'

'Why?'

'I have no idea,' she said, glancing back across at him. 'I'm a delightful ray of freakin' sunshine! What's not to love?'

His laughter sent an unexpected fuzzy feeling through her and her smile slipped a little. Suddenly it seemed she was surrounded by men who made her...*feel* things. A little voice inside her head gave a mirthful snort. *And look where that got you last time!* The reminder of Bryson quickly doused whatever remaining warmth she'd just felt. She wasn't going to let anyone make an idiot of her again. Nope, just good old-fashioned sex and fun times was all she was committing to from now on.

She found herself momentarily thinking about what Scott would be like in bed. Her gaze fell onto his hands holding the steering wheel. They weren't large, but they were meaty and kind of rough looking. There were lots of healed, scratch-like scars, which she assumed he'd gained during one of his jack-of-none trade jobs at some point in his past.

He was a bit of dark horse, this one. She thought about Hugo and his beefed-up, testosterone-fuelled Jeep, and realised that car actually suited Scott and his personality more so than Hugo. Hugo seemed more like a luxury SUV kinda guy. That thought reminded her of his mention of kids. She could see Hugo as a soccer dad—soccer on Saturdays and Nippers on Sundays. An image of a set of blonde-haired, blue-eyed kids running around out the back of his house flashed across her mind and almost made her gasp out loud. They wouldn't be *her* blonde-haired, blue-eyed kids, that much she knew for sure. Christ, she could barely manage to take care of herself at the moment.

The address she'd given Scott came up ahead and put an end to Quinn's musings. It was a modest brick house with a number of cars parked on the front lawn and in the driveway. 'This is the place…apparently,' she said, feeling unusually apprehensive about going inside. These were people she worked with, who had made her feel welcome from the very first day—she knew there was nothing to be nervous about, and yet she'd suddenly become paralysed with a very un-Quinn-like anxiety.

'Wait!' she heard herself say as Scott moved to get out and open her door, feeling a flutter of panic grab at her throat.

Chapter 28

'Everything okay?' Scott asked.

'Yeah, of course,' she said quickly, giving a small yet hollow-sounding laugh, her hand remaining on his arm from when she'd reached over to stop him getting out. Self-consciously, she removed it. What was wrong with her? She was never like this.

'Do you think your friends would mind if I invited myself along?'

She turned her head and looked at him, trying to cover the sudden flare of hope his words sparked. 'You'd probably be bored,' she said in as offhand a tone as she could manage.

'Vivian mentioned she was cooking tofu tonight and invited me to eat with them if I didn't have plans,' he said, wearing a comically desperate expression. 'Please let me come with you.'

Quinn chuckled despite her unease. 'Okay. I'm sure Tara won't mind.' She shrugged and instantly the heaviness of moments before lifted from her shoulders.

'I owe you big time,' he said, sounding relieved as he exited the car and walked around the front of it to pull her door open.

Somehow, she suspected he knew only too well who the real winner was in this situation. But she was grateful he was at least trying to pretend she was doing him a favour.

The front door was open when they reached it, and Quinn followed Scott's lead as he walked inside. The sound of voices led them into a kitchen hidden beneath an avalanche of shopping bags, packets of chips and bowls of salads.

'Amy! You made it!' Tara called as she entered through a back door and spotted them.

'Hi, Tara, sorry I'm late.'

'Nah, it's all good. There's no set starting time.' Tara waved off her apology, but eyed Scott with undisguised speculation.

'Ah, Tara, this is Scott,' she introduced quickly, sucking in a surprised breath as Scott's arm reached across her to shake Tara's hand, brushing her stomach. The brief contact rendered her momentarily silent before she shook it off. 'He's my flatmate. I hope you don't mind if I invited him along?'

'Of course not. The more the merrier. Besides, any friend of our Amy is a friend of ours,' Tara said, sliding Quinn a curious glance, which she blatantly ignored. 'Go on out, I'm just coming in to grab the nibblies out of the oven.'

She shooed away their offer of help, and Quinn knew there was no putting off facing the others. Taking a deep breath, she put on a bright smile and summoned her Quinn party girl persona.

With the introductions made, she was relieved no one made a big deal of her bringing a man along, but she suspected there would be considerable talk about it after she left and questions on Monday to answer. For now, though, Scott was being his amicable self and chatting casually with everyone, which helped cover up the fact she felt completely out of her element sitting here in a small suburban backyard scattered with children's play equipment and a smoky brick barbecue, which apparently required a small group of men to supervise.

After a few minutes, Quinn felt herself relax. She and Scott had taken up some vacant fold-out chairs in a circle with her colleagues, and listening to their familiar banter filled her with a strange, warm, tingly feeling. Maureen leaned forward to refill her plastic cup from a box of wine she'd retrieved from an esky beside her. While Quinn was staring in open-mouth shock at the whole wine-in-a-cardboard-box thing, the older woman caught her eye and asked if she'd like some.

'Ah, no,' she said quickly, trying to hide her horror. 'Thanks. I've got some...'

Scott picked up the bottle by her feet and snagged a couple of cups from the nearby table, before popping the cork and handing her a bubbling plastic cup of the champagne she'd brought along. It was certainly no Dom Pérignon, but it wasn't terrible. She was actually kind of impressed—she'd given the guy in the bottle shop the challenge of recommending something that tasted like it was worth two hundred dollars but only cost twenty. She hadn't been expecting to be able to drink it. Yet here she was, drinking cheap champagne from a plastic cup...and enjoying it.

'Figures you'd be a champagne tastes kinda girl,' Scott said a little later as she held her cup out for a refill.

'What's that supposed to mean?'

'I saw the way you reacted when your friend offered you cask wine.' He grinned and arched an eyebrow.

'Well, some things aren't supposed to come out of a cardboard box,' she muttered, shifting in her seat and feeling just the slightest bit tipsy. She frowned at that. *Tipsy?* This was only her third drink. Maybe her tolerance had lowered, because she'd been too broke to afford alcohol in the last few weeks. *Great.* It would take forever to build it back up again for her next big night out. Whenever that might be, she amended. She doubted any of her old friends would go out with her after her time served in purgatory. Did any of them even wonder where she was? A laugh nearby caught her attention, and she found her tetchy mood dissolve as she watched Tara and Janelle laughing together and reliving some clearly hysterical story. Somehow, she suspected if she suddenly disappeared now, *these* people would notice.

One day she *would* disappear. Her usual relief at reminding herself that this was all temporary didn't feel the same in this context. What were these people going to think of her once they knew the truth?

'Hey? I didn't mean it as an insult,' Scott said, jolting her back to the present.

'Oh. No, it's okay. I was just…doesn't matter,' she dismissed quickly, tossing down the remainder of her drink and reaching for the bottle.

'If you're going to drink, I think you're going to need some food,' he said, standing up. 'I'll be right back.'

'I thought he'd never leave,' Tara said, sliding into Scott's empty seat beside her, pulling Janelle onto her lap. 'We've been dying to interrogate you, but Mr Tall Dark and Handsome wouldn't leave your side.'

'So? Spill,' Janelle prompted.

'There's nothing to spill. He just gave me a lift here tonight, and I felt bad about sending him all the way back home.'

'I had flatmates in my day,' Janelle said dryly, 'but none of them *ever* looked like him.'

'He's pretty tasty looking,' Maureen added, joining the conversation.

'He's not a pizza,' Quinn protested.

'I'd order that one if I were thirty years younger,' Maureen said, following Scott's movements across the yard with narrowed eyes. 'Come to mumma,' she growled, to the amusement of the others.

'No wonder poor George looks worn out,' Janelle chuckled, and Quinn sent a glance across to the older man Maureen had introduced earlier as her husband.

'But seriously,' Tara said, cutting in, 'you can tell us—what's he like in bed?' She wiggled her eyebrows suggestively, which set the other women off once more.

Despite a reluctant tug of her lips, Quinn sent her friends a frown. 'I have no idea. He's just a friend.'

'You're just lucky I'm married to that mega babe over there,' Tara said breathily, eyeing her large New Zealander husband with doting eyes. 'Or I'd call your bluff.'

'I'm not bluffing,' Quinn protested with a laugh.

'Well, if you're not tappin' that, you should be. Good grief, woman, what's wrong with you?' Janelle asked, shaking her head slowly as they watched Scott heading back across towards them.

Scott hesitated slightly when he saw all eyes on him, and for a moment looked uncertain, but it was gone in the blink of an eye as he handed Quinn a plate of delicious-smelling meat and a huge helping of potato bake with a cursory side of salad. 'I know how much you like your meat,' he said, and the women around them exploded into howls of laughter, completely ignoring her warning glare.

'Thank you,' she muttered, taking the plate from him, relieved when the others moved off to get their own meals.

'What was that all about?' he asked, settling into his chair and positioning his plate on his lap carefully.

'You do not want to know,' she said, shaking her head. 'This looks so good,' she said, changing the subject hastily. And it did. The steak was tender and cooked to perfection, melting in her mouth at the first bite.

'Much better than tofu,' he added.

'God yes,' she agreed.

The food was helping with her earlier light-headedness and she was surprised at just how hungry she'd been.

'Are you glad you came now?' he asked after a while.

'Yeah, I am. Although you've created some great gossip by coming with me.'

'Ah,' he said slowly, knowingly. 'So that's what that was about before.'

'You'll be happy to know, if you're ever missing some female company, the majority of my colleagues will gladly help you out.'

'Good to know,' he said without batting an eyelid.

Quinn considered him silently for a moment as she chewed. 'So, *do* you have a girlfriend?'

'Why? You offering?' he asked, biting into his steak sandwich. His eyes crinkled in amusement as she sputtered the sip of wine she'd just taken.

'No,' she answered quickly. 'I was just curious. I don't exactly know that much about you, considering we live in the same house.'

'That's not true. You know a lot about me.'

She supposed that could be true; they'd talked about a lot of things the first night they'd gone out for pizza. He'd briefly mentioned his family, or lack thereof, and his crazy ex-flatmate who she was still not completely sure wasn't an ex-girlfriend, but she didn't know anything about what he did all day or where he went while she was at work. For a guy trying to start a new chapter, he hadn't moved forward much. He was always home when she was there and, apart from the occasional time she heard his car leave late at night, she didn't see him getting out much.

'Have you had any luck with a job yet?' she prodded.

'Yeah, had a few promising leads,' he said, finishing off his meal.

'Met any new people?' She wasn't sure why she was being so nosy, but she really felt she should be taking some interest in his life, since he seemed only too happy to drive her around the place at the drop of a hat.

Maybe he was just lonely. Something about that observation, though, did not add up. Even her friends had picked up on that swaggery, bad boy kinda feel she'd noticed during their first encounter. Whoever Scott was, he didn't seem like the kind of guy who was spending time alone because he had no other choice. Maybe he was taking a break from life to get over a broken heart or something—she better than anyone should understand that.

'Nope. I've been too busy applying for jobs.'

'Maybe I could see if there are any jobs going at the factory?' she offered.

'Sure. Worth a shot.' He shrugged. 'Another drink?'

She held out her cup and he tipped the last of the bottle into it. 'That's the last of it, princess,' he said, sending her a lazy smile.

She blinked a little uncertainly at the phrase, but his gaze had caught hers, the way it did sometimes, and once again she felt a weird sensation flutter to life inside her. How was it that one minute the man was the perfect flatmate she felt comfortable around, and the next, there were sparks of something very *un*-flatmate-like between them?

Hugo instantly came to mind, crowding her already overstuffed mind, and she felt a flicker of guilt. He'd wanted to come along tonight as her date and meet her friends, and she'd turned him down. Yet here she was with Scott. Admittedly, Scott wasn't a multimillionaire businessman who someone might recognise and put her in a pretty awkward position, and yet, she couldn't help but feel as though she'd betrayed Hugo by letting Scott come.

Scott is a friend, she defended weakly. If that was true, then why did she feel this attraction to him?

This was why she wanted to steer clear of all men. It was too confusing. Far too confusing to be dealing with it partially drunk on a twenty-dollar bottle of champagne.

Music blasted from a portable speaker on the back patio and kids ran around the yard, dodging adults and squealing in delight as they chased each other. The grown-ups laughed and seemed relaxed as they gathered in small groups, swapping stories as they drank and ate. This was so far removed from the kind of parties she usually attended that it was almost foreign. There were no hired waiters or bartenders, no extravagant decorations or elaborate gazebos, just a bunch of people gathered in a friend's backyard, enjoying the evening. It was so...nice.

In comparison, she hadn't realised how much effort it took to belong to her circle of friends. For starters, no one here cared about what people were wearing—had this been a party in her world, she would have had to consider her wardrobe choice on where she'd already worn something before or buy something new. She'd have had to visit the hairdresser and beauty salon and be conscious of what she was eating and how much, in case anyone made an unflattering comment. That said, it always amused her how all that went out the window by the end of the night, once everyone was too drunk to care about anything other than where their next shot was coming from.

Sometimes she found it hard to relate to the things she used to do. And not so very long ago. Had she really changed that much? If Gran called her right now and said everything was forgiven and she could have her money back, would she instantly go back to her old life?

Some things she knew she wouldn't return to. Her friends, for one. They'd shown their true colours when they'd deserted her, when she'd needed them the most. But as for the rest—a penthouse apartment, unlimited shopping and a nice car? Without a doubt she'd take them—and not even feel bad about not looking back. Well, she conceded, as she looked around at the friendly, familiar faces of her co-workers, maybe she'd feel a little bad. It was hard to unsee the blatant disadvantages some people had in this life.

So many good people had to work long, hard hours to make a fraction of what she'd had in the bank. Maybe this period *had* changed her perception of some things. She knew she'd look at money and how she spent it—*where* she spent it—a lot closer from now on. Without it, life was a lot harder, more uncertain, and she never wanted to find herself in that predicament again. Although it was kind of a moot point at the moment—she still had to earn back her inheritance and, at any point, it could still be taken away from her for good.

On the way home, Quinn watched the lights flash and blur as she stared out the window. The champagne had caught up with her and she was feeling drowsy. Scott had shaken hands with Tara's husband as they said their goodbyes and she recalled the warmth of his arm around her back as he led her towards the car across the dark front lawn. He'd fitted in with her friends like he'd been born to it. He probably had been—at least more than she had. Even Hugo probably would have been at ease there, having grown up in a small town without the millions he now had.

It was only her who seemed to feel like a fish out of water—like she didn't really belong anywhere.

Chapter 29

She felt his gaze on her from time to time during the trip home, but she didn't feel like talking. She was happy to stay floating in a semi-tipsy state. It was nice here.

At some point, she must have dozed off; her eyes shot open when she felt herself moving. In her scramble to right herself, she realised too late that she wasn't falling—Scott was carrying her. Or at least attempting to.

'Thank Christ you woke up,' he said, lowering her at the base of the stairs at the front of their house. 'I'm pretty sure we would have ended up in the Emergency Department if I'd tried to carry you the whole way up there.'

Quinn squinted and noticed the stairs looked like they went for miles—straight up. 'I can walk,' she declared indignantly. Anyone would think she was drunk or something.

'I won't stop you,' he agreed, holding his hands up in surrender as she placed a hand on the weathered old railing and began to climb.

Behind her, she could sense Scott—not feel him physically, but she knew he was there, close enough to catch her if she stumbled. She felt safe. She fumbled for the keys in her handbag and heard Scott's deep rumble of soft laughter as he helped guide the key into the lock after a few failed attempts to line it up.

The house was quiet as they went inside; Quinn giggled as she bumped into the coffee table on their way through the lounge room. 'Shh,' she said, and felt that it sounded very loud.

'I'm not the one knocking shit over,' he whispered back, righting a lamp from the side table she'd just passed.

'I'm not knocking shit over. It's falling over as I walk past,' she told him irritably.

'Okay, here we are,' he said as they reached her bedroom door. 'Bedtime for you.'

'But it's not even late,' she complained, eyeing the door he'd just opened for her.

'Can you manage from here?' he asked as she slumped against the doorway frame.

'I don't want to go to bed yet. I know,' she said, leaning forward but somehow overbalancing and ending up being steadied by Scott. 'Let's go and buy ice cream and sit on the beach and eat it.'

'It's too late for ice cream,' he told her patiently, and she liked the tolerant smile he wore as he looked down at her.

'You know, you should smile more often,' she said.

'It's pretty easy around you.'

'Smiling more often is not the same thing as laughing at me,' she corrected.

'I'm not laughing at you,' he said gruffly. '*With* you, maybe, but never *at* you.'

'I'm glad you came along tonight,' she said with a long sigh.

For a minute he didn't say anything, but his eyes moved across her face, lingering just a little on her mouth before meeting her gaze once more. 'Thanks for letting me come.'

'Thanks for letting me believe I was doing you a favour,' she said drolly. 'We both know you were just being a nice guy.'

'Yeah,' he scoffed lightly, 'that's me, Mr Nice Guy.'

'You *are* a nice guy,' she said, forcing herself to look him steadily in the eye.

'Get some sleep, princess,' he said softly, easing away from where he'd been leaning his shoulder on the doorframe opposite her. 'See you tomorrow.'

He waited until she closed the door before he took the three steps that put him at his own bedroom door. She knew because she found herself counting them each time he walked past. There was something comforting about knowing he was only three short steps away. Comforting and a little dangerous at the same time.

She didn't bother changing; that required far too much effort. Instead, she fell onto her bed and dragged the blankets over her. She didn't remember anything else, just a fluffy grey cloud that sent her floating into a nice, safe place.

***

Quinn squinted as she lifted her head off her pillow at the insistent banging on her door. 'What the hell?' she muttered, tossing back the covers and sitting up. 'What?' she yelled. She peered at the clock on her bedside table and tried to focus on the numbers. There was a seven and after that, well, it didn't matter what the others were—it was a bloody seven! On a Sunday morning—her day off!

'There's a guy at the front door,' Scott said from the other side of her bedroom door.

'So?' she said crossly.

'He's asking for you.'

In an instant, the hazy fog of her hangover abruptly cleared. 'Shit!' she whispered.

Hugo. She'd completely forgotten they'd arranged to meet up today. She stood up and looked around in a daze, one hand on her forehead as she tried to work out what to do first. She glanced in the mirror and gasped. She hadn't bothered taking her makeup off last night, and her hair looked like something you'd throw on a scarecrow.

She opened the door a crack. Scott was standing there, bare-chested, hands on his hips and looking less than thrilled.

'Distract him for a minute while I get decent.'

'Do I look like your personal secretary?' he growled, and she blinked at his snappy tone, but he'd already walked away and she didn't have time to ponder what his problem was. She slipped into the hallway and ran for the bathroom, frantically washing her face and brushing her teeth, then attempted to get her hair to look slightly less like a musician from the '80s. Realising it was the best she could do under the circumstances, she hurried out into the lounge room, where she heard low male voices. Hugo was seated on the edge of the old couch, talking to Scott, who stood across from him, looking no less impressed than he had a few moments earlier, arms folded tightly.

Her gaze fell on the tattoos on his chest peeking out from beneath his crossed arms—an Australian flag and a Lest We Forget insignia. She vaguely remembered seeing them the day of the bathroom incident, the first time they'd met, but it'd been overshadowed by the whole *meeting a stranger wearing her towel* ordeal. A clearing throat snapped her gaze away from Scott's chest and onto Hugo, who was rising from his seat.

'Morning, Amy,' he said, and sent a sideways glance towards Scott. 'I just met your flatmate.'

'I wasn't expecting you until later,' Quinn said, for want of anything better to say. The awkward vibe in the room wasn't helping her sluggish head.

'I thought maybe we could do breakfast. It's almost eight,' he said, checking his watch.

Almost wasn't eight though, she thought with a hint of annoyance. She'd been enjoying her sleep for the first time in a long time. Who the hell got up before eight on a Sunday? 'It was a bit of a late night,' she muttered.

'Your work party must have been a success then?' he said, and his gaze shifted to where Scott remained, watching on silently. Quinn also flicked him a glance, as a horrible thought occurred that he might have mentioned the fact he went along. That would be more than a little awkward to explain to Hugo after she'd turned down his offer to attend. 'Yes, it was…fine.'

'Hugo was just telling me about his company,' Scott said, thankfully changing the subject.

'Oh?' Quinn said, switching her gaze between the two men.

'Impressive,' he said, rocking back on his heels.

'I'm lucky to be able to make a living doing something I'm passionate about.' Hugo shrugged the comment off as humbly as always. 'Do you surf?' he asked Scott.

'No, but maybe I should take it up now I know a professional.'

'I'd be happy to take you out some time.'

She wasn't sure why, but the thought of these two men spending any time together was not something she wanted to encourage, then she felt bad, because she knew Scott didn't have any friends in the area. Still—did it have to be with *this* particular man?

She couldn't even put a label on what this thing was between her and Hugo, but getting a flatmate involved was just asking for trouble. What if she decided to stop seeing him, but he and Scott became best mates and kept hanging out together? That would be…messy. 'I'm starving, should we go?' she said, putting on a bright smile, effectively ending the conversation.

'Your chariot awaits,' Hugo said, stepping back to allow her to pass.

Scott gave a low whistle as he moved to the window and looked outside. 'Nice wheels.'

Hugo grinned. Male pride, likened to that of a proud parent accepting a compliment for their child, shone from his face, and Quinn rolled her eyes. Men and their toys.

'Nice to meet you, Scott,' Hugo said from behind her. 'Hope to see you around.'

'Count on it,' Scott replied confidently, his eyes meeting and holding hers in a strangely intense way that she was still pondering as they drove away a few moments later.

She really needed to stop drinking so much—hangovers were not as much fun as she once remembered.

***

She had to hand it to the guy. Hugo knew how to do things right—breakfast included. The swanky resort overlooked the canal and from their table outside on the deck they watched watercraft of every shape and description paddle, sail and motor their way out to the river mouth and beyond. The sun was out and, from behind her sunglasses, she was finally able to appreciate the endless blue sky that stretched overhead and the sound of the water lapping soothingly against the large pilings of the deck and wharf below.

'I was thinking maybe you'd like to come out on my boat after breakfast?'

'You have a boat?' she asked, then inwardly shook her head. Of course he had a boat. Probably a yacht, and a racing one at that, which he most likely entered into the Sydney to Hobart race every year or something.

'I don't always just surf,' he told her with a crooked grin.

Quinn stifled the little sigh his smile provoked. He really was good looking. She noticed a table of three women huddled together, sending pointed stares at them from across the room, and she froze as she recognised the younger one and self-consciously repositioned her glasses. Had they recognised her? No. How could they? She turned slightly in her chair and resisted the urge to hide behind a menu. Bloody Trudy Johansson. They weren't close, but they had friends in the same circles.

'Everything okay?' Hugo asked, noticing her fidgeting in her seat.

'Yep,' she smiled cheerfully. 'I'm eager to see your boat.' *And get the hell out of here.*

'I'm ready to go whenever you are. Are you sure you don't want another coffee or something?'

'Nope. I'm all good, thanks.' *Let's go, let's go!* she silently screamed. Maybe she was just being paranoid. Maybe the women weren't even looking at them. She risked another glance. Nope. They were definitely looking their way. *Damn.*

Quinn slid her hand into Hugo's and hurried him towards the doorway.

'I had no idea you were so keen on boats,' he said with an amused chuckle.

'Oh, I love boats,' she enthused, nodding furiously. She nervously waited for him to pay the bill and didn't dare look back at the table behind them, instead closing her eyes and fervently praying the women didn't come over for a closer look.

She didn't relax until they were back in Hugo's car and reversing out of the car park. Dropping her head back against the headrest, she let out a long breath.

'Are you *sure* you're okay? You seem a bit on edge.'

'Yeah. I didn't realise I'd drank so much last night. It's taking me a bit longer to shake it off.'

'Must have been a good night then.'

'Yeah, well, you know.' She hunched a shoulder nonchalantly. 'It was just a bunch of work people.'

She looked down when he put a hand on hers and held it as they drove. It felt so...nice. She couldn't remember the last time she'd had someone do little things like this simply because they wanted to touch her, be connected to her. Sure, the men in her life touched her, but it was usually during sex or for show in front of cameras. Not like this, when they were alone. Had her world really been that shallow and cold?

Her family weren't overly touchy-feely people, usually just a cursory double air kiss on greeting. When had that happened? As a child, her dad always hugged her, as had her mother when they were small. It had only been as she'd gotten older and everyone began having their own demons to battle that suddenly her family had grown distant; strangers with the same surname.

They pulled in at a marina and Hugo went inside the office, returning shortly afterwards to lead her down a long narrow wharf where rows of large, luxurious boats were moored.

She was no stranger to boats—her family owned a beautiful 150' Benetti for entertaining guests. They passed by a number of beautiful craft that were all as big or bigger than her family's boat, and she found herself excited to be back on the water in such luxury again—even if it was just for a few hours.

Chapter 30

'Here she is,' Hugo said proudly as he came to a stop.

Quinn looked at him, confused. '*This* is your boat?'

'Yep.' He grinned. 'Isn't she a beauty?'

The long, rather old wooden boat before her bobbed up and down merrily, dwarfed by its neighbours on either side.

'It's an ex-trawler that I rebuilt and refitted myself,' he informed her, reaching out to help her onboard. 'What do you think?'

'It's certainly something,' she managed. She'd never been on a trawler before.

'I plan to take her on a trip up to the Philippines next year.'

'Will it make it that far?'

'Of course she will. Here, I'll give you a tour.' He led the way inside and down a narrow set of stairs into a small lounge area with a row of bunk beds. They squeezed through a doorway into a small cabin that contained a double bed with a tasteful navy and white striped cover and white curtains hanging over the window above.

'There's a bathroom through there,' he said, pointing to the opposite end of the boat, 'and the kitchen and main dining area is upstairs in the bridge.'

'It's very cosy,' she said, looking around. She noted the interior was freshly painted.

'I looked at those other boats—the super yachts and whatnot,' he said with an almost disdainful air, 'but they lack something, you know?' He searched her eyes. 'A soul or something...I mean, they're pretty and luxurious and all that, but when I saw this old girl, I just thought, you know what? This is a boat with a story. It had a life. I was just drawn to it. So I bought it and renovated it over about a year or so, coming down here on weekends to sand her back and pull out old fittings, and each time I set eyes on her, I fell a little more in love.'

Quinn couldn't help but smile at the emotion in his voice. His passion was infectious. He had a way of catching you in his wake and bringing you along for the ride.

'I thought we'd head out and go for a bit of a cruise. Maybe have some lunch?'

'Sounds great.' She smiled, and found she genuinely meant it.

She sat up next to him as he expertly manoeuvred the craft from its mooring, and found herself admiring his quiet confidence as he worked. She took in his hands as they gently held the boat's wheel. They were large, capable hands; not manicured, office worker kind of hands, but not exactly rugged either—different to Scott's, she absently noted.

She frowned a little. Why was she comparing his hands to Scott's? Maybe it was seeing them in the same room together this morning? Still, why she was even thinking about Scott was weird. She wanted to ignore the niggle inside her brain that reminded her of the few incidents when she'd found herself feeling *things* around Scott. They weren't *important* things, she scoffed. It was simply that she found herself sharing a house with a man—a very *manly* type of man. She squirmed slightly, recalling the day he'd stood naked save for her towel in the bathroom. *See!* That's the weird shit she had to stop thinking about. Men were supposed to be off limits and, so far, she'd slept with Hugo, twice, and was having these annoying *thoughts* about her flatmate.

She distracted herself by taking a look around. The kitchen was through a doorway behind the bridge and, much to her surprise, was compact, yet had all the latest mod cons—even a coffee machine.

The table had a wraparound bench seating arrangement against the wall, but a glass door opened onto a small deck area, where another small table and two chairs sat for extra seating.

It was actually pretty cute. The fresh renovations made use of the limited room but still gave it a clean, open feel. No doubt a huge step up in the luxury department for a one-time working trawler.

They anchored in a small bay a little while later and Hugo began unloading an enormous amount of food from the fridge—enough to feed a small army.

'I didn't know what you'd feel like, so I got a bit of everything,' he said, piling the containers across the entire small kitchen bench.

With full tummies and the warm sun beckoning, they took a glass of wine upstairs to sit on a pair of sun lounges and sleep off their food comas.

'Happy?' Hugo asked when she swivelled her head to look at him.

'It's been an amazing day,' she said, and meant it.

'I was thinking...would you like to come away with me next weekend?'

'Away? Where to?'

He hesitated briefly before answering. 'To my parents' place.'

'Your parents?' she repeated faintly.

'I know it sounds like a big step—and it's probably crazy—but I've had this trip planned for a few weeks and I just keep thinking how much my parents would love you and how well you'd fit in out there. I wouldn't have brought it up this soon, only I'm already committed to go, and after the last few days...I don't want to be away from you that long.'

'Hugo,' she said, unsure where to start. A flat-out *No fucking way on earth* sounded a little harsh.

'I know,' he cut in hastily. 'It's crazy. I don't know what it is, but from the moment I met you, I've just felt this connection...' He sat up and leaned across to hold her hands. 'You can't deny the whole fate thing. What were the chances we'd keep meeting up?'

Admittedly, that *had* been really weird. *If* she believed in fate, which she didn't. But there was still the small matter of...

'Amy Sinclair, I think I've fallen in love with you.'

That.

He didn't even know her real name.

'You're everything I've been looking for—someone with a working-class background like mine. Someone who appreciates the value of hard work and earning what you've got, not some entitled, self-important socialite like the women I've seen in the past. They could never appreciate the life I've built and want to share with someone like you. I want to start a family with you—raise our kids to be decent and kind and keen to make this world a better place. We could do that,' he said eagerly. 'We could continue with the foundation work; travel and work side by side. I can give you everything you've ever wanted, Amy.'

Nausea began to replace Quinn's brief moment of earlier contentment. He didn't know anything about her. He knew Amy Sinclair, not Quinn Appleton, who was exactly the kind of woman he'd just said he detested. As soon as she told him the truth, it would crush him.

'I've freaked you out,' he said, giving a huge sigh and running a hand through his shaggy hair. 'Damn it. I should have kept my mouth shut. I'm sorry. It was too much too soon.'

'You just took me by surprise,' she said nervously.

'Look, just forget I said anything. It was stupid.'

His forlorn expression tugged at her heart. It wasn't his fault he thought he'd found the kind of woman he'd been searching for—hell, Amy Sinclair *was* freakin' awesome. She was a fighter. She had a job and purpose; friends she could count on, and who didn't have to spare a second thought about social suicide and gossip. She had no one to be accountable to except herself, and she was *nice*. People loved her for *her,* not for who her family was or for the money she had. Amy cared about people, not things.

Quinn Appleton, on the other hand, was a self-centred bitch who only did something if it required next to no personal involvement or attachment. She had trust issues and spent little time listening to other people's problems. All she cared about was her stupid inheritance.

The thought made her sick.

'Hugo, you deserve to find the woman you just described. You really do. But she's not me. You don't know the real me—and you wouldn't want to.'

'I *do* know you,' he protested, shaking his head slightly at her words. 'I see who you are.'

'You really don't.'

For a moment, he seemed lost for words, and she could see the confusion on his handsome face. She wanted to tell him the truth, but she couldn't. What would be the point?

'Do you mind if we head back?' she asked softly.

'Sure,' Hugo said, sounding defeated, which broke her heart.

The ride home was made in silence, and Quinn hated that she was the reason their perfect day had fallen apart.

When they arrived at her house, Hugo stopped her from getting out of the car. 'Can we just pick up where we left off before I opened my big mouth? I don't care about the weekend away. You don't have to come with me—meeting my family was way too soon—but can we just go back to the way it was before and build up to everything…slower?'

Quinn stared at her hands. 'Hugo, we come from two very different worlds.' How could she even *try to* explain how twisted and dysfunctional her family was? He'd said he didn't want a life partner who was self-centred and spoilt. How would he cope with his partner's entire family being *exactly* that?

'This isn't my only world. It's the benefits from my world that I've worked bloody hard to build. I come from working-class people, just like you. We're not as different as you think.'

Quinn gently touched his face and smiled sadly. 'Hugo, you are the nicest person I've ever met. I never wanted to hurt you, but I just can't do this.' She knew he wasn't going to take no for an answer if she continued to insist she wasn't the woman he thought she was. She needed a different approach. 'I'm just not interested in starting a family. I don't want kids—or a husband—I don't want the kind of future you want.'

'I don't understand,' he said, shaking his head. 'How can you not want those things?'

'Because I want to live my own life. Make my own choices. You're at an age where you're ready to settle down; I'm just starting to explore.'

'I'm not going to give up,' he warned.

'You have to. It's not going to happen, Hugo,' she said softly. 'I'm sorry.' She swallowed a lump of emotion and opened her door.

She didn't give him a chance to reply, slipping from the car and closing the door firmly. He didn't leave immediately; it wasn't until she'd walked into her room that she heard his engine start up and a tiny piece of her heart ran after him, frantically begging him to ignore the crazy woman who'd just turned him down.

At the beginning of all this, she would have jumped at the chance to become a millionaire businessman's wife without a second thought—it would have saved her from the humiliation of hitting rock bottom and being forced to scratch out a brand-new life. But that wasn't the person she was now. She wasn't entirely sure *who* she was, but she wasn't the same Quinn Appleton who'd been kicked out of her penthouse and forced to take care of herself.

As the sound of his Jeep faded, she turned from the window and sank onto the edge of her bed. She knew deep down she'd done the right thing, but it didn't stop her from feeling miserable. She'd just rejected a perfectly decent, perfectly *rich,* man because he was everything her family was not.

Chapter 31

Quinn smiled her thanks at the post office worker and stepped outside, moving her sunglasses from the top of her head to her eyes as the bright sunlight hit her face. With the latest sale of a Valentino evening gown that was now en route to Perth, she had a quite substantial nest egg. She was secretly proud of the fact she'd found a way to make some money all by herself. At first, she'd thought she would only sell a few of her dresses and some shoes, but the more she sold, the more she realised she really didn't feel...anything anymore. Once she would have thrown herself off a building if anyone had dared suggest she go without her beautiful wardrobe, but lately it just didn't seem as important as it once did. Besides, where the hell was she going to wear a Valentino in the next six months?

Today she had a plan. She was done taking the bus to and from work, and she'd asked Scott at least three times over the last few weeks if he'd found any cars that might be suitable for her to buy. Each time, he'd brushed her off with an offhand, 'Yeah, I'm following up a couple I've had my eye on.' She'd had enough of waiting. So today, she was going car hunting herself. How hard could it be?

There was nothing in her price range in any of the car dealerships along the main stretch of highway where car yards lined both sides of the road. She needed something to get her from A to B, just until she got her inheritance back and could afford something nice. However, when she found a few cheaper places that sold older vehicles, she began to wonder if maybe she *could* put up with the bus for a few more months. Down this end of Car Yard Row, *everything* became cheaper—the salesmen's suits, the offices. Everything except the price of the cars, it seemed.

She'd been about to leave the last yard when the rotund salesman, somewhere in his late fifties, she guessed, waved her into the small garage attached to the office. 'This was just traded in this morning,' he said, opening the door of an early-model Holden Barina and inserting the key. The engine turned over effortlessly and seemed to make the right kind of noise; at least, she couldn't hear any noticeable bangs or rattles, so that had to be a good sign.

'Now, I was planning to keep it for myself. I've got a little niece who's lookin' for a first car,' he told her earnestly. 'But I can see you're in a bit of a situation.' He rubbed his hairless chin thoughtfully. 'I reckon I could sell you this one for...four grand,' he said, nodding magnanimously.

Quinn eyed the little hatchback with its mismatched panels—three sides yellow and the right rear one white—and lifted a sceptical eyebrow. She might not be mechanical, but she wasn't stupid.

'All right then,' he finally conceded, 'make me an offer.'

'Five hundred.'

'A realistic offer,' he added.

'Nine hundred.'

'I have a business to run here.'

'Nine fifty, and that's as high as I'm going. I saw one of these listed on a buy, swap and sell site last night for eight hundred.' She put on her best bullshitter face—a fair copy of the one he was currently making.

He shook his head and kicked at the gravel beneath his faux leather slip-on shoes for a few moments, and she made to turn away.

'Okay, okay. I'm taking a loss on this, but I'll take nine hundred and fifty.'

Quinn doubted very much the guy had lost anything on the sale—he'd probably been about to send it to the wreckers for fifty bucks. 'Sold,' she said, reaching out a hand to shake his.

'You know,' he said, still holding her hand in his soft, fleshy one, 'you seem kinda familiar. You bought a car off me before?'

'Nope. This is the first one.'

He studied her, and she shifted uncomfortably, sliding her hand out of his and resisting the urge to wipe it on her shirt. Was he trying to use some kind of pick-up line?

'Well, you drive a hard bargain. I hope you don't come back to buy another one any time too soon,' he said with a hearty laugh, which ended in a bout of coughing as they walked towards his office to finalise the sale.

In the office, she reached for her wallet and pulled out her driver's licence to fill in the registration papers. As she withdrew the ID, a cascade of cards stored safely behind it tumbled out on the desk. Quinn scrambled to gather them up, her heart momentarily stopping as the salesman on the other side of the desk picked one up. Quinn practically snatched the loyalty card from his pudgy fingers and stuffed it back in her wallet with a flustered smile.

She knew she should have gotten rid of those cards, but in the beginning, she'd held on to them as some kind of secret rebellious snub—refusing to completely give up everything that had been part of Quinn Appleton. She'd forgotten they were even still in her purse, to be honest. It was odd to realise she didn't have that spark of rebellion anymore. However, after today, she'd be making sure she finally disposed of them. That had been a close call.

As she drove her new car out of the yard, she couldn't help the smile that spread across her face. Freedom. Slowly but surely, she was getting back the pieces of her life.

***

As she pulled into the driveway back at the house, Scott came down the stairs, staring at her with a look that she wanted to think was surprise, but deep down she knew was more like horror.

'I bought a car,' she announced as she got out and shut the door, turning to pat the bonnet proudly.

'You actually *paid* someone for this?'

'It's not pretty, but it's all I need to get me to and from work for a while.'

'I thought *I* was supposed to find you a car. Why didn't you call me to come with you before you bought it?'

'I did ask you—lots of times. Patience isn't one of my qualities.' She shrugged.

'Chuck me the keys and I'll give it a look-over,' he said, catching in one hand the small orange plastic keyring with Big Trev's Used Cars stamped on it and two silver keys attached.

'I'm starving,' Quinn said. 'I'll head up and order dinner. My shout.'

Scott already had his head under the bonnet and was too busy twisting and pulling bits and pieces to reply, so she left him to it.

'So?' she asked when he came upstairs after the pizza arrived. 'Does it pass?'

Scott gave a noncommittal grunt as he washed his hands in the kitchen sink before grabbing two cans of beer from the fridge and taking a seat on the lounge beside her. 'There are a few things that'll need to be replaced, but it looks all right for now.'

'In other words, I did okay?' she prompted smugly, accepting one of the proffered beverages.

'I can't believe you bought a car that you didn't have anyone check over first,' he said, shaking his head.

'It started. I can open all the doors and the radio works.' She shrugged. 'It's already got more things going for it than your car has.'

He elbowed her ribs and she snickered, licking cheese grease off her fingers. Maybe it had been kind of irresponsible to walk into a car yard and just buy one like that, but there she didn't have much choice. She simply couldn't go another day without her own transport.

'You should have called me to come and look it over before you bought it,' he told her, reaching for a slice of pepperoni, which had become their favourite ever since that first night they'd snuck away from the round table evening.

'As long as it gets me to work and back, I'll be happy.'

They ate in relative quiet; Quinn hadn't realised how hungry she was.

'I would have thought you'd have at least taken the boyfriend along—although he doesn't look like the kind who'd know much about cars.'

She finished chewing her mouthful before answering in as offhand a manner as she could muster. 'Hugo and I aren't seeing each other anymore.'

'Oh?'

Quinn concentrated on her pizza. 'He wasn't my boyfriend to start with.'

'I see,' he said, reaching for another piece. 'Whose decision was it? To stop seeing each other?'

'Not that it's any of your business,' she said, a little more snippety than she'd intended, 'but it was mine. We want different things.'

Quinn noticed he didn't seem overly perturbed about her reprimand, tilting his head slightly as he chewed. 'What do you want?'

She sent him an exasperated look that simply bounced off his curious expression. 'Not the same things he wants. Can we just drop it?'

'Sorry,' he said, not looking sorry at all.

'If you must know,' she found herself continuing, 'I just realised he was too good...for me.'

Scott squinted slightly, as though trying to understand, and she busied herself grabbing another slice that she suddenly didn't feel like eating. 'How do you figure that?' he asked. 'Because he has money?'

'No,' she said, glancing up briefly, 'I mean, he's *good*. Like *a saint* good. He does all this charity work, but because he wants to, you know? Not because it's just something rich people are obliged to do.'

'How do you know that? I mean, *really* know?' he asked, sounding sceptical.

'It's the way he talks about it. The passion he speaks with.' She shook her head. 'You can't fake that.'

'You'd be surprised what people can fake,' he muttered.

She eyed him warily. 'What do you mean?'

'Nothing,' he said, standing up. 'Want another beer?'

She declined and picked at her crust in silence. He returned, prising the ring off his can with a pressurised hiss before sitting back down.

'I mean, you haven't known him long, right? He could be just putting on this good guy front.'

She was usually a pretty good judge of character. At least, she thought she was. She hadn't seen through Bryson until it was too late. For a moment, she faltered. What if Scott was right? What if Hugo had just been *another* near-miss in her spectacularly crappy line of recent near-misses?

No. She wasn't wrong this time. She hadn't picked up on Bryson because she'd been just as fake and superficial as him back then.

She sighed as she sank back into the lounge cushions and wished she hadn't eaten that last piece of pizza.

'For what it's worth, I think you're selling yourself short if you think that guy was too good for you,' Scott said gruffly, staring at the beer can he cradled in his hand.

Quinn wasn't sure what to say to that. It was somehow the nicest thing anyone had said to her in a long while. The warmth from his thigh where it lightly rested against hers suddenly seared. Her gaze trailed along his forearms, wondering when she'd started finding the light dusting of hair on tanned skin such a turn-on. The big, bulky watch on his wrist only added to the masculine appeal. Maybe she was drunk? She glanced at the half-drunk can of beer that sat, growing warm, on the coffee table before her. Nope, that wasn't it.

The room seemed to have grown warmer and somehow smaller, as though the air around them was shrinking, drawing them closer together. Quinn risked a look at his face and her breath stuck in her chest as she clocked him watching her, silently.

Despite the fact he hadn't said a word, she could read his intention. He was waiting, leaving the next step up to her. Her mind replayed the last few months like a movie reel, and she viewed it as some kind of voyeur. Their first meeting when she'd been confused and angry and still very much old Quinn, then the gradual softening after his persistent—almost stubborn—reluctance to take no for an answer each time they ran into each other. She'd been so distracted with her own problems and then Hugo coming onto the scene that she hadn't stopped to realise how Scott had been slowly but surely worming his way into her life. Looking back now, she wondered if maybe she'd always been aware of him but had subconsciously ignored those feelings, knowing she already had enough crap to deal with.

Until now.

She could smell the subtle masculine scent of his deodorant—not some expensive cologne like Bryson baptised himself with, but a faint woody, citrusy suggestion that was sending out some potent pheromones she was definitely picking up on. There was nothing about this man that would normally make her look twice at him. His short, military-style haircut and slightly rugged—though not chiselled—handsome features were appealing, yes, but she'd preferred well-groomed and immaculately dressed over whatever the hell kind of style Scott's T-shirts and jeans could be called. And yet...here she was, undeniably attracted to the man.

It was more than that though, she was able to admit; despite the stirrings of lust she was doing her best to control, she trusted him. He'd been there, quietly listening to the edited version of her troubles and always on hand to act the knight in shining armour. She felt safe with him. With Scott, she didn't feel as though she was being judged, the way Hugo had sometimes made her feel. She could be herself—whoever the hell that was nowadays.

There was no denying the magnetic pull she felt as she sat beside him, surrounded by a swirl of sudden and potent desire. She'd barely moved—she wasn't even sure if she *had* moved—when she felt his lips on hers and was melded against him.

Her hands slid from his chest to his neck as she pulled him closer and their kiss deepened, changing from a probing throb to a hungry obsession.

He eased her backward on the lounge until his body covered her own. Clothes were hastily discarded, quickly replaced by the touch of heated skin on skin that sent Quinn's need into overdrive.

There was nothing delicate or gentle about this; it was nothing like being with Hugo. This was almost primal. It was need—fast and urgent. The need to find completion after all the pussyfooting about they'd both been ignoring for weeks on end.

Afterwards, Scott rolled off her, sitting on the edge of the lounge while she rested an arm across her forehead as her breathing struggled to return to normal. Scott's shoulders hunched as he stared at the floor between his bare feet.

'Are you okay?' she worked up the courage to ask when the silence had stretched on to the point of being unbearable.

'Yeah,' he said, but didn't lift his head to look at her.

Something wasn't right about this. She racked her mind to find the reason. Why was he acting as though he regretted it?

'Sorry,' he said, shaking his head, as he jagged his shirt from the floor and pulled it over his head before standing to tug up his jeans they hadn't even taken the time to properly remove. 'That was...'

'Pretty amazing,' she supplied quietly, which made him glance over at her, and she saw, with relief, his face soften slightly.

'Yeah. It was. I'm just sorry that I...well, went at it like a bull at a gate.' He shrugged awkwardly and Quinn found herself openly amused by his terminology.

'I mean it—that shouldn't have happened...like that. I usually show more control.'

'Maybe that's your problem?' she said lightly. 'Being too in control. Sometimes it's nice to act on instinct.' Once she had been the queen of spontaneity. She'd often decide to go away for the weekend on the spur of the moment, or throw together a party with a few hours' notice. But not anymore. It was harder to be spontaneous when you had limited funds and a job you had to show up for.

'We're flatmates,' he said, looking away briefly. 'This was probably a mistake.'

'Since when is being flatmates an issue?'

'Since...I don't know. All I *do* know is, I should have known better.'

Should have known better? What the hell?

'I should get to bed,' he muttered, not looking at her.

Quinn sat mutely, unsure what had caused his sudden turnaround. Until a few moments ago, he'd seemed more than eager to be a participant, and now he was acting like she had the plague and couldn't wait to get as far away from her as possible.

She watched him leave the room and struggled to make sense of his abrupt change of mood. *What just happened?* Confusion battled with uncertainty, and she felt the surprising sting of tears burn behind her eyelids before she clamped down on the emotion. She was not about to cry over some guy who'd just called sex with her a *mistake*. Anger quickly elbowed aside her uncertainty and Quinn finally emerged to take control of the situation.

She got to her feet and headed towards the bedrooms. Quinn banged her fist on his door and glared at the reluctant expression on his face as he appeared.

'I want to know what the hell your problem is,' she demanded.

'Amy, I—'

'Do not say you're sorry,' she warned.

He let out a deep sigh. 'I didn't want to ruin what we had. I really like spending time with you.' He shook his head. 'I don't have the best track record when it comes to women—I always manage to stuff it up.'

Quinn gave a small, harsh grunt. 'I can see why, if the first words that come out of your mouth after sex are, "This was a mistake!"'

'*You* weren't the mistake; my judgement—or lack thereof—was the problem.'

'Who made you the boss?' she snapped.

'Pardon?' His eyebrow lifted slightly.

'Why were you in charge of what was or wasn't the correct use of judgement? I happened to be part of it too, you know.'

'That's not what I meant,' he said, shaking his head.

'For your information, I also think it was a mistake, only I was being more polite about not saying it to your face,' she said, turning away and heading for her room.

'It's not you,' he called after her, sounding miserable.

Quinn spun back around, planting her hands on her hips. 'Oh, I know,' she spat. 'This is *all* you.' She saw him give a reluctant, self-reproaching smile before she turned and entered her bedroom, slamming the door.

Stupid, stupid, stupid! she fumed inwardly at herself as she pulled back the covers of her bed and climbed in. Every time she thought she'd learned a lesson about trusting a guy, she went and blindly allowed another one to stomp all over her again. What the hell was wrong with her?

Chapter 32

Never again would she take something as simple as driving a car for granted, she thought as she drove to work the next morning, passing her bus stop.

She'd been relieved when she hadn't bumped into Scott before heading off. She'd stubbornly pushed last night's events aside, doing what any well-adjusted adult would do and completely erasing the whole disaster from her memory. Denial worked perfectly fine.

This morning she was basking in the joy of freedom instead. God, she'd missed this. As she drove along the motorway, she took time to observe the other drivers in the vehicles around her. Everyone seemed to be on autopilot, their thoughts fixed on the day ahead.

She should be feeling the same. After all, she was driving towards a factory job she never wanted, but she found she really didn't mind it. She'd cut her own tongue out before she'd ever admit it to anyone—especially Gran—but she'd been coming to terms with her situation for a while, and once the anger and indignation had subsided, she'd found that she liked the daily routine.

Getting up early, going for a jog, coming home to take a shower and getting ready for work—her day suddenly had purpose. And she felt like she'd accomplished something at the end of it. Sure, it wasn't anything earth-shatteringly important—not like Hugo's kind of work—but it was work all the same. Besides, if she wasn't there to pack those boxes of Chocolate Heavens, what would countless numbers of people around the country—and the world, for that matter—do without their morning or afternoon tea fix?

She was also enjoying the comradeship she'd forged with her friends; they were such an odd bunch. She smiled at the thought. Maureen was old enough to be her grandmother—well, a younger grandmother than the one she had—but she was so feisty and down to earth.

Quinn would never forget the kindness Maureen had shown her from her very first day on the job. She'd never had older friends like these before—or friends with families. They had nothing in common and yet they had become incredibly important to her in such a short space of time. She couldn't imagine a day at work without them.

She glanced in her rear-view mirror and saw a bike had pulled in behind her. It was big and black, with shiny chrome, its loud engine drowning out the music on her radio (*which actually worked,* she thought with a smug smile, recalling that she'd pointed this out to Scott the night before).

The bike revved and she saw the rider pull out to pass her. When he drew level with her door, though, he simply stayed there. Quinn peered across at him. He was looking at her! A skeleton mask covered his lower face and a pair of black sunglasses shielded his eyes, and Quinn felt a twinge of discomfort. She checked her mirror again, searching for some reason why this guy would be maintaining pace with her in the next lane, but the road behind them was clear. As was the road ahead. *What is he doing?* Quinn slowed down a fraction more, but the biker adjusted his speed as well and continued to shadow her.

Now she was getting cranky. What game was this jerk playing at? He was ruining her perfectly good mood.

Maybe he was just bored and messing with her? Maybe he was trying to hit on her? She threw him a glare, just in case he thought he had a chance, but he didn't react.

Her exit was coming up, and she breathed a sigh of relief, waiting until the last moment to indicate she was merging into the left lane. She zipped quickly across and left the motorway and the big black bike behind.

When she pulled into the car park a little while later, she found that her hands were shaking and she took a minute to pull herself together before getting out. 'It was nothing,' she said firmly to herself in the mirror. 'Just some creep trying to get a reaction.' She hoped it would rain today while he was out riding, making him cold and miserable. His mood deserved to be spoilt just the way hers had been.

By the time she locked her car and headed in, she'd pushed the worst of her rattled nerves aside, and by the time she'd said her good mornings to everyone, she'd forgotten all about it.

***

That night, Quinn had just finished uploading her Lana Marks clutch purse to the fashion auction site, the same design Drew Barrymore had carried on the red carpet a few years ago, when a call flashed across her screen.

Private number. She hated those. They were always either salespeople or scammers. She disconnected the call, but immediately it called back, and she gave an impatient huff.

'Hello?' she snapped. *So help me if this is a scammer, they'll regret it.*

'Hey, Quinn.'

Her hand clenched the phone. 'Dad?'

'Yeah. It's me.'

Her mouth dropped open like a stunned mullet. 'What the hell?' she said, regathering her senses. 'I've been worried sick about you! Where are you? Where have you been?'

'Sweetheart, I can't talk long—I shouldn't even be calling.'

'What? Why not?'

He sighed. 'It's complicated.'

'Complicated? You think *your* life's complicated?' she said, her voice rising. 'You have no idea what I've been through.'

'I know,' he groaned, 'I know you've been thrown a curve ball, but...look, Quinn, things are...dangerous at the moment.'

Something cold clenched at her throat.

'I've really messed up this time, love.'

'Dad?' Her earlier relief mixed with anger subsided at the defeated sound of his voice. 'Where are you?'

'I'm fine. I'm safe. I just wanted to hear your voice.'

'Safe? From what exactly?' she persisted.

'I don't want you to worry. I'm making things right—that's all you need to know. I love you, Quinn.'

'Dad, none of this makes any sense. Why are you in danger? Let me help you.'

'You can't help me—that's why I left. To keep you and your brother and mother safe. Once this is over, I swear I'll tell you everything. But for now, just know I'm fine. I love you.'

'Daddy?' Quinn said as frightened tears clogged her throat, but the only reply was the sound of the dead phone line humming in her ear.

What was she supposed to do with this? Her father had just confirmed he was in trouble, but she still had no idea what kind of trouble or how to help him.

Scott.

She wasn't even aware of consciously deciding that was who she needed right now, she just knew he was the only one she could trust. Nothing about the night before mattered. In a crisis, she knew she could depend on Scott.

Quinn knocked on his door, but there was no answer. She hadn't heard him go out. She dialled his number as she turned back towards her room, but then stopped at the sound of a ringtone coming from Scott's room. Curiously, she opened his door and took a step inside. His phone was on the bedside table. *That's weird.* He wouldn't normally leave his phone behind if he went out, although it was plugged into his charger. She was about to close the door when something on the bed caught her eye.

A photograph had slipped partially out of a folder. She could only see part of it, but Quinn instantly recognised the outfit in the picture. Crossing the room, she slowly put her phone down on the bed as she reached for the folder, sliding out the photo and staring at it, dumbfounded. It was a photo of *her*, getting out of a car. She remembered the day it was taken; only a few days before Christmas, because she was carrying that cute bucket bag she'd picked up the same day at that chic little boutique that had just opened. She'd been wearing her favourite ripped jeans and a white top that she'd ruined by spilling coffee on, which could be clearly seen in the photo.

She glanced back down at the folder and flipped it open hesitantly to find more photos and paperwork. What the hell was this?

A chill ran up her spine.

Her dad was in danger. A memory of the carnage back at her parents' house replayed in her head. He'd left in a hurry. Fearful of his life.

'Amy.'

Quinn let out a small gasp and whirled to find Scott standing in the doorway, his face an expressionless mask as he clocked the photo still in her hand.

'What are you doing in here?'

'What are *you* doing with these photos?' she demanded, waving it at him.

His face changed, a small wince forming around his eyes. 'It's not what you think.'

'What am I thinking, Scott? That you're some kind of stalker? Why do you have all these photos of me?'

'I'm not stalking you,' he said calmly, taking a step into the room but stopping as Quinn recoiled. 'I know it looks bad—but I can explain.'

'So explain,' she said, watching him intently. If he tried to grab her, she planned on screaming. Surely Atticus or Vivian were home and would hear her...weren't they? She hadn't checked earlier. *Shit.*

'I can't,' he said, sounding genuinely regretful. 'I'm not at liberty to right now.'

'Not at liberty? What does that even mean?'

'It means, for your own safety, I can't tell you what's going on.'

Her mind scrabbled to make sense of this new situation, explanations slipping through her hands like grains of sand, until finally she latched on to one. 'You *know* what's going on with my dad, don't you? Are you somehow mixed up with everything that's been going on around here? Where is he?'

Scott held up his palms. 'I don't know where he is. But I do know he just called you.'

Quinn narrowed her gaze. 'How do you know that?'

'Because your phone's got a tap on it.'

'*What!*' She watched him warily as he took another step into the room. 'Who *are* you?'

He gave a slight shake of his head and a drawn-out sigh, and Quinn took advantage of his lowered defences and darted around him, running for the hallway.

'Amy, stop!'

She ignored him, making it to the front door and reefing it open, taking the stairs two at a time. She made for her car but remembered she didn't have her keys, changing trajectory to head for the supermarket a few streets over, where there'd be people and crowds and somewhere to call someone—she wasn't sure who yet, but someone.

Her legs pumped, her breathing loud in her ears, drowning out the sounds of traffic and noise around her.

She didn't turn to see if Scott was still following; she didn't think he was, at least not on foot, but it would only take a few minutes for him to go back for his keys and catch up to her in his vehicle. She had to make the shop before that happened.

She bounced impatiently on her toes as she waited for the cars to pass so she could cross the road, and from the corner of her eye she thought she spotted a car the same colour as Scott's rounding the corner. She was so distracted that she didn't notice the large van pull up beside her until the door opened and a man grabbed her, dragging her inside.

Chapter 33

She'd always imagined when watching this exact scene happen in a movie that the person would have time to get out of the way or call for help—anything to avoid being abducted—but, as she soon discovered, laying on a dusty van floor, pinned by the heavy weight of the man who'd grabbed her, she'd had no time to do anything. It had all happened in less than six seconds.

She heard another person scramble over the front seats, and saw jean legs and boots from her position on the floor, but couldn't lift her head to get a better look. That option was removed completely as something black was pulled over her head; she was flipped onto her back and her hands and feet were roughly tied. She heard a strange noise, like a squeak, and realised it was coming from her; a giant sob racked her body as she struggled against her binds.

She didn't know how long she fought, rolling around on the floor before she stopped, exhausted by her adrenaline surge. The ride seemed to go on forever. She tried to peer through the cloth covering her head; she could vaguely make out shadowy silhouettes of at least one person seated in the back with her, but it was difficult to tell and she certainly couldn't make out any recognisable features. Could it be Scott? It had to be, surely? After all, he was the one she'd been running from. But how had he gotten a van organised so quickly to grab her? *How has he been spying on you for months and you didn't know?* a little voice challenged. This was it, the final proof that she absolutely *sucked* when it came to judging people's character. First Bryson, now Scott. Of course, Bryson was only using her to get to her family's money, but Scott...well, she wasn't exactly sure *what* his game was, only that it somehow involved her father and he'd resorted to kidnap and God only knew what else was coming. *At least you didn't humiliate yourself by falling in love with Scott, like you did with Bryson,* another little voice pointed out helpfully. Which really wasn't helpful at all.

How could she be so oblivious to someone spying on her? *Maybe because you're a self-centred brat who is only ever wrapped up in her own problems?* Enough was enough! There would be no further commentary from her conscience!

The van slowed to a stop and instantly Quinn's heartbeat picked up in alarm. Where were they? What were they going to do to her? Maybe driving around aimlessly in the back of a van hadn't been the worst thing in the world. The uncertainty of what might come next was far more terrifying.

Within moments of stopping, the back of the van opened. Her wrist and ankle restraints were roughly removed and she was hoisted to her feet and propelled forward out of the vehicle. A hand none too gently guided her head down, presumedly so as not to hit it on the roof, *which was kind of nice of them, all things considered,* she thought.

With her sight gone, her hearing became more acute. She didn't think they were in the street, as there was an echoey vibe, as though they were inside a large building—maybe an industrial shed?—and she noted the smooth ground, like polished concrete, beneath her feet, which added to her theory.

The large hand holding her upper arm tightly jerked her to a standstill. The sound of something being dragged across the floor made her turn her head sideways, despite the fact she still couldn't see. Quinn yelped as she was forced down onto a hard seat, her newly acquired freedom to move her hands and feet short-lived as she was once more tied up. In a blinding flash of bright light, the hood covering her head was whisked away, and she found herself blinking like a startled owl as she tried to focus on the shapes before her.

She was scared, but she was also angry. The longer she'd had to think about what an idiot she'd been to fall for Scott's friendly, good-looking, boy-*quite-literally*-next-door act, the more furious she became. Fury outweighed fear as her eyes finally adjusted to the glare and she was ready to take on Scott, or whoever the hell he really was. In fact, he was just lucky they'd tied her up, because right now, if he was standing in front of her, she would do her best to scratch his lying bastard eyes out.

Unfortunately, as she searched the increasingly terrifying and, quite frankly, *ugly* faces of the men in the room, her bravado began to slip.

None of the faces belonged to Scott.

'Miss Appleton.' The raspy voice of an obviously heavy smoker dragged her attention to the other side of the room, where a large-chested man in a black leather vest and black jeans was perched casually against the edge of a desk. 'Nice of you to join us.' She judged his age to be somewhere in his late fifties. He had a world-weary, hard-edge kind of look, with permanent crease marks around his eyes and forehead that added ten years to his face, and a nasty-looking silvery scar that ran from his mouth to his chin.

'Who are you?' she snapped, ignoring the few sniggers the man's greeting caused, and looked him up and down quickly.

'Who I am isn't really important. It's who you are that matters.'

'What are you talking about?'

'You're an Appleton.'

Ah, so that's what this was. She gave an unamused snort. 'You're after some kind of ransom? You guys should have planned this a couple of months earlier. Haven't you heard? The Appletons are skint.'

'Oh, we know all about the debt your daddy got himself into.' There were a few grunts around the room following that, and Quinn frowned in confusion. 'We're not interested in ransoming you—at least, not for money. But we are interested in trading you.'

'Trading me?' *What the hell does that mean?!*

'We'll trade your freedom—*and your life*,' he added offhandedly, 'for your dad's location.' He shrugged one shoulder and folded his tattooed arms across his chest.

Her *life?* 'I don't know where he is,' she told him simply.

The man pulled a face, shaking his head. 'Well, that's going to be a problem.'

'What do you want with my father?'

'Probably best you don't worry about that,' he advised, cocking his head slightly as he looked at her.

'I think I have a right to know what's going on.'

'You actually have no rights. All you need to do is tell me where your father is.'

'I told you, I *don't know* where he is. The last time I saw him was on Christmas Day. I've been trying to find him for months.'

'I don't believe you,' he said, unfolding his arms and picking up a long, serious-looking knife from the table beside him she hadn't notice before. 'I think you *do* know where he is.'

'I don't. I've been wanting to call the police to report him missing, but...' Her words faltered.

'But what?'

'My family didn't want it getting out to the media.'

'I can see why. It would be embarrassing to hear all about how the rich and famous Jethro Appleton was now nothing more than a drug runner.'

Quinn stared at the man in horror before giving an incredulous glare. 'I hardly think so,' she said, trying not to laugh at the absurdity of it all.

'Better believe it, sweet cheeks. Your daddy has been workin' for us for almost twelve months.'

'You're lying.'

He shook his head, but smiled smugly. 'He came in pretty handy with his yacht and his private jet.'

'Why would my father want to work with a bunch of...' She stopped, partly because she couldn't decide between the words *criminals* and *scumbags*, and partly because she suddenly realised said criminals and scumbags were currently holding her captive with at least one sharp knife. 'It doesn't make any sense that he'd work for you.'

'When you rake up that much debt, you'd be surprised what a desperate man will do,' he said, staring at her intently.

Quinn swallowed nervously as the gravity of her situation dawned on her. Maybe she'd been so full of excess adrenaline before that she'd been unable to fully appreciate how much trouble she was in.

She took in the three other men scattered about the room. All were clad similarly to the man before her, in black jeans of questionable cleanliness and black leather vests. A memory of the biker following her to work a few days ago suddenly sparked a connection. 'You've been following me,' she blurted.

'We had some trouble finding you,' he admitted gruffly. 'Until you bought that car. Big Trev is an old friend of ours and he was the one who recognised you.'

Typical—of all the people who could have outed her, it had taken a used car salesman to figure it out. Damn those stupid cards she'd held on to.

Then another thought emerged. She narrowed her eyes at the man. 'If my father's working for you, why do you need to find him?'

The calm expression promptly left the older man's face, and his jaw clenched, the scar running from the corner of his lip to his chin turning white in the process. 'Your daddy made a very stupid decision.'

His voice, although cold and hard and sending a shiver of apprehension through her, didn't stop her curiosity being stirred. If her father was mixed up in a drug ring with these bikers, he was clearly not with them now—and it certainly explained why he needed to leave in such a hurry. 'What decision did he make?'

'He decided to call our bluff, and now we've got to show him what the consequences of that will be.'

It didn't take much guesswork to figure out *she* was the consequence. So much for sparing her life if she told them where he was.

'Now, once more—where is he?'

'I told you, I don't know.'

He looked over her head and lifted his chin towards one of his men behind her. Quinn heard movement, and a man appeared in front of her. The blow to the side of her face stunned her into silence. It was immediately followed by a high-pitched ringing in her ears and an intense sting.

'We're going to keep doing this until you tell us what we want to know.' The man's calm tone did nothing to reassure her.

'I don't know where he is. I spoke to him,' she said quickly, eyeing the man who was about to take a step towards her again. 'Today. But he didn't say where he was. He didn't say anything except that he was safe.'

'You don't have your phone on you,' the big biker said, frowning. 'Why?'

Her mind flew back to where she'd dropped it on Scott's bed. 'I wasn't expecting to get dragged into a bloody van by a bunch of thugs or I would have come prepared.'

'It's a pity we've met under these circumstances. I kind of like you.'

Whack. Another hit sent her head sideways; tears sprang from her eyes.

'I think you're lying. I think,' he continued, prowling the room, 'that you *do* know where your father is and that your phone probably has his number on it. Which brings me back to the question of why would you have left your phone behind when you left the house? Were you on your way to meet him? Did he think your phone was being tracked? Did he tell you to leave it behind?'

'No,' she snapped. Her face hurt and she felt sick to her stomach. 'I wasn't expecting to leave the house.'

'So why *did* you?' he asked, leaning in close to her face and breathing on her. She really did feel like puking now. Christ, his breath stank—like old cigarette smoke and tuna.

'Because I was trying to get away from—' She stopped, recalling Scott's part in this afternoon's horrific shitshow. This was all Scott's fault. If she hadn't been running away from him, she wouldn't have been out on the street and completely at the mercy of these freaks in leather.

'From who?' he persisted.

'From my flatmate,' she snarled. 'I don't know who he is. He had photos of me, of my family. I panicked and ran.'

There were a few odd glances swapped before he narrowed his gaze at her. 'How long have you known him?'

'Not long. He moved in a few days after I did.'

'Feds?' one of the men asked, which sparked more frowns.

'Could be,' the older guy muttered. His narrowed gaze settled on her thoughtfully.

Feds? The word pinged about in her head. As in, Federal Police? If that was the case, why on earth would an AFP officer move into her house? The sudden, horrible realisation that maybe this man hadn't been lying about her father drained the remaining colour from her face. *No.* She wouldn't believe it...and yet, the evidence kept piling up.

'I think we need to bring this flatmate of yours here for a bit of a visit,' he mused, stepping away from her and giving a toss of his head towards the door. 'Get a few of the boys to go over there and bring this prick to me. I wanna know what his story is.'

'Yeah, but Jimmy, if he's a Fed...' a biker with bad acne scars started, before his protests petered out at the cold glare his boss levelled at him.

'Then it'll be one less dog out there givin' us grief, won't it?' Jimmy finished pointedly. The men hurried to the door without further objection. Clearly, they weren't keen to argue the point too hard.

How the hell did she end up in this mess? One day, life was cruising along perfectly, and the next, she was tied to a chair in a stinking industrial shed. Her cheek throbbed now that the shock had worn off and she could almost feel the bruise beginning to form. She supposed she was lucky he hadn't broken any bones...yet.

Fear clutched at her throat. These men were going to hurt her. She knew that, simply by telling her as much as they had, they would have to kill her. The thought terrified her. She didn't want to die. She'd miss her friends and her horribly cramped bedroom in that dump of a house. She'd miss her job...okay, that was clearly the stress talking, she wouldn't miss her stupid job, but she *would* miss going to work. She gave a silent scoff at that. Who would have ever thought Quinn Appleton would miss going to work? Somewhere along the line, she'd discovered it felt good to be doing something useful. She'd gotten used to her new life, her new identity. Amy Sinclair's life was so much easier without all the drama and shallowness. She had real friends, not the fake, fair-weather kind Quinn had. Amy was real. She was free to do whatever she wanted without the pressure of her family name hovering above her, defining who she was.

Only, she realised now with a sinking heart, Amy *wasn't* real. These men had taken her because she was an Appleton, because of whatever her father had done to them. Her bloody family, even now, had managed to drag her back down when she thought she'd found real happiness.

Outside, bikes started up, their thunderous revs grating on her already stretched nerves.

'While we wait for the boys to deliver your friend, we should get better acquainted,' Jimmy said, coming back across the room, bringing a chair and taking a seat so they were at eye level. Quinn's gaze moved to his hand, which still held the large hunting knife that now rested on his thigh. 'I really didn't want to have to resort to this, you know,' he said, almost apologetically. 'I don't like involving women or children in business, but your father didn't listen.'

'If this is about the money he owes you,' she started, but was cut off by the man's slow shaking head.

'It's not about money. This is about honour. Your father has none.' He shrugged. 'So, we have to send him a message—convince him he needs to come out of hiding and do the right thing.'

'What's the right thing?' She knew she should just keep quiet, but she couldn't help the curiosity. She'd been looking for answers and this was likely her last chance to find them.

'Pay the price for his betrayal.'

'How did he betray you?'

'That's not really any of your concern—that's between your father and I.'

'I'd have to disagree with you there,' she snapped. 'Seems like I'm pretty involved now.'

Chapter 34

A loud bang sounded and the door flew open. Smoke suddenly filled the room, making Quinn cough and wheeze, followed by orders to 'Get on the ground!' being yelled by a stream of men in black armour. The air was thick with swearing and shouts of outrage as the bikers put up a short-lived fight with the heavily armed officers surrounding them.

It all happened in less than a minute, and yet somehow, it felt like an eternity as Quinn watched on helplessly from her chair. From behind her, someone undid her bounds and her hands dropped to her sides, her arms aching from their abrupt release. A painful tingling sensation flooded her extremities as feeling returned.

Strong hands helped her to her feet and a muffled voice behind a mask asked if she was hurt.

Quinn felt numb. It had all happened so fast. She managed to shake her head before the man carefully led her out of the room, around the now-prone bodies of her captors, who were lying handcuffed and helpless face-down on the floor.

Outside she was handed over to a pair of paramedics, who carefully examined her face. It hurt to touch but was nothing more than superficial bruising. Superficial still hurt like a bitch though, she decided, wincing as she held the cold pack the male paramedic gave her to her cheek.

With the shock subsiding, indignation began to flare up. She wished she'd been able to go back inside and give that arsehole Jimmy a hard kick to the ribs. She was feeling a lot braver now that she was surrounded by all these armed police.

The scene looked like something out of an action movie—patrol cars and armoured vehicles parked haphazardly inside the high-fenced security gates of the industrial shed, while other vehicles arrived to take the bikers away shortly after.

Two men approached the ambulance, both with IDs stating 'Australian Federal Police', and Quinn immediately started. *Scott! What had happened to Scott?* 'They sent men to my house to get my flatmate,' she told the officers, fear gripping her at the thought of the bikers breaking into the house. *What if they hurt Viv or Atticus in the process of finding Scott?*

'It's all right,' one of the officers said, holding a hand out to calm her. 'We intercepted the three men on bikes leaving here prior to the tactical team intervening. We'd like to go over a few things with you, if you're feeling up to it?'

Quinn nodded, relief sapping the burst of energy from her body, and she sank back down onto the edge of the ambulance bed gratefully.

'They were looking for my father,' she said as one of the men flipped open a notebook.

'Were you aware that your father had connections with these men?'

'No,' she said. 'Did you plant an AFP officer in my house to spy on me?'

The first man seemed taken aback by her question. 'Why do you ask?'

Would they admit Scott was one of their own? Even at this point when everything had seemingly blown up? Maybe they weren't allowed to.

'My father wouldn't have been working for these men,' she said instead.

'We're still investigating the claims.'

'How did you know I was here?'

'We've had the club under surveillance for the last few weeks and then we were informed about your abduction.'

'My father is missing, and these men kidnapped me to prove some kind of point to him, but I still don't understand how he's mixed up in all of this. It has to be some kind of mistake.'

'We're aware of your father's disappearance and the matter is an ongoing investigation. We'll be going through this place and hoping to turn up some evidence that will help find him—or at least explain any part he may or may not have had in the illegal activities the motorcycle club has been recently involved in. If there's anything you think of that might help us, we'd be happy to hear it.'

'They didn't say much. Just that Dad was in debt and he was desperate. Wait,' she said, looking back at the other officer with a confused frown, 'what do you mean you were aware of my father's disappearance?'

'We've been working with your family for the last few months to locate him.'

'My family?' She eyed him doubtfully before suspicion turned to realisation. 'My grandmother told you he was missing?'

'It's an ongoing investigation and we can't discuss a lot of the finer details,' the more senior officer said, gently but firmly. 'Rest assured, we will do everything we can to locate your father, Miss Appleton.'

Gran had been working with the police? All this time, Quinn had been begging her to go to the authorities about her father and Gran had already done it? Why the hell wouldn't she have said so?

After the officers left, Quinn thanked the paramedics and exited the ambulance. She breathed in the cooler air outside and felt a little better. Glancing around, she spotted a familiar face standing next to a black car and slowly walked towards it.

'Are you all right, miss?' Lionel asked, his brow creasing as he took in her bruises.

'I'm okay,' she said, trying to smile but wincing as the action pulled at her swollen cheek. 'You should see the other guy,' she joked without much enthusiasm. It shouldn't have surprised her that Gran had sent a car. Obviously, she was all over the situation. As usual. 'I'd like to go back to my place, Lionel.'

'Your grandmother requested you return to Appleton Park.'

'Tell Gran thank you, but I'll take a taxi home.'

'It's not safe for you there,' Lionel said, holding open the car door.

Quinn let out a long breath. Thoughts of Scott and the photos implicating him in God only knew what seemed too much to deal with if she went back now. Despite the fact she had a burning need to know why he had them and who he really was, the actions of the afternoon were rapidly taking their toll. She couldn't be bothered to fight anymore. She was too tired.

Sliding into the back seat, Quinn accepted the pillow and throw rug Lionel produced from the boot gratefully, and was asleep before they'd even turned onto the motorway.

***

When Quinn arrived at Appleton Park, she found Gran seated in the drawing room, waiting. She caught the flash of alarm as Gran took in Quinn's appearance, and her throat tightened at the unexpected sympathy that showed on her grandmother's face.

Quinn hesitated briefly before reaching for her grandmother's outstretched hand and battled to keep the sting of threatening tears at bay. She had to hold it together, especially in front of Gran.

'Oh, my poor dear, what did they do to you?'

Her soft voice caught Quinn off guard. It was so unexpected to hear any real emotion coming from her— other than the usual anger or disappointment.

'It looks worse than it actually is,' she said, trying to brush it off lightly, but a glance up at the large oval mirror on the far wall told her it *did* look pretty horrific.

A movement across the room drew Quinn's attention, and she found herself staring, stunned. 'What are *you* doing here?'

Chapter 35

'I asked him to come,' Gran said, cutting in.

There, across the room, stood the last person in the entire world she'd ever have expected to find in her grandmother's drawing room.

Scott.

'What the hell is going on?' she demanded, dragging her gaze away from a noticeably silent Scott to her grandmother.

'I didn't want to involve you in any of this, Quinn,' she started wearily.

'In any of what?'

'Your father's trouble.'

'You went to the police about him even though you told me not to. Why?' she demanded. 'Why didn't you tell me?'

'Because we couldn't afford any publicity.'

'For the family?' Quinn asked incredulously.

'For your father's life,' Scott intervened.

Quinn stared at her gran, waiting for an explanation when it seemed Scott wasn't going to add anything further. 'Your father agreed to give evidence against a very large drug ring. He went into protective custody when they found out he was passing on information to the authorities.'

Quinn gaped, then turned her attention back to the man standing with his arms crossed, watching silently from across the room. 'Who are you? Where do you fit into all this?' The Scott before her wasn't the same Scott, the flatmate, she'd gotten to know. This Scott was remote; detached. Instead of his usual jeans and faded '90s band T-shirts, he was dressed in a pair of black tailored trousers and a white button-up shirt, looking every inch the professional businessman.

'Mr Scott here works with a private security firm I've hired.'

'To do what?'

'Protect the family. Investigate, whatever needs to be done,' he supplied smoothly.

'So you moved into the room next door to protect me?' she asked dryly.

'We knew people may try and come after the family,' Gran said in a tone far calmer than Quinn thought reasonable under these circumstances.

'So this whole Amy Sinclair disguise thing wasn't really about my trust fund,' she said flatly.

'Oh no, it was definitely about the trust fund,' Gran confirmed. 'But it was also an added measure of protection.'

She needed a drink. A very large, very strong drink. Now.

Walking over to the booze cabinet, she reached for a glass and poured a large shot of tequila, tossing it down and wincing as it burned her throat, but it went a long way to help numb her bruised emotions.

'So you,' she said, turning back to face Scott, 'were sent to spy on me day and night posing as a flatmate?'

'It seemed like a good cover opportunity.' His expression was almost unreadable—a mask of indifference so unlike the man she'd begun to feel something for.

'You were very convincing,' she said, trying to match his composure but fearing her anger might be giving her away.

'He was doing his job, dear,' Gran interrupted. 'No point in blaming the man for that.'

'Oh, I don't blame *him*,' Quinn said, whirling around, 'I blame you.'

'Blame me all you like. It's my job to make sure this family is safe and that's what I did.' She watched as Gran briskly brushed imaginary lint off her skirt. 'Now, why don't you go up and have a nice hot bath and get some rest.'

'I'm not staying. I have to get home. I've got work tomorrow.'

'I'm afraid that's not going to be possible,' Gran said. 'Today's events have been all over the news. Your identity has been well and truly revealed.'

'What?' Shock reverberated throughout her entire body. 'But how?'

'There was a security leak somewhere. Anyway, it's put us all in a very vulnerable position. I'm afraid it's far too dangerous for you to be living alone, and going to the factory is out of the question now that everyone knows who you are.'

'But why? I mean, why should it make any difference?'

'You *want* to go back to the factory?' Gran asked, arching a sculptured eyebrow doubtfully.

'Well, not the *job*, exactly,' she said. 'I just...I don't know...I'm used to it now, I guess.'

For a long moment, Gran studied her thoughtfully. 'You can't return now. Not as an Appleton. It would only make things...awkward.'

'Let me get this straight. I was good enough to work there, but only as long as I didn't use the Appleton name? That sounds a little hypocritical to me, Gran. What happened to an honest day's work?'

'This is not the time or place to be having this discussion,' Gran snapped.

'Not in front of the employees,' Quinn challenged, sending a scornful glare at Scott, who didn't so much as bat an eyelid at the remark. She wasn't sure why she was so defensive and angry, all she knew was that suddenly everything that had started to feel comfortable was being taken away from her—again. She was tired of being told what she could and couldn't do.

'What about my things back at the house? I can't just leave Viv and Atticus high and dry without a boarder—without *two* boarders,' she added meaningfully.

'We'll compensate the house owners and explain the situation, and your belongings will be packed and brought back here for the time being. This is the safest place for you until we find out what happens with your father and the trial.'

'There's a trial?'

'There will be,' Scott said, stepping in calmly. 'The AFP has been building a case on these guys for a long time. Your father's information has been vital and his evidence is essential. For now, though, he has to remain in a safe house and under protection.'

Lionel came in and picked up the remote. 'You wanted to know when the news was on,' he said, selecting a channel on the TV screen that magically unfolded from behind a painting.

Scott crossed the room and stopped just behind her. She swallowed hard at the smallest jolt of nervous anticipation that followed his nearness.

Just stop it! He was lying to you this whole time!

'In a scene that could have come straight out of a Hollywood movie, the heiress to one of Australia's richest family fortunes, Quinn Appleton, was abducted earlier today in a brazen act allegedly backed by the outlaw biker gang The Brotherhood of Rebellion Motorcycle Club.' An image of Quinn dressed in a long, off-the-shoulder, royal blue Prada evening gown filled the screen. God, she loved that dress. It was one of the designs she hadn't been able to part with yet.

'Sources close to the Appleton family say police have since managed to negotiate the release of Ms Appleton, who suffered only minor injuries in the incident.'

Footage of the aftermath played, showing the bikers being led out of the industrial shed and then a battered and bruised Quinn being led to an ambulance. Her breath caught at the unexpected close-up.

'Ms Appleton, a regular on the society circuits, hasn't been spotted recently, and appears almost unrecognisable in these images.

'The Brotherhood of Rebellion Motorcycle Club leader, Jimmy Logan, known in criminal circles as Pick Handle Logan due to his infamous method of killing, is currently in custody. Authorities have not released the motivation behind the abduction. Speculation surrounds the Appleton family and rumours that Jethro Appleton, son of Lady Elizbeth Appleton, head of Appleton's, one of Australia's oldest family-owned businesses, has fled the country after leaving a trail of outstanding debts. Investigations are ongoing.'

'Turn it off,' Elizabeth snapped from her seat. She leaned forward and picked up her teacup. 'So much for keeping everything quiet,' she muttered.

'Maybe if we knew what was going on this wouldn't have happened,' Quinn retorted, eyeing her gran furiously. 'I came to you begging for help to look for Dad. I told you I knew something was wrong, and you dismissed my concerns like they were nothing. I can't believe I was stupid enough to fall for it all.'

'It was to keep you safe.'

'It was to keep me in check. You used this entire situation to get exactly what you've always wanted — another Appleton under your control.'

Any other time Quinn would have been terrified by Gran's stony silence, but not now. How dare she manipulate Quinn's entire life the way she had. 'Well, I hope you're happy. You can keep your money. I don't want anything to do with this family anymore. I'm done.'

'You've had a traumatic day,' Gran said, managing to snip each word out briskly. 'Nothing constructive can come from this now. After you've rested, we can sit down and discuss things with calmer heads tomorrow.'

'I'll escort you to your room,' Scott interjected swiftly.

'I don't need an escort,' she all but snarled.

'I have to do a check upstairs anyway, it's on my way.'

Quinn didn't want to stay down here with Gran anymore, and the lure of a hot bath was too strong to ignore, so she allowed herself to concede, just this once, reluctantly following him from the room.

They didn't speak as they trudged up the winding staircase past the first floor to the second, but as they approached Quinn's bedroom door, Scott held his arm in front of her, moving past her to inspect the room before returning to allow her to enter. 'All clear,' he announced.

'Oh, I'm so glad,' she said, sarcasm dripping.

She saw his frown and gritted her teeth against the small pang she felt in return.

'I would have thought after today's events you'd be taking this more seriously,' he said.

'I *am* taking it seriously. I just can't work out who you're pretending to be today.'

'I wasn't pretending.'

'Right.'

'I was undercover.'

'You were lying.'

'I couldn't tell you anything,' he protested.

'So was making out with the boss's granddaughter part of the role? I hope you got paid extra for that.'

'That wasn't…' He stopped, a frustrated sound gargling in his throat. He put a hand out to touch her arm, stopping her from turning away. 'Everything that happened today was my fault. I let my guard down and you got hurt. I can't forgive myself for that.' His voice had lost that cool, measured tone of earlier, and for a fraction of a second, she saw the Scott she knew. There was real pain in his eyes. Then it was gone. 'If I'd kept my head in the game, you wouldn't have found out about any of this and those bastards wouldn't have taken you.'

'Maybe if there hadn't been a *game* to start with, none of this would have happened at all,' she snapped.

'After meeting Jimmy, you have doubts this game is legit? Your father's life is in real danger. The Brotherhood of Rebellion is only a small part of the organisation your father got himself mixed up in. You're still not safe—none of you are.'

'Well, that's comforting.'

'There'll be extra security posted inside and out, and this house will be in lockdown.'

'For how long?' Quinn asked.

'Until it's safe. There won't be any more slip-ups; I can guarantee you won't ever be put in danger because of me again.'

Quinn heard the slight shake in his voice and held his hard gaze, her anger beginning to melt away. Her abduction had affected him more than she'd realised. It wasn't simply ego, that he'd been negligent in whatever he thought his duty had been, it was real fear and pain he'd felt. The old Scott was still in there.

'It wasn't your fault,' she said softly. He blinked uncertainly. 'They were waiting. They would have taken me on the way to work, or while we were out jogging.' She shrugged. 'Even if you'd been there, they would have done it.'

'I'd have killed them first if I'd been there.'

'Or they'd have killed you,' she said dryly. 'It was me they wanted and you would have been expendable. I couldn't have lived with that.' She swallowed a lump of emotion and realised just how true that was. Scott had become important to her. He'd been there all this time, watching over her—and while she found it alarming that she hadn't even suspected, it was also humbling. He'd been willing to put his life in danger to protect her.

'Get some rest,' Scott said, his voice low and husky, which had the effect of wiping away any fatigue she may have had, replacing it with an entirely new sensation.

Reaching up onto her tiptoes, she gently touched her lips to his. He hesitated briefly before he returned her kiss. Quinn slid into his arms and ignored the protest of her aching muscles, needing his warmth and strength against her. The kiss deepened, becoming an almost savage hunger, before pain made her flinch, having forgotten how tender the side of her face really was. Immediately, Scott stepped back, uttering a harsh curse, followed by a swift apology.

'No, it's okay, it really doesn't hurt that much,' she protested.

'You need to get some rest,' he said, taking a further step away and lowering his gaze. 'Goodnight, Quinn.'

That was the first time he'd used her real name, and in that instant, she felt real grief, as the last link between them as Amy and Scott had been effectively severed.

'Wait,' she called, making him stop and turn back, almost reluctantly. 'What's your real name?'

He smiled. 'Peter Scott. Everyone just calls me Scott though.'

She felt marginally better that at least that much was true.

'Night,' he said, then walked away once more, moving swiftly down the hallway.

Quinn closed the door behind her and dropped her head wearily. It was hard to imagine that today had started out so normally. She felt as though she'd aged a good few years since breakfast.

Quinn peeled off her T-shirt and jeans and grabbed the fluffy white dressing gown that hung in her wardrobe before heading into the ensuite. As she waited for the bath to fill, she inspected her face properly. It wasn't pretty. No wonder Scott all but ran to get away. Her cheek was puffy and the bruise was an angry shade of crimson, but at least her eye wasn't swollen shut.

A flash of memory replayed of the sharp, ugly knife and those cold, hard faces staring at her, and an involuntary shiver went through her body. Had the police not shown up when they did, things could have turned out a lot worse than a bruise on the side of her face. She rubbed her arms to ward off the sudden chill, but it didn't help. Her whole body felt cold, and she quickly stepped into the bath, sinking into its blissful warmth and letting out a long, slow breath. The flashbacks continued before her eyes each time she shut them, so she reached for something else to replace them, settling on Scott and the kiss they'd just shared.

There'd been something almost desperate about it. It had been explosive, yes, but just beneath that, there was something else...another emotion she couldn't put her finger on.

She was still angry at Gran—and him, to some extent—for not telling her the truth about her father and what he was really doing, but that paled in the face of the danger she'd faced this afternoon. Now it seemed pointless to waste time being angry. Scott's words came back to her as she let the warm water drizzle through her fingers. *We are still not safe.* Until her father was able to give his testimony, his life was still very much in danger—as was hers, if these people tried to get at her again.

Eventually, the water cooled, and she reluctantly climbed out of the tub, drying herself before donning the fluffy gown and stumbling towards her bed. She didn't even bother pulling back the covers before sinking into the huge soft pillows and falling asleep.

Chapter 36

Quinn sighed as she rolled over on the huge king-size bed and stretched. Her shoulders and arms still hurt—in fact, probably more than they had the day before. It was like the day after a return from a long hiatus to the gym, only with bruises.

If she was completely honest with herself, she didn't miss waking up on her small, hard mattress back home. She blinked at that. When had her rented share house become home? While she was pondering that, her phone buzzed, alerting her to a message. It was from Tara.

Saw you on the news. I can't believe it. Are you okay? Please just let us know you're all right.

Quinn's lip trembled a little. She tried to reply, typing out a few words before erasing them and starting again. She wasn't sure how to answer. She wanted to say she was sorry for not telling them who she was, but then she'd have to explain the reason and, despite the real fact being that it was supposed to help protect her identity, the actual reason she'd believed had been in order to collect her trust fund. She felt ashamed now when she remembered how miserable she'd felt on her first day—angry with Gran for forcing her into a job she had no intention of enjoying, with people she'd felt were below her, doing menial, unimportant work. God, what an absolute and utter dick she'd been. She'd entered that factory a spoilt, entitled little shit. But she'd come out something different. She wasn't the same person anymore. Amy had taught her how to be someone people wanted to be friends with. How to be independent and...happy. But she couldn't be Amy anymore, and that frightened her. She didn't want to go back to being Quinn Appleton, socialite. She wanted more out of life. She wanted to *do* something, make a difference. She wanted to help people and earn an honest living. She wanted these things, but she was terrified of falling back into her bad habits and being swept from the path she so wanted to take.

She looked down at the curser flashing on her screen.

I'm fine. Just a little bruised. I'm sorry I didn't get a chance to say goodbye. Thank you for everything. Please pass on my regards to the girls.

She reread it a few times before hitting send then dropped the phone on the bed beside her. She owed those women so much more than *regards.* Maybe once everything settled down, she could catch up with them and explain it all...but by then, they might not even care. And could she really blame them?

***

Later, she walked into the drawing room looking for Gran and found her seated at her small desk. In the far corner was a woman wearing dark trousers and a white shirt under a loosely cut jacket. On her hip was a revolver in a holster.

'Oh, you're up? I thought I'd let you sleep in. Your breakfast is in the kitchen if you're hungry.'

She was actually starving, but more concerned about why there was an armed woman in the drawing room.

Gran glanced at the woman and gave a small smile. 'Quinn, this is Monica. She'll be here with us until things settle down a bit.'

'Where's Scott?'

'Mr Scott assigned Monica and her other colleagues outside to replace him.'

'Why?'

'I don't know, dear,' Gran said, dismissing her questions with a hint of impatience. 'But Monica would like to go over a few things with you before you eat. So I'll leave you to it.'

The woman walked across the room and extended her hand. 'Monica Bond,' she said, and Quinn shook it briefly, raising an eyebrow.

'Bond. Monica Bond,' Quinn quipped lightly, but the woman apparently didn't see the funny side, pursing her lips together and continuing.

'I just thought it might be good to introduce myself and go over any concerns you may have. I also wanted to reiterate the protocols Mr Scott put in place so we're all on the same page.'

'Sorry? Where is he again?'

'He was reassigned to another client.'

'By who?'

'By himself. He's the boss.'

'So he reassigned himself from working with my family?' Quinn asked slowly.

'From working *this* part of the family,' Monica answered tactfully.

'In other words...with *me*.' She waited for Monica to confirm, but she remained stubbornly silent. 'Why?'

'I couldn't really say what the reasoning was behind it, Ms Appleton.'

'Because you don't know or because you can't say?'

'Because I'm not paid enough to get involved in my boss's personal life,' she said dryly.

So it *was* because of her. After last night, she'd thought maybe they'd at least talk about this new thing between them. Surely, after everything, he owed her that much? Clearly not. Her family paid him to do a job, and he'd done it.

'It would be preferable that you don't leave the house unless it's for some kind of emergency. If you can work from home, that would make life for everyone and, more importantly, your security and safety, easier.'

'Can you contact him if you need to?' Quinn asked.

Monica blinked. 'Do I *need* to contact him?'

Quinn considered the woman quietly for a moment. 'I'd like you to get a message to him to contact me.'

'If I hear from him, I'll be sure to pass on your request.'

'What if you don't hear from him? Quinn asked, narrowing her eyes.

'Then he's probably extremely busy working,' Monica said with thinly disguised exasperation. 'In much the same way I'm trying to.'

'Okay. Sorry,' Quinn said. 'Yes, all right. Stay in the house. Don't go anywhere. Work from home.' She gave a small, dejected snort. She didn't have a job to go to now anyway. She glanced at her watch and realised it would be morning tea. She was really going to miss gathering around the staffroom table with a cuppa and listening to the gossip and latest news of each of the women she worked with.

'If you need to go out, you must always inform one of us and we'll organise transport and accompany you.'

'Okay,' Quinn agreed tonelessly.

'I can't emphasise enough the importance of making sure you never leave the house alone,' Monica said, eyeing her sternly.

'*Okay,*' Quinn stressed, holding the woman's serious gaze. 'I get it. Is that all? Can I go now?'

'I'll be nearby if you need me,' she said with a hint of irritation. Clearly, Monica thought Quinn was just being difficult. The truth was, she had no intention of trying to leave the house. For one, she had nowhere to go. And secondly, after her encounter with Jimmy and his boys the day before, she had very little desire to find herself in that situation ever again. She was more than happy to hide away.

***

When Quinn came back downstairs later, she was confronted by Lionel explaining firmly into the phone that the family had no comment then hanging up, only for it to immediately ring again.

Quinn raised an eyebrow at Lionel, who shook his head irritably. 'The press has been rather insistent about getting a quote.'

'Is Gran in the study?' she asked, and at Lionel's nod headed down the hallway to find out if there'd been any news about her father.

Gran looked up as Quinn entered the room and gave a disgruntled harrumph as the phone shrilled. 'You would think there had to be some other newsworthy story out there,' she said.

'This one's got all the hallmarks of a juicy scandal though.' Quinn smirked, taking a small triangle sandwich from a platter on the table nearby.

'We're having a visit from some detectives to update us on yesterday's incident. I believe they would like you to be present to go over a few things from the statement you gave yesterday. All routine apparently. And you've had a number of calls.' Gran handed over a small stack of paper with names and phone numbers. Flicking through the pile, Quinn tried not to roll her eyes. Funny how, all of a sudden, her old friends were interested in her welfare. More like they just wanted some of the inside scoop on the unfolding drama.

When she saw the last name, though, she hesitated.

Hugo.

A wave of regret flowed through her. She could only imagine his reaction to seeing her on the news last night. She bit her lip as she took in his simple message: *I get it now*. That everything made sense to him gave her a small sense of relief, but also made her incredibly sad. She crumpled up his message and held it in her palm. Hugo was a good man, who fell in love with a woman who didn't exist. Yet another victim to the carnage her father had brought upon the family.

She dropped his note, and the rest of them, into the bin beside the table and took a seat in the small window nook that overlooked the side garden.

'I'll be away tomorrow all day with meetings,' Gran was saying, which drew Quinn's attention briefly.

'What are the meetings about?'

Gran glanced up from her writing and looked surprised. 'To do with the automation plans for the factory.'

Quinn frowned. So the rumours were true, and the fears of everyone on the floor were well founded. 'It's really going ahead, then?'

'It's something we've been working towards for a number of years now.'

'But you'll be replacing all those jobs with machinery.'

'Yes, there'll be some job losses unfortunately, but the long-term financial gain far outweighs the short-term losses,' Gran pointed out logically. 'I'm afraid the price of progress often has more than its share of casualties.'

'There has to be ways we can reduce the number of job losses. These people are from low-income families. They *need* their jobs,' Quinn said, getting up from her seat. 'You can't just replace them all with machinery.'

'There's a bigger picture here, Quinn,' Gran said, replacing the lid of the elegant pen she'd been using, gently setting it down on the desk before her. 'The company has to keep up with the times. We need to run it to make a profit. It won't do anyone any favours if we don't upgrade our systems for greater production.'

'But these people have been loyal employees. Aren't you the one who's been telling us all this time that Appleton's is all about family?'

'Yes, dear, but there's a fine line between holding on to the past and moving forward. Unfortunately, in order to move forward, we have to make some hard decisions. Not everyone will lose their job. Many of the employees can be retrained as operators—machinery will always need people to oversee them.'

Quinn thought about the people she'd worked with and, while some would happily adapt to a more technical job, there were many who wouldn't. 'Gran, I know the company needs to stay relevant to new technology—I get it—but there has to be something that can be done to keep jobs. This factory is the main employer in the area. Some families have both parents working there—can you imagine what that will be like? The effect it will have if both income providers in the same household lose their jobs?'

Gran's expression softened slightly, and she gave a small nod. 'I do understand your concern. It's also one of mine. I've thought long and hard about this for a long time now, but there just isn't any way around it. We have to go ahead with the full automation.'

Quinn thought frantically for a way to buy some time before everything became official. 'I think we should call a meeting with the employees and get their perspective on it. There are people who've been with the company for over thirty years. Surely they've earned the right to at least give their input?'

'Darling, while it warms my heart that you've suddenly developed an interest in the business, this isn't something that I see has a lot of options.'

'Well, can you at least give me a chance to offer up another solution?' Gran opened her mouth to protest, but Quinn cut in quickly. 'Not about the automation,' she clarified, as clearly the company had already made up its mind about that, 'but in regards to job losses. If I can come up with a proposal to use the employees somewhere else, would you at least consider it?'

'Well, I don't know...'

'Gran, you put me in that factory to learn about the business,' she stated, holding her gran's gaze steadily. 'I'm asking you to give me the chance to do something important. I want to make a difference.'

'Does this mean you want to stay on at Appleton's...moving forward?' Gran asked curiously.

It seemed pointless to deny it. She really cared what happened to the business and the people who worked for it. 'I think there's some really great opportunities to do some good out in the world and we have the resources.' She shrugged, thinking of Hugo. Maybe Appleton's would never be the type of philanthropist Hugo was, but they could do better.

'So, yes, Gran. I'd like to stay on.'

Chapter 37

Quinn chewed the inside of her lip uncertainly as she waited in the front parlour two days later for her guest to arrive. She didn't like that the meeting place was here, but she had little choice at the moment, being pretty much under house arrest. It wasn't so much any real threat on her life she was worried about, it was more so the unrelenting interest from the media that made going out anywhere in public a nightmare at the moment. She didn't want to subject anyone else to that particular circus.

The front gate buzzed, announcing an arrival, and Lionel spoke into the intercom. Her hands began to sweat a little.

Quinn paced the room, waiting for the sound of the doorbell so she could greet her guests before Lionel could go all butler pomp and ceremony on her. The last thing she wanted was for her friends to get introduced like they were going to some bloody ball at Downton Abbey. However, hot on her heels was the ever-diligent Ms Bond, who reached around her at the last minute and stepped in front to open the door.

'You don't need to be here,' Quinn whispered harshly, tussling over who was opening the door.

'It's my job,' Monica hissed back.

'Your men at the front gate already vetted them, or they wouldn't have gotten through.'

'I still need to check all visitors.'

Quinn rolled her eyes. 'What are you going to do, frisk them or something?'

When the woman simply continued to hold her gaze, Quinn's face shifted into one of steely resolve. 'You are *not* going to frisk my friends,' she snapped. 'I don't care what Scott told you to do—if you lay one finger on them, I swear to God, I will have you kicked out of here faster than you can blink.'

'Your safety is my priority.'

'*Your* safety should be your priority right now,' Quinn countered, bumping the woman aside and swinging the door open with a bright smile on her face.

'Hi,' she said, and felt her smile waver slightly at the lone visitor on the front step. 'Tara. Just you today?'

'Yes,' she said, and Quinn hadn't realised just how much she'd missed that New Zealand accent until now. 'The others...' Tara hesitated briefly, 'they just need a little bit more time,' she finally said, clearly figuring there was no way of softening the blow so she might as well just say it.

'That's all right,' Quinn said, forcing her smile to widen despite the disappointment. Deep down, she hadn't expected *any* of them to turn up.

Tara sent a curious glance towards Monica, who still stood close by and lifted an eyebrow slightly.

'This is Ms Bond,' Quinn introduced, ushering Tara inside and around the security woman, sending Monica a pointed glare. 'She was just leaving. Come inside. I'm really sorry we had to meet here. I would have preferred some place a bit more normal, but...'

'I know you said you were okay before, but are you really?' Tara asked as they entered the parlour and Quinn shut the door behind them.

'I am,' Quinn said, and this time her smile was warmer. The bruising wasn't as noticeable now—not with makeup covering the majority of it—and it wasn't as sore. She still found herself a little jumpy at times, and sometimes her heart felt like it was racing for no apparent reason, but she was hoping it would eventually settle down on its own without a visit to the doctor and a prescription of some kind.

'I still can't believe it. I just wish you could have told us—we'd have put you up with us, made sure you were safe. You didn't have to deal with all that on your own.'

'I wish I could have,' Quinn said sadly. 'The last thing I wanted to do was lie to you all. I've never had friends like you before.'

She saw Tara roll her lips together slightly after she took a seat. 'The girls think this whole thing was some kind of play to report back on the workers,' she admitted.

'What? No,' Quinn said, startled by the news. 'I swear this had nothing to do with that. It was...' It sounded so stupid to explain now. 'This was something my gran insisted on—like a way I had to prove myself to her. That I was willing to start at the bottom and earn my way into a job.'

'At the bottom,' Tara repeated dryly. 'With all the common folk.'

'That's not what I meant.' Even though that's exactly how she'd felt in the beginning, she felt somewhat ashamed now. 'If you believe nothing else about all this, please believe that. This was not about anyone else. I wasn't there to deliberately trick anyone.'

'But that's how we all felt once we found out. Like fools,' Tara said. 'We took you in as one of us and all the time you were just pretending to be something you weren't.'

Quinn had replayed this moment in her head many times since learning that her identity had been revealed in the press. She knew this grilling was no more than she deserved, and the girls had every right to hold her to account. She'd always known that one day she'd have to face them—even if everything *hadn't* come undone the way it had—but she'd deliberately tried not to think about it, unable to face the guilt and hurt she'd unintentionally caused. Now, though, she had to face it—front on.

'I may not have started out intending to care about anyone or anything in the beginning,' she admitted, lowering her eyes from the accusing expression on Tara's face. 'But I did. I found friends I'd never imagined finding, and pride in doing a job I'd never thought I would do.' She shook her head, still amazed by the fact. 'I *wanted* to be Amy. I wanted her life. She had everything I never even knew I wanted until I had it—and then it was gone. But I'm not the same person I was. I don't want to go back to how I used to be. I want my friends to stay in my life.' She stopped abruptly and blinked back tears. 'I understand that you all feel betrayed, but I just hope that, in time, maybe after I've proved myself, you might give me another chance.'

Tara cleared her throat and gave a small sniff. 'I can't make any promises,' she said, and her voice sounded a little huskier than normal. 'But I'll tell the girls what you've said. It'll be up to them to make up their own minds.'

'Fair enough,' Quinn said, taking a deep breath. At least Tara hadn't yelled at her and stormed out of the room.

A knock sounded at the door and Quinn looked up to find Lionel entering with a tray. 'Thank you, Lionel. This is my friend Tara,' she said as he set the tray down on the table before them.

'Nice to meet you, Miss Tara,' Lionel said, smiling politely before leaving the room.

'Was that a *butler?*' Tara asked, her eyes widening as she stared in the direction Lionel had gone.

'Yes, although he's also my gran's driver and event coordinator.'

'An honest-to-God *butler,*' Tara repeated, her tone dripping in awe.

Quinn decided now might be as good a time as any to bring up her ideas about an action plan for Appleton's. 'Actually, Tara, while you're here, I really want to discuss something with you.'

Quinn went over the news that meetings were already underway about the automation side of things, and she hurried to explain what she wanted to do. 'So, I've managed to convince Gran to consider a proposal for keeping on as many staff as possible.'

'Which is?' Tara prompted warily.

'I haven't actually *got* any idea what the proposal actually *is* at the moment. That's kind of where you come in.'

'Me? How am I supposed to help?'

'I need you to help me brainstorm some ideas. I want to put something back into the community. You're always saying there isn't enough affordable day care and after-school care for kids, which makes it hard for families to have both parents working. What if we had something like that? A subsidised day care with an after-school program attached?'

'Well, that would be great. But how?'

'Appleton's could fund it with a bit of creative shuffling of funds, but we'd need people to retrain as childcare workers to staff it.'

'That would only be a handful of new jobs though,' Tara pointed out, looking at Quinn thoughtfully for a few moments.

'Which would bring us to phase two—addressing some of the socioeconomic issues we have in the area. I've been doing some research, and one of the biggest issues is the growing number of childhood diseases caused by unhealthy eating that doctors have seen appearing. We've got unlimited numbers of fast-food restaurants, but as a result, kids and adults are missing out on healthy, homemade meals, because meat and fresh food has become so expensive.'

'You're not telling me anything I don't already know,' Tara sighed. 'With four kids, my grocery bill is through the roof once I add fruit and meat. It's scary how expensive it's gotten.'

'I was looking at how popular the meal box industry has become. You know the ones that deliver a box of ingredients to your door with a week of healthy meals ready to prepare?'

Tara nodded slowly. 'But most of them are too expensive to be feasible for low-income families,' Tara put in with a frown. 'I really wanted to try them, but there's no way we can afford it.'

'I'm suggesting we start up a division of Appleton's to cater for this market, which is largely ignored. We promote it as fast food that's healthy. The meals will be bigger, feeding more than just the current two or four people per box. We do *real* family meals that kids will actually eat, not waste time on fancy recipes and ingredients that are advertised as "restaurant quality". We focus on making it affordable and healthy. It would need manual packers, buyers, nutritionists, marketing, kitchen staff, delivery drivers. All sourced from current staff. We'd get them into the major supermarkets in prominent, convenient spots near the front of the store, so it's just as easy to stop in and grab them as it would be to go to a drive-through. We could even look at making them click and collect, maybe?' Quinn was getting more excited by the idea as she spoke.

'It all sounds interesting,' Tara said thoughtfully, 'but do you really think Appleton's would be on board with it? Sounds like there'd be a lot of money needed to start all this up?'

'Let me worry about the finer details. I won't lie, it'll be a hard sell, but if I have all of you behind me—if you think it's something that might work—I'll fight for it.'

Tara sat in quiet contemplation. 'I think if it worked, it would be amazing,' she finally said. 'It would save a lot of jobs and be something positive for the area. But I'm not sure you'd be able to convince the company to invest that much money into it.'

'I'm arranging a meeting with the board and I'd like to have some representatives from the floor come along to put forward their opinions. Do you think you can get the girls to come along? Will you talk to them?'

Tara slowly nodded. 'I can try.'

Quinn sat back and gave a grateful smile. With Tara on board, she was sure the others would at least listen to her idea. She picked up a plate of daintily cut sandwiches and cakes and offered it to Tara.

There were so many possibilities ahead of them and she couldn't recall the last time she'd felt so passionate about something. Gran and the board had to see the value of this venture—so many of these people were depending on its outcome.

She pushed away the prospect of failure that hovered on the fringes of her mind. There was no room for negativity. There was a lot of work to do before they presented these ideas to the board and she had to concentrate on that right now. She'd worry about the what-ifs later.

Chapter 38

The next two weeks went by in a blur of activity. Police came and went; their routine updates to her grandmother bringing both good and bad news.

Her father *had* been working in a multinational drug ring and he was going to be charged with a number of offences that would see him do time in prison.

The news had hit Quinn hard. It seemed impossible that her father—the man she thought she knew—had managed to get himself tangled up in a web of crime and debt. The news broke and, once more, the press swarmed around the front gates, bombarding them with interview requests.

Shares were taking a hit, and Gran looked frailer than Quinn could ever recall seeing her.

Never had there been a worse time to approach the company to pitch a new business idea. Gran was in constant talks with accountants and solicitors, department heads and marketing, in an attempt to stave off the majority of the damage the company was absorbing.

The one good thing to come of it all was the fact her father had agreed to turn witness against the drug ring, which would lead to a number of international and high-profile criminals finally being brought to justice. In return — and only because of the sheer enormity of the case —they were dropping a number of the more serious drug-related charges that would have seen her dad locked away for life. He'd still have to do time, but it would be considerably less than it would have been due to the investigation discovering he had been working with the ring against his will. Blackmail and extortion evidence had been found in a number of raids that had been carried out.

It was a good outcome—of sorts. Nothing really felt like a win though, when there was so much of her life that still felt as though it was in tatters. Her desire to make changes within the company continued to burn within her, but the chances of it unfolding were growing dimmer by the day. Gran was fighting just to make sure the company didn't fall apart completely.

Which was why it was so unexpected when Gran called her into her office and Quinn found herself seated at a table with a number of serious, besuited individuals.

'Quinn, your idea—the food boxes. I'd like you to explain it to us, if you would,' Gran said, holding Quinn's owl-like gaze.

'You would?' Quinn couldn't have been more surprised by the request than if Gran had just told her she'd taken up pole dancing.

Gran lifted an eyebrow pointedly and Quinn snapped out of her stupor, quickly organising her thoughts and launching into the pitch she'd been mentally practising for the last few weeks but hadn't expected to deliver this soon. When she finished, she looked across at her grandmother anxiously, receiving a small nod of approval as a low murmur went around the table.

'Yes, I think that would work,' one of the men at the far end announced after a few minutes.

'I agree,' Gran said, closing her notebook firmly. 'Quinn, I'd like you to work alongside a team of people Mr

Bowbridge will put together, and make this happen. Time is of the essence, so you'll be starting tomorrow.'

'Tomorrow?' Quinn gaped.

'You have something else taking up your time?' Gran asked almost sarcastically.

Of course she didn't—she had no job, no social life, nothing but these plans she'd been consumed with. 'I mean, so soon? Why the hurry?'

'We need something positive to counteract the damage your father's troubles have brought upon the company recently.'

The man she assumed to be Mr Bowbridge interjected swiftly. 'We need to show the public we care about communities and the welfare of our employees. This idea of yours,' he said, waving a finger towards her, 'to reintegrate our current staff to avoid job losses, this is exactly the image the company needs right now.'

Quinn fought the protest she felt rising at their almost pompous tone and reasoning—surely they'd want to do it for the simple fact it was the right thing to do? But then she remembered that, up until this very minute, she'd feared her idea wouldn't even stand a chance, and quickly bit down on her reaction. *Baby steps*, she thought. She'd make changes, she'd just have to chip away at it. She forced a smile and listened to the plans that were unfolding around the table, trying her best to contain her excitement.

Her fingers itched to text Tara—so much so that she had to link them together on the table to stop herself from doing it—but the minute the meeting broke up, she went outside and sent a message. She did a happy dance on the spot as Tara called back immediately and asked a million questions, for which she had no answers.

But none of that mattered right now. Things were finally looking up.

***

Quinn paused before walking into the boardroom and took a deep, calming breath. She could do this.

Inside, her grandmother sat at the head of the table as regal and composed as the queen she was. At least in here.

Placing the folder of notes she'd been busily preparing for the last few weeks on the table before her, she took a moment to collect her thoughts before launching into her presentation.

'Ladies and gentlemen, my name is Quinn Appleton, and I'm here to present the exciting new direction Appleton's is about to take.'

The presentation went off without a hitch, but Quinn was struggling to remember much of it as it passed by in a rush of nerves. She wasn't even sure anything she'd said made sense, but everyone around her seemed upbeat and cheerful, so clearly it must have.

She sank into her seat gratefully and took a sip of water, but there was a hum of energy running through her body. She felt alive, like she'd never felt before. The last few months had been exhausting, as she'd worked hard to get the idea from an outline on paper to the finely honed business plan it now was, but right at this very moment, she forgot how tired she felt.

As the meeting wrapped up and people began to gather around the tables set up with coffee and food, Quinn crossed to where Maureen, Janelle and Tara stood, having all spoken as representatives, looking slightly uncomfortable in a room full of management.

'Thank you so much for your input,' Quinn said, feeling nervous as she approached the small group. She knew there was still a lingering sense of betrayal there that even the last few months working together hadn't completely quelled. It had been an awkward first meeting, but Tara had played the peacemaker, and while it wasn't the easy friendship of before, it was a working relationship and, over time, she'd managed to win back at least their respect, if not their complete forgiveness. She could wear that. She *had,* after all, betrayed them by pretending to be someone she wasn't.

'You did all the hard work,' Maureen pointed out, but her tone was a little less stilted than it had been in their previous meetings.

'I couldn't have done it without you guys.'

'Rubbish,' Maureen brushed off.

'I wouldn't have been so aware of some of the issues in the community without listening to you all discussing them.'

'The beauty of being an undercover boss, I suppose,' Janelle said with a sniff, reaching for a scone.

'That's not how it was. I was never spying on you. It had nothing to do with the job. There was a lot going on back then, and the truth is, I didn't expect to actually like my job or make friends. I wasn't a very nice person before all this started, and I feel like you guys were part of the reason I was able to see everything differently. Without you, none of this would have been possible.'

'It must be nice to be back where you belong,' Maureen said, and Quinn was about to go on the defensive until she saw the genuine look on her friend's face.

'It's nice not to have to hide who I am, but I'm not sure I really fit in anymore.'

'Maybe that's a good thing,' Maureen said gruffly, but her eyes softened. 'You're not that same girl we used to read about in the magazines in the lunch room. You've come a long way from that. Don't go back.'

Quinn gave a wry twist of her lips. 'No,' she said. 'There's no chance of that happening. I've found where I belong now—I'm really excited about our future here and I'm so happy that we get to continue to work together. I missed you all.'

'The place wasn't the same without you there either,' Tara said, smiling.

'And I hear they sent Darrell packing too,' Janelle chuckled. 'Good riddance.'

'I think Darrell got a bit too big for his boots. He'll be much happier down in the Melbourne office...once he's finished his compulsory communications and teamwork course.'

Maureen gave a delighted chortle. 'I can just see him now, fuming at the indignity of it all. Serves him right.'

'There's still hope for him,' Quinn said. 'Look at me. Who knew I could come out the other end of all this practically a new person.'

'I reckon your gran had a fair idea what was hiding inside you all this time,' Maureen noted with a knowing nod.

'How are you two getting along now?' Janelle asked, as their gazes turned upon the woman holding court at the end of the room.

'Better than I expected,' Quinn said, catching her grandmother's eye and smiling slightly before looking away. 'I think she's just happy there's at least one of the younger generations finally happy to be part of the company.'

'The right one, if the latest stories in the trash mags are any indication,' Janelle added with a disapproving sigh.

'Oh no, what did I miss?' She hadn't looked at a magazine in weeks. She realised, to her surprise and somewhat horror, that she kind of missed them!

'You didn't hear about your cousin?'

Quinn blinked. For the last few months, she'd done nothing except eat, breathe and live with this proposal and the launch of their new product. 'No, why? What's she done now?'

'Her manager just absconded with her fortune.'

Quinn stared at her friends blankly. 'What?'

'Yep. Wiped her accounts out apparently. She's destitute.'

'Except for the couple of million-dollar mansions in Los Angeles and some other exotic place,' Tara said dryly.

'Maybe Gran can give her a job at Appleton's?' Quinn joked, then paused as she clocked their three shocked faces before they all burst into fits of giggles.

'One Appleton on the factory floor was enough, thank you very much,' Maureen groaned.

Quinn made a note to look into the Greta debacle later—much later—she'd had enough of family catastrophes for a while. No, for now she was just going to enjoy the success of launching their new business line and be grateful for the amazing people she had in her life.

Chapter 39

Quinn parked her old Barina in the circular drive of Appleton Park and climbed out, feeling happy but tired after a huge day. She knew the car annoyed Gran, which was why she got a malicious little kick out of leaving it there.

'You've made your point,' Gran had bitten out a few weeks earlier when she'd greeted Quinn coming in from work. 'It's time to get yourself a decent vehicle. Not...that thing.' She'd barely been able to look at the little multicoloured hatchback.

'I'm not making a point about anything, Gran,' she'd said with an innocent smile. 'You were the one who confiscated my car originally. I did what you told me to do—I went out and earned one.'

'Yes, all right, well done. But now it's time to get rid of that and replace it with something more suitable.' She gave a small, impatient huff. 'You hold a position in the company now, dear—what are people going to think when they see you driving around in *that?*'

Quinn shrugged, then kissed her gran's cheek lightly. 'Maybe they'll think you don't pay me enough,' she joked.

'That's not funny,' Gran had called after her. The truth was, she'd grown attached to her little car. It wasn't pretty, but it was reliable—so far it hadn't missed a beat. There was a lot to be said for having dependable things around you.

Footsteps sounded on the gravel nearby, and she looked up and froze.

'Scott,' she whispered, wondering if she looked as shocked as she felt.

'Quinn,' he said, sounding far calmer than she had.

'What are you doing here?'

'I've just finished in a meeting with your gran.'

'Oh.' She tried not to search his face for any sign of the old Scott—knowing she'd only be disappointed when she didn't find it like last time—but couldn't help herself. It still hurt to realise this cool, professional man before her could have faked being that laid-back, reliable guy she'd fallen for. She pulled herself up quickly. She hadn't fallen for him; they'd shared a moment, that was all. She'd been someone else back then too. None of it had been real.

'Well, I'd better get inside,' she said, making to move past him but stopping when he said her name, the almost urgent-sounding plea prompting her to face him once more.

'I'm sorry I couldn't be honest with you...before.'

Quinn tried for an offhand kind of nonchalance but was horrified to realise her throat had tightened and discomfort prickled behind her eyelids. *Oh. Hell. No.* She was not going to cry. Not *here*. Not now.

'I understand that you probably hate my guts—I get it, I don't blame you,' he said, lowering his head to stare at the gravel beneath his feet for a moment. 'But I just wanted to tell you...it wasn't all part of the job. I, ahh,' he stammered slightly, before swallowing, 'I kinda scared myself at how personally involved I allowed myself to get. It almost cost you your life. It was unforgivable.'

'It wasn't your fault,' she managed, unsettled by the raw emotion on his face.

'If we hadn't argued that day...if I'd been thinking clearly...none of it would have happened.' He looked up and held her gaze with an unwavering intensity. 'I let my emotions get in the way of the job I was doing. I'm sorry.'

For a moment, they looked at each other, before Quinn blurted, 'Was any of it real? Honestly?'

'A lot more than was supposed to be,' he said with a small, tormented smile. A twitch at the window caught her eye, and she smothered a groan at the sight of Gran standing there, barely bothering to disguise herself behind the curtain, curiously watching them.

'Will you come with me somewhere?' he asked, having also noticed their audience.

She only briefly hesitated before nodding, and followed him towards a dark, rather boring-looking sedan. 'So even your car was fake?' she asked, feeling more dismayed by this thought than everything else.

'No. That was real. This is the company car.'

She bit back a smile at that; maybe Gran had the same talk with Scott as she'd had with her about appearances and cars.

They drove in silence for a while, Quinn feeling nervous, like on a first date with a stranger—which, in many ways, was exactly what this man beside her was. After a while, she relaxed back in the seat and tried to work out where they were going.

'I'm not angry about the whole flatmate thing,' she said, breaking the silence. 'I wasn't being honest with anyone either about who I was.' She realised she wasn't angry at his deception anymore—hadn't been for a long time. She simply missed *her* Scott.

'Maybe we both need to start over…as who we really are this time,' he suggested, glancing at her briefly before turning his attention back to the road.

'You may not like this version of me,' she said simply. 'I'm not Amy, the working-class factory worker.'

'Maybe you're more Amy than you realise,' he countered. 'I'm still Scott. I'm just not the unemployed jack of all trades.' He shrugged.

'I kinda liked him,' Quinn said wistfully.

'He's still in here.' He held her gaze for a moment, and she swallowed over the unexpected emotion. They turned into a driveway with a large set of gates, which Scott pressed a remote to open, and drove through.

'What's this place?' she asked, taking in the high-set Queenslander before them.

'This is where I live.'

Quinn turned back to the house and studied it more thoughtfully. The white paint looked fresh, and the wide timber steps leading up to the front door seemed new compared to the rest of the house.

'It's a work in progress, but I'm getting there,' he said, meeting her at the base of the steps as she walked from the car.

'It's beautiful.' And it was, with its wraparound verandah and carved posts, cast iron balustrades, gables and timber louvres. The battened screening at the top of the staircase provided privacy, and the authentic leadlight glass in the front windows added a heritage quality that Quinn fell in love with on sight.

'Did you do all this renovating yourself?' she asked, turning her gaze from the house to Scott in admiration.

'Yeah—like I said, jack of all trades.' He grinned.

'Exactly what trades have you acquired?'

'Before the army, I started a building apprenticeship, but while I was in school, I'd help my uncle in his plumbing business on weekends and in school holidays. I don't know,' he said somewhat modestly, 'I guess I'm just a quick learner—I've seemed to pick up a lot of useful skills over the years.'

Quinn turned back to the house and shook her head slowly. 'This is amazing. It's gorgeous.'

He seemed pleased by her reaction, then led the way up the front stairs. Inside, the hallway floor shone as it was bathed in the late afternoon sun, which picked up the golden-brown hues of the polished timber.

Quinn followed him through the house, passing some rooms with a strong smell of fresh paint and drop sheets covering furniture, out to the rear verandah, where a large timber table and chairs sat and an impressive-looking barbecue stood in the corner. Quinn thought briefly of her dad, knowing these two would probably be able to talk for hours about their manly barbecues.

She took a seat on a comfy-looking outdoor lounge setting while Scott went back inside to get drinks, returning with two bottles of beer and sitting beside her.

'Do you think Amy and Scott had a chance? If none of this had happened—if that's who we really were?' she asked as a familiar, comfortable silence stretched between them, almost like old times.

'I think they would have. I think they still could.'

'Everything's different now,' she said softly.

'Nothing we can't get used to.'

'I don't even really know what you do.'

'I run a private protection and security business.'

'So, you're a private detective for rich people?' she asked.

'Among other things. I don't only work for your family. I supply protection for companies with staff working in dangerous places. We do training for companies to teach their employees what to do and not to do in certain countries where safety could be an issue. We handle hostage negotiations on behalf of major companies if they find themselves in that kind of situation. Lots of stuff.' He shrugged.

'And you own the company?'

He nodded, easing back in his seat. 'I was in the army until I decided to get out and use my skills doing something a little more lucrative.'

'You left without saying goodbye,' she said, and knew that it sounded like an accusation, and she guessed it was. It still hurt.

'I had to get my head straight—something I couldn't do around you.'

'Well, thanks so much for leaving me there with Agent Bond. She was a heap of fun,' Quinn said, rolling her eyes.

Scott fought back a grin. 'I had to fork out a fortune on stress leave after she finished that assignment.'

Quinn thought he was joking, but wasn't quite sure. She dropped her gaze, toying with the material of her blouse. 'Where did you go?'

He paused briefly before answering. 'I was on protection detail with your father before his trial.'

Quinn's head snapped up at that. Scott was among the men and women who had risked their life protecting her father in a safe house during the trial? She knew there'd been two attempts on her father's life in the lead-up to the trial, since it involved a number of high-profile criminal families overseas. That only came out recently after the trial had ended.

'Thank you,' she said, swallowing a sudden lump in her throat. 'For keeping him safe.'

'How's he doing?' Scott asked, shrugging off her gratitude, but she sensed it had meant something to him.

'He's doing really well,' she said, smiling as she thought about her last visit to the rehab centre he'd been court-ordered to attend to address his gambling problem. 'He seems different—happier.' For the first time in years, he seemed like the father she'd known as a little kid. 'He's talking about returning to the company when he's finished his sentence.' The threat of some kind of retribution following his testimony was always going to be something hanging over his head, but he seemed to have reached peace with the situation—living day-to-day with a new appreciation for the second chance he'd been given in return for risking his life to bring such a big crime ring down.

'I guess it's good news for your company,' she added dryly. As a result, they would always have a bodyguard whenever they were out in public and on the grounds of

Appleton Park, until such time the threat to her father's life was deemed over.

'It's a priority I take extremely seriously,' he said with a slight frown.

She didn't want to talk about the dark side of her family legacy. Standing, she walked across to lean against the railing. She'd learned there were some things that were simply out of her control and there was no point stressing over something that might never happen. She was done with living in the shadows and hiding. She had too much to live for now.

'I see you've been doing big things,' he said, sensing her withdrawal and changing the topic. 'Your gran is pretty proud of you, you know.'

His words warmed her. She and Gran had been working closely over the last few months and Quinn was seeing a whole new side of the woman she thought she'd always known—but clearly hadn't. She was in awe of her grandmother's business savvy; the calm yet firm way she'd waded through the crisis as it had unfolded, guiding the company through each storm with the experience of a seasoned captain.

'I'm actually pretty proud of her too.'

'So you've forgiven her?'

Quinn eyed him warily. 'I guess so.'

She watched as he stood and joined her at the railing. 'Do you think you can forgive *me*?'

'I already have. You were just doing your job.'

'I was serious earlier—I'd really like to start over, see how we go without any secrets hanging over our heads.'

Quinn studied him quietly; her heart thudded almost painfully against her chest. 'I'm not sure we can,' she said, and instantly saw the hopeful glint in his eye fade a little before she hurried on. 'I still have one last secret.'

For a moment, he froze, his gaze searching her face intently. 'What secret would that be?'

'I think I liked you more than a flatmate should have liked you.'

His shoulders seemed to relax slightly as he rubbed a hand over his upper lip. 'Yeah? Well, that could be a problem, I guess.' He paused. 'Unless, of course, I also liked *you* more than a flatmate should have.'

A smile stretched across her lips at the familiar banter, and her eyes met his as she leaned towards him.

She delighted in the heat of his skin through his white business shirt as she spread her fingers wide across his chest and up around his neck. The short, close cut of his hair felt soft yet spiky against her fingertips, and she inhaled deeply, the heady scent of something incredibly masculine and slightly spicy filling her senses and making her a little light-headed as he ran his hands along her back and down past her hips, pulling her tightly against him. It reminded her just how perfectly they fit together.

She pulled back slightly and smiled. 'There you are,' she said softly.

His tender smile made her heart clench in relief. She'd thought they'd left Scott and Amy behind in that old run-down house with the rickety stairs, but here they were. Reunited and free to move on without any more secrets between them.

Epilogue

'Are you sure you want to do this?' Quinn whispered as they walked up the front steps and through the front door.

'Absolutely,' Scott whispered back. 'Stop worrying. How bad can they be?'

Quinn opened her mouth to tell him exactly how bad, but stopped when Lionel appeared and graciously led them into the drawing room.

Decorations hung around the room like a scene from a Victorian Christmas card, and soft festive music filtered through the air.

It was easy for the uninitiated onlooker to be fooled into thinking this was some perfect family gathering—how could it not be? Only this year, there was something different about it. She found her father standing beside his mother and a smile touched her lips. Over the last few months since his return from prison and rehab, her relationship with her dad had fallen back into the kind they'd had when she was younger. Quinn was proud of the courage he'd shown, giving evidence at the trial despite the danger involved. While he still had a long way to go, Quinn knew he would succeed. He had her and Gran to help him through it.

And while she missed her mother, it was clear the toxic nature of their relationship had done nothing for their happiness. Both seemed far happier apart. She only wished they'd realised it sooner.

Quinn was planning a visit to Bali to see her mother in the new year. Their relationship wasn't as easy as the one she shared with her father, but it was better than it had been, and there was always hope.

'There she is, our little businesswoman of the year,' Uncle Tobias announced as he crossed the room with dramatic flair.

Quinn rolled her eyes. 'Uncle Tobias, this is Peter Scott,' she introduced, the name no longer sounding strange on her lips.

'Just call me Scott,' he said, leaning across to shake her uncle's hand.

'Well, isn't this a delightful twist to the tale. I've been hearing a lot about you, *Mr* Scott,' Tobias said in a purr-like tone. 'It's just like a scene from *The Bodyguard*. You even look a little bit like a young Kevin Costner. I always did fancy him,' he added, wiggling his eyebrows wickedly.

Scott didn't give the slightest indication he was alarmed, although she did see him glance down at their still-joined hands pointedly after the moment threatened to stretch on a little too long.

'Oh, what a shame—all the handsome ones are taken.' Tobias sighed heavily, reluctantly releasing Scott's hand.

'I wouldn't let Claude hear you say that too loudly,' Quinn murmured, glancing across the room at a younger man dressed neatly in a suit. The year before, Tobias had been heartbroken at the thought of having to give up the man he loved, but a year away from the family had done them the world of good. Tobias and Claude had returned married.

'I'm so happy for you both,' Quinn said, smiling.

'I believe we have you to thank for twisting the old girl's arm for an invitation to Christmas dinner this year,' he said, almost slyly.

'There wasn't much twisting needed. I think you'll be surprised at how much Gran has mellowed.'

'It's certainly a start.'

Not *all* the bridges had been mended since the great Christmas disaster of the year before, but the lessons learned served to remind them of how important family really was. It took almost losing her dad to show how truly insignificant the loss of everything material in her life had been. Things could be replaced, but nothing could replace her father.

Scott slipped his arm around her waist and she tried to ignore the flutter of excitement that immediately set off. It didn't matter whether it was a brush of his hand against hers or the touch of a kiss—her body was tuned into his, and the slightest contact still managed to make her giddy.

Her smile disappeared, though, as she spotted the seductive swagger of her cousin making her way towards them.

'I've been waiting to meet the man who managed to sweep my cousin off her feet. Kind of like déjà vu, don't you think?' Greta asked sweetly as she reached out a hand towards Scott. 'I'm Greta.'

'Nice to meet you,' Scott said, giving her a brisk nod but ignoring the outstretched hand. 'I'll get us a drink.'

'I'll help,' Tobias offered quickly, sending a wink to Quinn as he watched Scott walk ahead of him.

Quinn took in her cousin's expression and groaned silently. If Greta hadn't thought Scott was a challenge before, she most definitely did now.

'So, tell me, Quinn, how does it feel to be a working girl?'

'I'm loving it actually.'

'Come on, there's no need to hide the truth—I won't tell Gran.'

'I'm happier than I've ever been,' Quinn said, glancing over at Scott.

'I have to say, the rough-around-the-edges ones can be rather fun for a bit of a fling.'

'Like Bryson was, I suppose?' Quinn said, trying to keep her tone even.

Greta gave a scornful snort. 'Bryson? God no. He was a bore. What on earth did you see in that twatwobble?'

'*You* married him,' Quinn shot back.

'It wasn't serious. Just like our rather rugged bodyguard over there will just be something to stop me falling asleep at another boring family gathering.'

Quinn knew she was only trying to get a rise out of her, but the memory of how Greta so brazenly—not to mention, easily—had stolen Bryson away from her still hurt.

'Why do you do it?' Quinn found herself asking.

'Do what?'

'Always try to take what's mine.'

Greta smiled scathingly. 'Because it's so easy,' she said.

'But why? What did I ever do to you to make you hate me so much?'

For the briefest of moments, something in Greta's eyes flared, before that detached, impossibly cold expression returned. 'You don't have to *do* anything. That's the point. Quinn can do no wrong.'

'What?'

'Oh please,' Greta scoffed. 'That innocent little wide-eyed act won't work with me.'

'Greta, I seriously have no idea what you're talking about.'

'You've always been Gran's pet. She's always favoured you. Perfect little Quinn,' she mimicked.

'Do you even *remember* last Christmas?' Quinn asked sarcastically. 'Clearly, I wasn't being favoured then. Or after,' she added dryly, recalling the culture shock of suddenly having no money or social pull anymore.

'And yet, here you are,' Greta said with a bitter twist of her lips. 'Heading your own department in the company. Sitting on Gran's right-hand side. While I still don't have my trust fund reinstated. Go figure.'

'Gran made it clear she wanted everyone to show more respect to the company if we wanted the perks.' Quinn shrugged. 'Turns out it was the best thing I ever did. I love what I'm doing now.'

'Well, I suppose if you haven't got any special talent for anything else, you may as well work for the company.'

Once upon a time, not so long ago, Greta's comment would have cut Quinn deep. As she studied her cousin now, though, she saw through the perfectly made-up face that women all over the world envied, and saw the petulant, spoilt child Greta had been—and had never grown out of. *How sad.* And how lucky that she'd been saved from the same fate. She couldn't even relate to the woman she'd been before Gran's shake-up the year before. That girl was a stranger now—one she was happy to never see again.

Her gaze moved across the room to rest on the two men standing comfortably talking together, and felt the last traces of animosity for her cousin fade away. Her father and Scott had spent a lot of time together while in the safe house. It was dangerous work, considering her Dad had a bounty on his head. She suspected Scott had done it as self-punishment for the day she'd been kidnapped. She'd be forever grateful that the two most important men in her life were home safe and that the danger had now, hopefully, passed.

Scott looked over and caught her eye, sending her a wink and the ghost of a smile—a promise of what they'd no doubt be doing later, once they were back home, alone. How different this Christmas was to the last one.

'Excuse me, Greta, I really don't have time to listen to any more of your crap,' Quinn said, cutting off her cousin's bitter tirade mid-sentence, effectively shocking her into silence as she walked away. No one had the power to make her feel inadequate anymore.

After all, she was Quinn Appleton, and she was already making a difference.

Acknowledgements

To Jess and Kaitlin, Louise Langley, David Ross, and my Facebook friends and readers who helped brainstorm whenever I put out the call for help—thank you so much for all your support!

Accidentally Working Class was pretty aptly named, considering it came about purely by accident. I strongly believe the stories sometimes pick us and not the other way around, and this book was determined to be written.

It started out as women's fiction, then took a bit of a rom-com twist before morphing into something unique and special. Quinn and Scott wormed their way into my heart, and I hope you've enjoyed their journey as much as I enjoyed being taken on the ride right alongside them.

You can find more books by Karly Lane at all good book shops and online, or head to www.karlylane.com.au

Also by Karly Lane:

North Star

Morgan's Law

Bridie's Choice

Poppy's Dilemma

Gemma's Bluff

Tallowood Bound

Second Chance Town

Third Time Lucky

If Wishes Were Horses

Six Ways to Sunday

Someone Like You

The Wrong Callahan

Mr Right Now

Return to Stringybark Creek

Fool Me Once

Something Like This

Take Me Home

Once Burnt, Twice Shy

Burnt

Guardians of the Crossing Series

Reign of Secrets

Blood of Kings

The Lion's Prey

The Operation Series

Operation Summer Storm

Operation Willow Quest

Operation Swift Mercy

Operation Date with Destiny

Printed in Great Britain
by Amazon